A superb storyteller, one of the very finest writing today ...
'. [he] has demonstrated that not only can he make any period of history his own but that he can also master a new genre entirely'
FOR WINTER NIGHTS

'Wrap up warm! ... this is a book which drags you in to its lethal environment'

*Also by Giles Kristian*

**THE RAVEN NOVELS**

Raven: Blood Eye
Sons of Thunder
Óðin's Wolves

**THE BLEEDING LAND**

The Bleeding Land
Brothers' Fury

**THE RISE OF SIGURD**

God of Vengeance
Winter's Fire
Wings of the Storm

**THE ARTHURIAN TALES**

Lancelot
Camelot

# Where Blood Runs Cold

## Giles Kristian

PENGUIN BOOKS

TRANSWORLD PUBLISHERS
Penguin Random House, One Embassy Gardens,
8 Viaduct Gardens, London SW11 7BW
www.penguin.co.uk

Transworld is part of the Penguin Random House group of companies
whose addresses can be found at global.penguinrandomhouse.com

First published in Great Britain in 2022 by Bantam Press
an imprint of Transworld Publishers
Penguin paperback edition published 2022

Excerpt on p. vii from *The Collected Poems* by Robert Frost © 1969 Holt
Rinehart and Winston, Inc., published by Vintage Books. Extract
reproduced by permission of The Random House Group Ltd.

A CIP catalogue record for this book
is available from the British Library.

ISBN
9780552178518

Typeset in Sabon LT Std by Jouve (UK), Milton Keynes.
Printed and bound in Great Britain by Clays Ltd, Elcograf S.p.A.

The authorized representative in the EEA is Penguin Random House
Ireland, Morrison Chambers, 32 Nassau Street, Dublin D02 YH68.

Penguin Random House is committed to a sustainable
future for our business, our readers and our planet. This book
is made from Forest Stewardship Council® certified paper.

If you've ever asked yourself the question, *how far would I go?* this book is for you.

*The woods are lovely, dark and deep,*
*But I have promises to keep,*
*And miles to go before I sleep,*
*And miles to go before I sleep.*

Excerpt from 'Stopping by Woods on
a Snowy Evening' by Robert Frost

# 1

ERIK LIFTED HIS eyes to the rear-view mirror. Sofia was holding a finger against the window, tracing the staccato movement of a snowflake as it melted and journeyed across the glass, leaving something of itself in its wake until it was gone.

Even as he looked back to the road, he knew that Sofia had sensed his glance, and so he looked to the mirror again and this time their eyes met. Just for a second, then she turned her face back to the window, her gaze fixed on an old red timber farm and outbuildings that passed in a snowy blur.

It had been a game once, with Sofia's sister. He'd glance at Emilie but she'd look away immediately. Was Sofia remembering now too as she watched the snow-laden pines and the dirt-blackened drifts whir by? He knew she was.

The sat nav said they'd be arriving in sixteen minutes. They would fill the boot with supplies, then head up to the cabin. Elise was determined that they would sit down and eat together before bed. Comfy clothes. Candles. He would get a fire going. Some music. A cosy family dinner. The first night in the mountains. The start of something new.

The drive from Tromsø had been easy enough. Two and a half hours, including a toilet and snack stop, and the thirty-minute Ullsfjord ferry crossing from Breivikeidet to Svensby. On the near-silent crossing, he had lost himself gazing at the summits and upper slopes of the snow-cloaked mountains cast in the pink blush of dawn. The sky the infinite blue of azurite copper ore, the water before the bow of the ferry still black, fathomless and indifferent, a dark mirror between worlds.

It had been snowing on and off for three days, the ploughs shaping canyons of cleared snow along the roads while people slept. He had lain awake listening to them, welcoming the interruption of the deathlike stillness of the night. Now the only snow on the roads was whipped by the wind across the black asphalt in ghostly swirls before the headlights.

The whole idea of coming out to the Lyngen Alps was to escape the last ten months. Not to forget – who could forget? – but to feel something else. To breathe again. And they needed it. So Elise had told him over and over, and no doubt she was right. She usually was.

Her employer, Friends of the Earth Norway, couldn't have been more understanding. They had welcomed Elise back to work, had orchestrated this posting to ease her back into the job. And hadn't Erik himself suggested they rent a cottage away from everything and everyone? Fresh air. Ski trips. The Northern Lights.

More than once he had seen Elise's eyes flick up to the mirror. Seen her looking at the empty back seat across from Sofia.

'There must be something going on today,' Elise said, breaking into his thoughts. They were coming into town already.

'Never thought it would be so busy,' he said, leaning forward over the steering wheel, searching for somewhere to park.

'The demonstration.' Elise was peering at a throng of people a hundred metres ahead, gathered before a makeshift stage in the small town square. 'Karine told me about it, but I forgot it was today.'

'Who's Karine?' he asked, anticipating the eye roll that followed.

'Karine Helgeland,' Elise said. 'She did say I should come to the protest if we arrived in time.'

He knew that Elise had been chatting online with this local Sami campaigner, been kept up to date about the mining company which had bought land and an old copper mine around here somewhere.

'You've got a few days off before you start work, though, right?' he said when they were parked up. His tone had sounded more confrontational than he'd intended.

Elise turned to him, frowning. 'I told you, we'll have the week's holiday before I start.'

He glanced up at the rear-view mirror. Sofia was staring out of the window. He needed to get out. The car was full of tension. Most of it his own.

'I can do some research in the evenings,' Elise said. 'Maybe speak to a few people. But we'll have the days.'

He said nothing, then twisted around to give Sofia a smile which felt like a stranger on his face. 'Let's get some supplies. Some chocolate?'

Sofia's smile was her answer, as she plucked her woollen hat from amongst the clutter of bags and Amdahl family belongings and pulled it onto her head.

'Stay close,' he called to Sofia behind him as he forced a way through the crowd, his arms wrapped around the bag of groceries.

'I see her, Pappa,' Sofia said, pointing.

'Keep up, Sofia,' he said, pushing his way to the front of the crowd. A group of men and women stood holding signs saying things like: SAY NO TO NOVOTROITSK NICKEL and WHAT HAPPENS IN THE ARCTIC DOESN'T STAY IN THE ARCTIC. One sign in particular caught Erik's eye. It bore a photo of a Sami herder and a reindeer below the words WHERE WILL WE GO NOW?

The protestors, some in the bright blues and reds of traditional Sami dress, thronged around one of their number who stood at a microphone, addressing the crowd. Her words were clear, even through the screech and squeal of the low-rent PA system. Novotroitsk Nickel would reopen the old copper mine, she said, and destroy more of the ancient reindeer grazing land. This corporation's greed was yet 'another assault on the fragile Arctic environment'.

Elise would be right in the thick of it. This wasn't the biggest of battles that she and Friends of the Earth were fighting on behalf of the natural world and its myriad species. But better that Elise was here, rather than eight hundred kilometres away, lobbying against the transportation of used nuclear fuel from the Gulf of Finland to Siberia, like her last job. Better that they were together.

'There, Pappa!' Sofia pointed again as she squeezed between a knot of phone-zombie teenagers, and caught up with him.

'I see her, Lillemor,' he said.

'Pappa!' Sofia said, trying to look crosser than she was at his use of her pet name. *Little mother*. He suspected she still quite liked it now and then.

Elise stood to the side of the stage, looking up at a larger woman who was making her way down the rickety metal steps towards her, smiling and waving at Elise as though they were old friends.

Erik headed forward again, then stopped dead. A man had stepped hard and fast into his path, face to face, so that some of the shopping spilled out onto the filthy snow between booted feet in the crowd.

He shook off the man's gaze, cradled the bag in one arm and bent to pick up a pack of minced beef.

'Watch where you're going,' the man said, glaring down at him.

*Fuck. Really?* Erik thought. He put the bag down on the slush and ice and stood to face the man. Fought to subdue the adrenaline rushing through him.

'You walked into me,' he said, his tone calm and matter-of-fact.

'Pappa,' Sofia said.

'You couldn't see over your shopping bag,' the man said. Russian, at a guess. Wiry and young. Short peroxide blond hair and noisy cobalt blue eyes. A restless face out to prove

5

something. The kind of face any father should probably pretend he hadn't seen.

Too late for that. Erik held his eye and straightened up. He knew he was being challenged. Also knew it would be a mistake to turn his back on this man.

'Pappa,' Sofia said again. More urgently this time. Fear in her voice.

Erik shook his head and stooped again. 'Help me, Lillemor,' he said, and Sofia bent and gathered up a couple of tins and put them in the bag.

'Allow me,' came a voice. Another man from the crowd dropped into a squat beside them, picking up a can of beer that had broken free of the pack. He swept the dirty water off the can and Erik saw a tattoo on the back of his hand. A wolf's snarling face beneath a parachute. Wings, or maybe fire, on either side. 'I prefer Ringnes myself,' he continued. The same accent as the other man. 'An Oslo beer but owned by the Danes. Like Norway used to be.' He handed Erik the can. Erik placed it back in the bag with the other items, and the two of them drew themselves up to full height.

Erik nodded in thanks.

The man smiled. As he stood, Erik noticed a pale scar running through his lips onto his chin. He was tall. Not that far off two metres. Lean face. Eyes as fixed and steady as the other man's were unmoored and adrift.

'I apologize,' the tall man said, gesturing at his white-haired companion, who seemed pissed off at being dismissed out of hand. 'My brother is . . . clumsy. And his manners could do with some work.'

Erik glanced at the man, who shrugged inside his coat, huffed warm air into his busy hands and dipped his head in some sort of acknowledgement-cum-apology which he didn't mean. Erik nodded to the tall man again, wrapped his left arm around the shopping bag and held out his other hand to Sofia, who took it tightly.

The audio speakers on the stage squealed. 'We must protect what is ours,' the Sami protestor said. 'Doing nothing would be a betrayal of our ancestors, our children and our children's children.'

'Let's find Mamma,' he said, squeezing Sofia's hand, and together they continued through the crowd until they reached his wife, who was standing with the other woman.

'Erik, this is Karine,' Elise said, smiling at her friend.

'Pleased to meet you, Karine,' he said, letting go of Sofia to shake Karine's hand, then wrapping his arm around the shopping.

'And this must be Sofia.' Karine stepped back to examine Sofia, who said a shy hello. 'I've heard all about you,' the older woman said, nodding in approval.

'Karine has been helping me prepare for the investigation into Novotroitsk Nickel,' Elise told Erik. She glanced at Karine. 'I don't know what I would've done without her.'

He suspected Karine had been helping Elise with other things too. There was usually wine or a stiff G&T involved in these late-evening Skype calls. And a week or so ago, when he'd gone into the study to take Elise her usual cup of green tea, he could tell she'd been crying. He hadn't said anything. If Elise could open up to Karine Helgeland, well, that was good, wasn't it?

'Quite a turnout,' Erik said to Karine, nodding at the press of people around them.

'We're doing what we can,' she said. She looked to be in

7

her late fifties, and though an outdoor life had weathered her face, giving her a stern air, her eyes still held a youthful mischief.

'Isn't Mrs Helgeland's *kofte* beautiful, Sofia?' Elise gestured at Karine's traditional felt dress with its ribbons of contrasting colours, its pewter embroidery and her red wool bonnet.

Sofia nodded.

Karine smiled at her. 'I usually only wear it on Sami National Day—'

'The sixth of February,' Sofia interrupted.

Karine gave Elise an impressed glance, then turned her bright eyes back to Sofia. 'But today is a day to be proud of our heritage and to speak up for the land, which cannot speak for itself,' she said. Then, to lighten the tone, she took off her hat and leant towards Sofia. 'Although, to be honest with you, this can get very itchy.' She scrubbed her short brown hair with thick fingers, then straightened and put a hand on Elise's shoulder. 'We are so grateful to have Elise here,' she said, raising her voice above the loudspeaker a metre or so away. 'Together we must make sure that the land is protected.' She and Elise shared a look of solidarity and determination.

'But you've just arrived after a long journey,' Karine continued. 'You'll want to be settling in up there,' she added, looking up at the snow-covered mountains to the west of the town. 'Why don't you come for dinner Saturday night?' She turned her head, fixing her dark eyes on Erik. 'If you don't already have plans.'

Before he could answer, Karine turned away to greet a handsome man with silver hair rattling the stairs of the platform as he descended towards them. A warm smile spread across his sun-browned and wind-beaten face.

'This is my husband, Lars,' Karine said. 'Lars, this is Elise Amdahl and her husband Erik.'

Lars nodded to Elise and shook Erik's hand firmly.

'And who is this?' Lars asked, stepping back and holding his arms out towards Sofia. 'A young adventurer coming all the way up here to see how we mountain trolls live?'

Sofia glanced at her mamma for reassurance. 'I'm Sofia,' she said, looking back to Lars Helgeland.

He dipped his head. 'You must be what, fifteen? Sixteen?'

'Almost thirteen,' she told Lars.

'Ah, so! I'm glad to meet you, Sofia.'

Karine and Elise shared a smile. 'The Amdahls are coming for dinner on Saturday,' Karine told Lars, who raised his eyebrows, as surprised as Erik at how fast this had happened.

'We look forward to it,' Elise said, smiling. 'Message me with the time and if there's anything we can bring. We'll see you Saturday.'

Erik had already turned away, but he lifted a hand in farewell. Then, through a gap in the crowd, he caught sight of the tall scarred man who had helped him pick up the shopping. Their eyes met and the man nodded cordially, then Erik turned to Sofia.

'Come on, Lillemor,' he said.

Sofia loved the drive up to the cabin, especially when they left the roads cleared by the ploughs and had to fit the snow chains. He let her help him attach the levers and clips. It added a half-hour to the journey but it was worth it to see her face when she got back in the car, huffing into cupped hands, cheeks red from the cold.

Sweeping her hat off and rubbing her own hands together in the warm air from the AC vent, Elise smiled at him in a way he realized he'd been missing. They continued along the twisting track climbing up into the mountains, towards Jiekkevárri, at nearly two thousand metres the highest peak in Troms county. Past half-hidden shacks and winter cabins built forty years ago, between fields dense with snow and tall spruce bent and burdened with it, as though cursed by some spell and frozen in time. The Mitsubishi's gasoline engine purring now, generating power for the electric motors. The chains rattling on the wheels, biting into the deep snow. They came like pilgrims from the new world seeking to make their sacrifice to the old.

Now and then they passed other vehicles on the road – the 4x4s of other cabin owners, most with a Thule ski box on the roof like their own, or the occasional yellow plough with flashing lights, creating its own blizzard as it hurled snow into drifts either side of the road. Three thousand kroner a year would see one of these keep the track to your cabin open.

'We owe someone,' Erik said when they took a left off the road and saw the track ahead cleared. On the roof, though, the snow was piled a metre deep. It overhung the gables, defying gravity, as if suspended in time by the same magic that made ice sculptures of the water that should have been gushing down rock faces, and held the trees unnaturally still beneath their thick white burdens.

The same spell that held him too.

It was two-fifteen and already growing dark when Elise

turned the key in the door and pulled it open. The smell of the pinewood interior took Erik back to a hundred vacations boy and man, by fjord and mountain. Lamps were switched on, candles were lit, and he set a fire in the Jøtul wood-burning stove in the lounge while Elise made filter coffee and Sofia introduced herself to her bedroom. He had cleaned the soot from the glass of the stove before making the fire, and now leaned forward watching the flames, their tentative questing then growing hunger as they fed on the kindling and licked at the seasoned birch, whose leprous white bark caught like paper. The cold sits in the walls, his grandmother used to say. Only now did he truly know what she had meant. Soon, the fire was softly roaring, tongues of flame caressing the glass, and the iron stove started to ping and tick as the metal expanded with the heat. It was a ritual, this waking up the cabin. Saying to the place, *we'll get to know each other, but for now just know that you are ours and we are yours.*

He felt a calm which had evaded him these past ten months. A settling in his stomach and in his heart. But no sooner had he acknowledged this welcome change than the memory of the scream came back to him. The twisting in his gut as he watched. The lurch forward, far, far too late. He shook his head hard to dislodge the vision, swallowed back the bile that had risen to burn his throat, shoved himself out of the chair and headed outside to fetch more logs for the fire.

In the morning, after four cups of coffee to offset another night's broken, haunted sleep, he dug out two snow shovels from the shed. He and Elise set to work clearing a path from the car to the cabin door, where the plough had not reached.

Sofia helped out for a while, emptying last night's ashes from the stove, filling the log basket from the pile under the eaves which someone had restocked at the end of last winter, and bringing the skis and snowshoes from the roof box on the car to the porch. She arranged them neatly, a set between each of the pegs on the wall of the porch. After that, she disappeared inside while he carried a ladder from the shed along the path which Elise was still busy clearing with the scoop. He'd decided to clear at least half the snow off the roof before lunch.

'Please don't fall,' Elise shouted to him as he reached the top of the ladder and prepared to haul himself onto the roof.

Her needless warning struck him like a blow to the chest. For a moment he held tight to the ladder, not wanting to look down at Elise. Knowing she would be inwardly cringing at her own words.

He pulled himself up onto the roof, then took two tentative steps to retrieve the shovel he'd already thrown up there. He could hear the thrust and cut of Elise's scoop as she resumed her own work, and was just trying to guess where the roof ended and the overhang began, when he caught movement from the corner of his eye and looked up. Dressed in her Helly Hansen gear and snowshoes as if ready to join one of Amundsen's polar expeditions, Sofia was setting off up the slope towards the pine woods behind the cabin.

'Where are you going?' Erik called down to her.

Sofia stopped dead. She stood with her back to him for a moment as if she had known she would be challenged. Then she turned around. 'I'm just exploring,' she shouted, lifting a gloved hand in which Erik knew would be the pocket knife she had so desperately wanted for Christmas. A Victorinox

Huntsman multitool with fifteen functions, it had been the only thing she had asked for, but Erik's toes crunched up in his shoes every time he saw her opening and closing the sharp blades and gadgets.

'No, Sofia, I want you to stay here,' he said, gesturing with the shovel.

'But, Pappa, I just want to look around,' she called back.

'And I'm telling you I want you to stay here where we can see you,' he shouted.

'Because you don't want me to die too,' she said. Her words were quiet, but sound travels far across snow, and he heard it. Elise had too. They looked at each other, making an unspoken agreement not to react.

'What if she promises not to go far?' Elise said, looking at the sky and then at her watch. He guessed it was around midday. 'It'll be light for another two hours,' Elise said. 'It's a shame if she can't make the most of it.'

'No,' he said, more forcefully than he'd intended.

Elise gave a slight shake of her head, then turned, dropped her shovel onto the snow beside the path she'd been clearing and set off towards the porch.

'Where are you going?' he asked.

'Somebody has to make lunch,' she said, disappearing from view.

His daughter followed, head to the ground, fists clenched. A moment later, he felt the vibration of the door slamming shut below his feet and was surprised it hadn't cleared the snow off the roof and him along with it.

'Shit,' he said. It was only the first day and already Sofia was sulking with him and Elise was pissed off. So much for the cosy family trip to the mountains. 'Shit,' he said again,

13

thrusting his shovel into the snow and hurling a wedge of it over the side of the roof. *And I'm hiding up here on the damn roof,* he thought, *like that's going to help anything.*

Down came the shovel. Off flew the snow. He lost himself in the task. Truth was, he enjoyed the repetitive drudgery of it, the heat blooming in his arms and lower back. The rhythm of his breath and the pulsing of blood in his ears. Peace in movement.

It was in stillness that his mind beat madly, like a bird trapped in a room, hurling itself against the window glass.

# 2

HE'S HAVING THE dream again. He knows he's dreaming and still he cannot steer its course. He never can. The figure is more shadow than man. More dark presence than human form. More of a sensation, like the heaviness in your gut when you've lashed out and hurt the feelings of someone you love. Or the clenching tightness in your chest when something is broken that you know can't be fixed.

He feels all this even in the dream. Knowing he's in the dream. But this time it's different, and despite the dread, he moves closer.

*What are you?* he asks.

He sees in the dark form the outline of a face. An eye. And Sofia is here too. *Here I am!* he shouts to her but she can't hear him. The terror is on him now. In him. Its claws sinking into the soft meat of his heart. *Sofia!*

She's moving towards the figure. *No – stay away! Sofia, stay with me!*

He hears his daughter scream.

'Erik!' He woke with a start, Elise's voice bringing him back. The fuzzy blue display of the alarm clock sharpened as he swung himself out of bed, heart racing, knowing that the scream had been real. Three twenty-two a.m.

'She's having a nightmare,' Elise said, already on the landing. Erik stumbled after her and through the doorway. Elise pushed open the door of their daughter's bedroom.

'Shh, darling. It's just a dream,' she soothed, as she sat on the bed beside Sofia and took the girl's hands in her own. 'Just a dream.'

Erik exhaled sharply, still trying to blink away his own dream, which clung to his mind and body, heavy as wet clothing.

'Pappa,' Sofia said, half awake, half dreaming still.

Erik sat on Sofia's other side, gently running a hand through her sweat- and sleep-tangled hair, pushing it back from her face. 'It's OK, Lillemor, Pappa's here.'

'I'll bring her some water,' Elise said, leaving Erik with Sofia.

'It's OK. You go back to sleep now. I'm here.' He leant and kissed her on the forehead, holding his lips there a moment. 'We love you so much.'

She smiled and squashed her head back into the pillow as he stood.

'Love you,' she said, her words slurred as if she was already drifting off.

The next morning, he got up early and set to work clearing the rest of the roof. When it was done, he found Elise at the dining table, laptop open, coffee beside her, those two vertical

16

furrows between her eyebrows and nose as subtle as a *do not disturb* hanger on a hotel room door.

She didn't need to look up to know what he was thinking. 'I just need an hour or two,' she said, frowning at the laptop screen as her fingers danced across the keyboard. How she could type and speak different words at the same time was a mystery to him.

He couldn't help himself. 'I thought you weren't starting for a week?' he said.

Her right hand left the keys, index finger pointing up. 'You were on the roof.'

'You were still in bed,' he said.

She took a weary breath and looked up at him now, the creases of her concentration frown melting away. 'It's my first job back with them. I want to be prepared.' She gestured at her laptop. 'And it's important.'

So he and Sofia drove into town to the Vinmonopolet to buy wine. Once back in the car, he turned, taking a moment to look at her.

'I can't believe you're going to be a teenager,' he said.

She raised her eyebrows, no doubt recalling all the times they had called her a sulky teenager long before the eve of her thirteenth birthday.

'I mean it.' He shook his head. 'Where has the time gone?'

'Pappa,' she said, staring ahead through the windscreen, 'you promised to take me on the Long Ski when I was thirteen. Remember? A proper trip. Sleeping in snow shelters and everything.'

He kept his eyes on the road. A knot tying in his stomach.

'You promised, Pappa,' Sofia pushed.

'I know,' he said. 'But that was a couple of years ago.'

*Before Emilie died*, he left unsaid, though it was loud enough in the silence.

'I'm thirteen tomorrow. I'm old enough.'

'I don't think we can do it this time,' he said.

'But you promised,' she protested. 'Emilie asked you, the Easter before last, and you told her to wait until I was thirteen and then the three of us would go together.'

'I know what I said.' His words were sharper than he'd intended. Just the mention of her name. 'But so much has happened since then. It's different now.'

He glanced at her and she shook her head and turned her face to stare out of the side window.

He remembered that day in crisp detail. Emilie had borrowed her grandfather's well-thumbed maps, still marked with pen from his own trips, and plotted a five-day, four-night ski tour through woods and across frozen lakes. She had been so excited. But Sofia had been too young to go. And so Erik had told Emilie that they would wait until Sofia was thirteen and they could all go together. He had known how disappointed Emilie was. And yet she had explained the route plan to Sofia, who had listened wide-eyed and announced to the whole family that she would remind Erik of his promise the day she turned thirteen. He had known she wouldn't forget.

But it wasn't Easter now, with its fourteen hours of daylight, when the crisp sunlight offered warmth for the climb and gently melted the snow's surface, creating perfect conditions for the descent. It was only just February, and the days were short and cold.

'Let's give it another year, Lillemor,' he said. 'Just one

more year and then we'll go on the Long Ski. A real adventure, I promise.'

Silence. Another promise he wasn't sure he could keep.

'Thank God for the directions you emailed me,' Elise told Karine as they'd stood in the Helgelands' front porch, stamping snow off their boots and hanging up coats and hats. Turning on the happy family show like throwing the light switch at a winter fair.

'We're expecting more snow,' Lars said, leaning out to look up at the grey cloud blanketing the sky. 'In a few days you won't be able to get up here in that.' He was pointing at the Mitsubishi. 'Snowmobiles are the only way when we get a heavy fall.'

Karine and Lars were perfect hosts, generous and welcoming, and Lars clearly enjoyed a beer, which gave him enough in common with Erik to see the evening off to a better start than he had expected.

Elise asked if it ever worried them, being so remote, but Lars just chuckled.

'We love living out here,' he said, gesturing towards the window. The curtains were open and the snow beyond the glass glowed gently in the black night. 'We're not city people, as you can tell.' He looked over at Karine, who was in the kitchen showing Elise her recipe for *fiskeboller*. The air was fragrant with the scent of the creamy white sauce and potatoes, taking Erik back to his childhood and his mother's kitchen. 'If we wanted visitors all the time, we'd live in Tromsø,' Lars said, a mischievous smile on his face.

Lars must have been in his early sixties, Erik guessed, but

he was still broad-shouldered and solid, his hands tanned from so many summers of outside work, even now after the long winter.

'Ah, there are cabins being built all the time,' Lars added. 'Beautiful things of cedar wood. Even the roofs are cedar. Inside, everything cladded in oak. Huge windows with views of the mountains and the sea. Built to follow the contours of the landscape and laid out . . . just so,' he said, waving a broad hand. He rubbed the bristles on his cheek. 'Well, you know all this. Karine tells me you're a carpenter? You must be a busy man with all the houses springing up these days.'

'Actually, I'm taking some time out,' Erik replied, feeling Elise's eyes on him from the kitchen doorway. *Time out.* When was the last time he fitted a staircase, window frame, or skirting board? Or looked at a set of blueprints? Ten months ago he had hung a digital *Sorry . . . Temporarily Closed* sign on his website, and there it hung still. Amdahl Carpentry shut down for business until further notice.

Once dinner was underway, the conversation inevitably turned towards Novotroitsk Nickel, and how the locals felt about the Russian-owned company buying the mineral rights to the old Koppangen copper mine west of town. Lars, Karine and Elise shared their fears about waste being dumped in the fjord. About how the Sami Council was ignored, and how the government was willing to destroy the indigenous land in the north of Norway.

On and on it went, and he listened. Barely. Swirling the wine round his glass as Karine retrieved a letter from her cork board beside the fridge.

'This came yesterday,' Karine said, handing it to Elise.

He saw the logo of Novotroitsk Nickel on the letterhead,

two blue Ns interlinked like a pair of mountain peaks. 'They said it was just an exploration project at first,' Karine said, 'to see if the old mine had industrial potential. This was about a year ago.' She gestured at the letter in Elise's hands. 'That outlines their intention to explore the abandoned tunnels further and dig three new test pits, pending the results of a feasibility study.' She pushed her plate away as though talk of the mine's reopening had soured the food.

Truth was, he was bored of the conversation. Angry too, because he knew this was what Elise cared about. Her obsession. And he'd been wrong to think they could find each other again here in the mountains. Plus, the wine had gone to his head in all its euphoric *fuck-it* brilliance, and so he told them that the world needed copper if it wanted electricity. That it was how electricity worked.

'We're all for electric cars, right?' he said. 'If we're going to electrify the world to save it, then maybe we have to be prepared to lose some of the old ways.'

'Are you joking?' Karine asked him, her aspect hardening, suddenly expressing all the cheer of a granite rock face.

'It's just the wine talking,' Elise said, a smile on her lips but anger in her eyes.

Karine suggested they talk about something else, and Lars stood, telling Sofia he had something to show her.

Elise left the table too, carrying dishes to the kitchen. And so he sat alone, watching as Lars showed Sofia the contents of a beautifully carved wooden box that sat on the windowsill. Beyond it, the night loomed, filling the world with black nothingness. Sofia seemed genuinely interested in the old photos of the Helgelands' ancestors. In the other treasures too: a comb made of reindeer antler which Sofia said looked just like the ones she'd seen in the Viking Ship Museum in Oslo. A horn needle case engraved with little reindeer. A leather purse with tin thread embroidery which had belonged to Karine's great-grandmother. And most exciting, judging from Sofia's wide eyes, a huge knife which Lars took down from the stone mantlepiece over the stove.

'We call this a *stuorraniibi*,' Lars told her. He smiled at her frown. 'It just means big knife.' He shrugged for comic effect, before drawing the blade from the reindeer leather sheath and making a chopping motion with it. It was nearly twenty-five centimetres long. 'Long and wide enough to cut firewood or small trees to make shelter poles. Strong enough to split reindeer bones.' He turned it around to hold it by the spine of the blade. 'Feel the handle.' He offered it to Sofia. She touched the wood. 'Birch,' he said, 'for a better grip in cold and snow.'

'I have a Swiss Army knife,' Sofia said, and no sooner had she spoken the words than the knife was in her hand and she was easing the little blades and tools out one by one, and now Lars was shaking his head as if he had never seen anything so wonderful, much to Sofia's delight.

Sofia looked more engaged, more interested than she had about anything her father had done with her for a long while. What exactly *had* he done with her in the last year? They'd gone hiking a few times, picking late summer berries along the trail. He'd taken her to the Alfheim Stadium to watch Tromsø IL lose to Rosenborg in the fourth round of the Norwegian Cup. Oh, and there was the funeral of her sister. That had been a family day together.

Erik got up, grabbed hold of the three empty wine bottles and carried them to the kitchen counter.

'Will you have coffee?' Karine asked them, fetching mugs down from the cupboard.

Elise glanced at him and he knew the answer. At least they could still communicate without words.

'No, thank you,' Elise replied. 'Our little girl turns thirteen tomorrow. We have a big birthday breakfast to get up for.' She smiled.

Erik looked over at Sofia. She stood at the window, looking west into the night as Lars told her about Karine's brother, Hánas, who was a reindeer herder.

'Right now, while we are cosy and warm,' Lars said, 'Hánas is somewhere up there on the plateau with his herd.' He pointed out at the night and the dark shape of the mountain.

'Sometimes we see a light in the dark and we know it is Hánas in his tent,' Karine said, coming over to join her husband and Sofia at the window.

'It must be beautiful up there,' Sofia said.

'But so cold.' Elise mimed a shiver as she put a hand on Sofia's shoulder.

Sofia didn't seem to notice. She was still looking up at the mountain. Elise and Karine shared a smile, acknowledging the girl's preoccupation.

'So have a very happy birthday tomorrow, Sofia,' Karine said, 'and make sure your *mor* and *far* spoil you all day, starting with a special breakfast.' She looked out of the window and nodded to the dark distant peaks. 'Did you know, on my thirteenth birthday my father took me up there and taught me how to lasso a fully grown reindeer? A big bull, he was. I can still see him in my mind. Antlers like this.' She threw her hands up. 'One and a half metres.'

'Ha!' Lars exclaimed, wafting her words away with a hand.

'Were you there, husband?' she asked, lifting her chin in challenge, so that Erik could see the stubborn young girl she once was. 'Whose story is this anyway?'

Again, Lars batted the air with a big hand.

'So after many attempts I lassoed the bull over his great big antlers, and my father had to help me hold the rope – like this,' she said, miming the action, 'or that bull would have carried me off and I would probably still be hanging on now. But then we had to get home before dark because we didn't want to meet a *stallo* up there.'

Sofia screwed up her face. 'What's a *stallo*?'

'Sofia is too old now for stories of stupid great *stallos* and trolls,' Lars said. He was standing by an antique cocktail cabinet, pouring himself a brandy in the soft light from the interior.

'I was just telling Sofia what I did on my thirteenth birthday,' Karine said. 'You have to have adventures when you're young.'

Erik was watching Sofia as she turned to look at him. He knew what she wanted to tell the Helgelands – that he had promised to take her on the Long Ski when she turned thirteen. Her silence knotted him up inside.

After declining Lars's offer of brandy, he and Elise thanked their hosts for a lovely evening, said their goodbyes and crowded into the porch with Sofia to put on their coats, boots and hats.

'Sofia,' Lars said, coming out after them, 'I have something for you.' They turned and waited as he tramped through the snow after them, their warm breath pluming around their faces. 'Here, Sofia, for your birthday,' Lars said.

Sofia held out her hands and took the *stuorraniibi* he offered her, looking at her mother and father for reassurance.

'Of course, you must only use it with your parents' permission,' Lars said, nodding at Elise, then Erik. 'But I thought ... well ... you have your modern pocket knife, which can do everything you can possibly think of, but you should also have something from the past, to remember those who came before us.'

Sofia stared at the gift in her hands, open-mouthed. Not knowing what to say.

Erik looked at Elise. Surely *she* knew what to say. Like, *what the hell's wrong with you, Lars, giving a bloody great Sami knife to a thirteen-year-old girl? Who does that?*

'You lucky girl,' Elise said, putting her arm around Sofia's shoulder. Subtly trying to squeeze a *thank you* out of her.

'Thank you, Mr Helgeland,' Sofia managed, tearing her eyes away from the knife to look Lars in the face.

'Take care of a good knife and it will take care of you,' Lars said. Then he raised his hand. 'So, see you all again.' He turned and walked back to the house. 'And happy birthday, Sofia,' he called, his breath fogging in the glow of his porch light.

# 3

HE KNEW HE'D been ungracious at the Helgelands'. Even if he hadn't known it at the time, which he had, he'd have been in no doubt after. Elise's silence in the car had been as relentless and deliberate as the wipers sweeping falling snow from the windscreen, her fixed gaze ahead more a containment of anger than a second pair of eyes on the hazardous road.

At least she had waited until they got back and Sofia was in bed before confirming it.

'You knew how the Helgelands feel about the mine re-opening,' she said. 'You knew how worried they are, how upset they are.' She tilted her head on one side, her eyes slits of accusation. 'And you know the damage it'll do.'

'I was saying that it might not all be bad,' he replied, sitting on the edge of the bed, pulling off his socks. 'Maybe it'll help the Helgelands . . . if they can look at the positives. That's all.'

'But worse than that,' she said, ignoring his explanation, 'you know it's the whole reason we're here.'

They both fell silent for a moment, the seconds marked by the ticking of the clock over the bedroom door.

'The whole reason?' he said, like a man dropping a weighted lure into a hole in the ice. 'We came as a family because we knew we needed to spend some time together.'

She shook her head. 'You know what I mean,' she hissed, shutting the wardrobe door too hard, then holding still, listening to see if Sofia had woken. 'This is my job.' She turned to him, throwing her nightdress on over her head. Then she pulled the gown down and just stood there, eyes brimming with frustration and emotion.

He knew whatever he said would be wrong. Because she was right. He should say sorry. Take her hand. Hold her. But he said nothing.

As the clock made its relentless trek into the night, one step at a time, he felt her awake in the dark beside him.

'This is just a silly one from me,' he said, handing a present to Sofia as she stood another card at the end of the zig-zag line extending along the table between the breakfast dishes. Waffles and cloudberry jam, slices of cheese and salami and cured lamb, rings of green pepper, boiled eggs, a dish of crispy bacon and a loaf of poppyseed bread.

Sofia took a moment to admire the wrapping, which looked like a hedgehog had found some paper by the bins and wrapped itself up to stay warm. A little something extra, he'd only remembered about the present two minutes before she'd come into the room.

It was a pink merino wool hat with little outlines of igloos and snowflakes and polar bears, some of them ice skating, others sitting on their backsides, holding fishing rods.

'It has a fleece lining so it's not itchy and will keep you really warm,' he said, realizing now that the hat was too young for Sofia. Even at nine or ten she probably wouldn't have chosen pink, though the polar bears would have been OK. But at thirteen? Her current hat, a shapeless, scruffy thing, was urban camo.

'I can change it,' he said.

She shook her head. 'No, I like it,' she said, folding it neatly and placing it on the table beside her cards.

They ate breakfast. After opening a few more presents, Sofia unwrapped her gift from them. The moment had a weight to it which he knew they all felt, and he watched Sofia's face as she tore the paper off the light blue trekking backpack.

'We'll go hiking in the spring,' he said.

She frowned at that suggestion. Then nodded. 'Thank you,' she said, putting the rucksack down on the floor beside her.

'It's designed to be more comfortable for women,' Elise said, lifting an eyebrow at Sofia and patting her own hips.

'I love it,' Sofia said.

'We can try it later,' he said. 'If you like, we could ski to the glacier. Maybe take a picnic. As long as we're back before it gets dark.'

Sofia nodded. Picked up the headphones she'd unwrapped earlier. 'Can I go and try these?' she asked.

'You've not finished your breakfast.' Elise gestured at the barely touched boiled egg and the slice of bread and Jarlsberg on her plate.

'Not hungry,' Sofia said.

Elise nodded and the girl turned and was gone.

He waited a moment, reached for the coffee jug and said, 'I think I should take her. On the Long Ski.'

'You think she's ready?' Elise asked.

He thought about it, holding the coffee jug in mid-air over his mug. Thought about the trip to England. That climbing wall. Saw Emilie lying there on the blue landing mat which should have broken her fall but somehow had not.

A clatter of plates brought him back. Elise had begun clearing the table, and he watched her for a moment as she scraped the leavings into an empty dish. She was already thinking about her work, he knew. As soon as the breakfast plates were gone, her laptop would be on the table, and he would no doubt find some job that needed doing, or think of supplies that needed fetching from town. So much for the family holiday.

He heard himself call Sofia's name. Once, then a second time. There was a pause, then the thump and creak of her coming back down the stairs.

'What is it?' Sofia said, standing in the doorway. Her blue eyes lingered on them both in turn, but settled on him.

Maybe some open space would be good for him. And some time with Sofia, just the two of them.

'Pappa?' Sofia said, bringing him back to the moment. She lifted her chin impatiently.

He looked at her face. Really looked. She had suffered so much, and what had he done? Added to that suffering by keeping her wrapped in cotton wool when she was growing up, when her horizons should have been expanding, not closing in. She deserved better.

'I've been thinking about the Long Ski,' he said. 'I'll take you.'

# 4

THEY STOOD IN the predawn dark, Sofia shivering with excitement, Erik adjusting the rucksack on his back and tightening the hip strap one last time. Behind them, the yellow glow of the cabin windows. Before them, the winter night. Silent. Still. Clinging to the land like some residue of the long polar dark. He looked to the west, where the clouded sky was hazed white by an unseen moon whose diffuse glow softly lit the snow on the jagged peaks.

He was excited too. His whole body thrummed in readiness. He felt strong. Felt young in a way he hadn't for a long time. Maybe even since his military service, when he was eighteen and they had done their cold weather training in Bardufoss. When he had been a young man with everything ahead of him.

'Are you ready, Lillemor?' he asked, turning to Sofia, who was pulling on her lobster claw mittens. It had snowed the night they'd driven home from the Helgelands' and almost all the next day, and he breathed in the crisp scent of it. Lying before them, a world of fresh powder snow. Near-perfect conditions.

'Yes, Pappa,' she said, and he heard the slight tremor in those two words. Only natural when it's ten below, and you're about to leave a warm, cosy cabin and set off on skis, and the chances are you won't see another human being for days.

'Feels good, doesn't it?' he said, readying to attach the harness of the pulk into which he'd packed the tent, the portable stove, their sleeping bags and various other things they would need on the trip. When he'd stowed the first aid kit, he'd found Emilie's old teddy bear tucked down deep under the blankets. A tatty, moth-eaten bear wearing a short-cropped red sweater. Emilie had called it Crow, though he'd never known why, and he hadn't seen the thing for years, but Sofia must have rescued it from soft toy purgatory in the loft and snuck it into the pulk when he wasn't looking. He didn't mind the extra ten ounces or whatever it weighed. Maybe it was Sofia's way of taking Emilie on the trip with her.

Her mother was trudging towards her, bundled up in her duvet jacket and hat.

Sofia thrust her poles into the snow, and Elise held out her arms, taking Sofia's hands in her own.

'Promise me you'll be careful,' she said.

Sofia smiled. Then, seeing the solemnity in her mamma's face, she killed the smile.

'I promise,' she said, dipping her head.

'Have fun,' Elise said. Spoken like an instruction.

'We will.' The plumes of Sofia's breath mixed with those of her mother.

'And look after your pappa,' Elise said.

31

The smile crept back to Sofia's lips, settling there like a cat in a basket.

'I will, Mamma,' she said, pretending to be embarrassed by the attention.

Elise pulled off a glove, thrust a hand into her coat pocket and pulled out a folded piece of paper. 'Just a little note for later,' she said, unzipping a pocket on Sofia's green jacket, sliding the folded sheet inside and zipping it back up again. Then she put her hands either side of Sofia's pink birthday hat and pulled her head towards her, planting a kiss on both cheeks and her forehead.

'Maybe we'll all go next time,' he said, looking at Elise as he pulled a glove off the ski pole stuck in the snow in front of him.

She lifted one eyebrow to meet the rim of her woollen hat. 'We'll need a bigger tent,' she said, which wasn't a *no*, and he smiled, thinking she looked beautiful. She came over to him and put her arms around him and they held each other.

'I love you,' she said, her skin pressed hard against his cheek.

'I love you too.' He sent the words into the rough fabric of her hat.

They stood like that for a moment, then she pulled away so their eyes could meet in the dark.

'Ready?' he asked Sofia.

'Yes,' she said, resolute. Mittened hands clenching and unclenching around the grips of the poles.

He tried to imagine Emilie standing there on her skis, leaning forward on her poles, eager to set off. For a terrible, aching heartbeat the image formed and he saw her. And the pain of it flooded through him. He could bear it no longer and so he turned and looked at the pulk at the end of the poles three and a half metres behind him, running an inventory in his mind of everything he had packed for the trip.

'Give me a second,' he said. Because first he needed Emilie to go. Needed that ground beside Sofia to be undisturbed again, a pristine patch of snow in the darkness. And so he started whispering the things they needed. 'Sunglasses. Ski goggles. Sun cream. Spare rope for the pulk. Spare socks. Snow probe.' It had taken them most of the previous day to prepare and pack for the trip. Thermal base layers, microfibre layers, shell jackets, shell pants, woollen ski socks, their down jackets. An ice axe, a snow shovel. He gave each item its own moment. A reverence. *Cooking stove, spare gas, matches, first aid kit.*

'OK, I'm ready.' He lifted a ski pole into the air to signal that this was it.

Thrusting the pole into the snow, he pushed down with his weighted leg while kicking forward onto his gliding leg, and they were off, with the pulk hissing through the snow behind him.

They moved across the snow as smoothly as shadow. Kick and glide. Kick and glide.

'Be safe!' Elise shouted, the words hanging in their wake.

Erik lifted a pole in answer. And then it was just the two of them out there in the moon and snow-silvered dark. Making tracks where before there were none.

They skied west as the day crept up on the world behind them, then followed a valley that snaked north between hills cloaked in snow-laden pines. Sofia skied well and he was proud of her. The two of them lost in the rhythm, their diagonal stride fluid and efficient and eating up the ground, Sofia following in the tracks he carved through the deep snow.

They skied for three hours, with just one break to rest their legs, throw back a cup of black coffee each and share a *Kvikk Lunsj* chocolate bar, which Sofia enjoyed infinitely more than the coffee. Then on, two specs of colour in a white world, their tracks stitching the virgin snow.

For lunch they stopped amongst the trees, where Erik took the shovel from the pulk and dug a bench in the snow for them to sit on as they ate cheese and salami sandwiches. He didn't mind the silence between them but wondered if she did.

'You warm enough?' he asked. He could feel the sweat cooling on his own skin and didn't want her to get cold now they were no longer moving.

'I'm fine,' she said.

He looked at her skis and poles where she had stood them neatly next to his. She had watched him wax his skis, then he had watched her wax her own, and she had done it with great care, reverence almost.

'Do you still want to sleep in the tent tonight?' he asked. He had planned a circular tour, skiing around the western edge of the Strupbreen glacier, up to Blåvatnet Lake, then heading east to Stor Reindalstinden, going around the great mountain before following the edge of the fjord back south to Koppangen.

'Yes,' she said, frowning at him as though she feared he was changing his mind.

'Because there's a hut at the foot of Tvillingstinden. It would be warmer.'

'I want to stay in the tent,' she said. That frown line between her eyes. Just like her mother's. 'You said we could. You said that at least for one night we could stay in the tent. And the first night would be best because we're fresh and everything's dry.'

He raised a hand in surrender. 'We can,' he said, smiling. 'Of course we can.'

She nodded. Relieved. When they'd finished, they put on their rucksacks and clipped into their skis and Sofia asked if he thought anyone else would sit on the snow bench he had made.

'I think it'll snow again before anyone comes this way, and it'll be covered,' he said. Her expression was inscrutable. He couldn't tell if she was disappointed it would be gone or pleased that it was theirs and theirs alone. 'And anyway,' he continued, 'it's another three weeks before people start coming here to ski. Only the serious skiers come out here in February.'

A look of pride on her face. That at least he could read.

'Look, Pappa!'

He followed her outstretched arm to see an eagle soaring above the open ground across which they had come.

'Maybe it's hunting,' he said. They scanned the horizon for the bird's prey, but saw nothing. Suddenly the eagle partially closed its wings and entered a low-angled glide, picking up speed as it drew its wings tighter. Just above the snow, its wings opened, its tail fanned and it thrust its feet forward and they heard a sound like a thunder clap from those great wings whipping the air.

'Can we go and see?' she asked.

'We can go a bit closer,' he said. They skied out of the

trees into the open, beneath the heavy sky, keeping within their own tracks to save energy. But the eagle saw them or sensed them, and beat up into the wan day, silent as snowfall.

With the great bird an ever-decreasing speck in the distance, they skied to the spot where the eagle had landed, and there they found a mountain hare in its white winter coat. Wads of its fur lay scattered around, shivering in the breeze, though the hare itself was still. They stood there, the two of them, gazing down at it, broken and dead, its life crushed by the eagle's talons.

Three spots of blood lay on the snow, bright and startling in the overcast day. He wondered if Sofia was thinking about Emilie. If she recalled the sight of her sister lying broken on the rubber mat at the foot of the climbing wall in south London.

He remembered the look on Sofia's face as she had stared at Emilie. At the bone poking through the broken skin. At the blood. The impossible angles.

'Let's go,' he said.

As the day retreated, they turned to the north and started to climb. Twice they stopped and attached skins to the undersides of their skis. One ascent was so steep that they spent forty-five minutes laboriously side-stepping up the hill, pushing the metal edges into the snow to keep from sliding back down.

It was hard going for a young girl, and several times she stopped to catch her breath and he knew she was frustrated and that the muscles in her thighs would be raging. But she didn't complain. And he didn't make a fuss of her when they reached the summit and stood looking back at the many hundreds of marks they had made in getting there.

'Do your jacket up, Lillemor,' he told her, because she had got warm with the effort of the climb and unzipped her windbreaker. They shared the rest of the coffee in his flask, and Sofia asked if they could make a fire later, and he said they could. Then they skied on towards the Koppangsbreen glacier, looking for a good place to make camp for the night.

'Do you think the eagle found the hare again?' she asked.

'I'm sure it did,' he said.

'But it would be harder to see because it wasn't moving,' she said.

He thought about that. 'It would see the blood.'

'And our tracks,' she said.

'And our tracks.'

They found a good place, away from the base of any slope to avoid the possibility of a snowslide, where a bank of fir trees offered a windbreak. The snow was too thick to dig out with the shovel, so they put on their snowshoes and spent a while stamping it down, then gathered firewood while waiting for the snow to firm up.

He let Sofia choose how to orient the tent and she did it right, with the entrance across the wind, which was gathering strength now as darkness came upon the world. They dug the pegs in horizontally and stamped down the snow around them, letting the wind freeze them in position for fifteen minutes before tightening the guylines. With the shovel he built an arrow-shaped wall pointing into the wind, so that if it snowed, and he thought it would, the snow would be blown against the wall or else right over the tent instead of burying it. But he told her that if it got even quieter in the night, she should wake him, because it might mean the wind had changed and snow was covering the tent and he would have to clear it off.

They piled snow around the skirt of the tent to stop wind or snow getting in underneath, then set to work inside, digging out a hole in the vestibule so they could sit on the edge with their feet in the trench and organize their gear.

As they arranged their sleeping bags and other equipment, he realized he'd been wrong to go back on his promise about the trip. It would have been unfair to deny her this. He knew she was capable, and that his fears were not her fears.

When it was all done, he was hungry and saw she was shivering, so he stomped down an area near the tent for a fire and made a platform with some of the sticks they had gathered. Then he feathered some dead wood with his knife and Sofia arranged the kindling in a tepee around it. Soon the fire was crackling and flames were questing in the dark and they sat on their mats and watched it as if it were a god being born and they were the first humans.

Later, when the flames had died down but the fuel was hot, they emptied a brick of frozen beef and vegetable stew into a pan and set it over the fire until it was bubbling. Even though they had only been skiing for a day, both agreed it was the best meal they had ever eaten. They made a pact not to tell this to Sofia's mother.

After dinner, he scoured out the pan with snow and boiled water for hot chocolate. They sat in their sleeping bags, cupping their mugs in their hands, blowing and slurping at the chocolate as if it were some mysterious elixir they had chanced upon in a glacial crevasse.

'How are your feet?' he asked her.

'Fine,' she said, wiggling them in the bottom of her sleeping bag.

'No blisters?'

'I don't think so. My legs ache from the climbing,' she admitted.

'Mine too,' he said.

The wind was getting up. Moving across the canvas like hands trying to get inside. He had put their rucksacks on the other side of Sofia, as a buffer against the tent wall. In his military training, when they had built igloos and snow holes to sleep in, they had always put the least experienced recruits in the middle of the group, away from the ice walls. But there had been another reason why he had lain the rucksacks there and not in the vestibule. He'd not wanted it to be obvious that there was room for another ground mat, another sleeping bag. Another person. He told himself he had done it for Sofia, but he knew he had done it for himself.

'Can you show me how to feather sticks for the fire, Pappa? In case we have another one tomorrow night.' She showed him her watch. 'It's too early to go to sleep.'

'We'll be in a warm hut tomorrow night,' he said.

'But still, I should learn,' she said. She was deploying her most disarming smile, the one she knew took four or five years off her, and so off him too. A smile from simpler times. 'We could have a fire in the morning?' she suggested. 'To make your coffee?'

It was getting cold. Their breath was clouding inside the tent and though she hadn't seemed to notice the temperature drop yet, or at least hadn't complained of it, it might not be a bad idea to give her something to do, something else to think about.

'We'll use Mr Helgeland's knife to split the wood,' he said.

'You mean my knife,' she corrected him, already up to her elbows in her birthday rucksack. Looking for it.

'Your knife,' he agreed, pulling on his ski boots.

He went outside to fetch some of the sticks lying beside the still-flickering fire. He looked up at the sky. It was all cloud. Moving fast into the east. The wind in his face and hissing into the dying fire had more spite in it now. He knew that if he'd brought the thermometer from the tent it would show a fall of two or three degrees.

They had checked the weather forecast several times the previous day, and though there had been mention of a winter storm in Greenland, the experts had been almost certain it wouldn't spread towards Iceland and the Norwegian Sea. He hoped they were right, because tomorrow they would be crossing the glacier and there would be nowhere to hide from the wind out there.

He split and feathered the first stick to show her again how it was done, then handed her the knife. She stood the piece of birch on its end in the foothole he had dug in the vestibule, then set the blade along the top of it, making sure there was plenty sticking out beyond the log. She took another piece of birch and brought it down upon the spine of the knife, striking it repeatedly, driving the blade in to split the wood, just like he had shown her. But then the blade must have come to a knot in the wood, because it stuck fast. She grabbed the hilt, trying to free the knife from the grip of the wood, and he was telling her to stop, but it was too late, and she slipped, and the blade sliced through her cotton gloves into the pad of soft flesh below her thumb. She didn't make a sound.

'Shit,' he said, taking her hand towards the lantern and carefully pulling off the glove. They both looked at the cut and he swore again.

'Sorry, Pappa,' she said. Her eyes were wide with shock. Not pain. Not yet, because the knife was sharp, but the pain would come soon, he knew.

He took her other hand and put it around the cut. 'Hold it tight.' He fetched the first aid kit from the pulk, glanced over his shoulder. 'Tighter!' he said. Blood was spilling out from under her hand. He could hear the *tap, tap* of it on the ground mat. His stomach knotted.

'It'll be OK,' he said, tearing open the packet with his teeth and unspooling the dressing. He took her hand again. 'The knife was clean. We'll stop the bleeding. It'll be OK.'

She looked away, to the back of the tent.

'Do you feel faint?' he asked.

'No,' she said. Then she said, 'A bit.'

He wound the dressing around her hand, nice and tight. It needed to be tight.

'I feel dizzy, Pappa.'

'I'm nearly done.'

He tied off the bandage, then lifted the lantern and brought it closer to see if the blood was soaking through. It wasn't.

'I was telling you to stop,' he said.

'I'm sorry,' she said. She was crying now.

'It's not your fault,' he told her.

'It hurts.'

'I know it does,' he said.

He saw that she was shivering. 'It's my fault. I shouldn't have let you use the knife.'

She was holding the injured hand in her other hand, and tears were rolling down her face.

'Wait here,' he said. He went outside into the dark and strapped her skis and poles to the pulk. He fetched their sleeping bags and put them in the pulk too, along with Sofia's rucksack and a few other things from the tent.

'Where are we going?' she asked.

'The Helgelands aren't far from here,' he said. 'Five or six kilometres west.'

'That's a long way,' she said.

'It's nothing,' he said.

Then he helped her into her boots and her jacket, pulled her hat onto her head, and she got into the pulk and he covered her with the sleeping bags. She couldn't ski because the bandage around her right hand was thick and she wouldn't be able to grip the pole.

'We'll be there soon and then we'll take a proper look at that cut,' he said.

'But it'll be heavy,' she said from the pulk.

'No, it won't,' he said, doing up the harness. 'It's a good sled. It runs like butter off a hot knife.'

They set off into the night. Into the cold wind, which dragged tears from his eyes and ran them across his cheeks, because it was too dark to wear his ski goggles. He looked over his shoulder, trying to fix in his mind the shadowy landscape and the tent within it, so he could come back in the morning.

He had left the lantern on, and its light made a soft bloom that touched the canvas walls but did not penetrate into the night beyond. And he thought that, sitting there in front of the frozen fir trees, the tent looked like a fragile little sanctuary at the end of the world.

But now it was in the past, and only the child in the pulk mattered to him. He skied hard. Adrenaline gave him strength and anger heated his blood. He should not have taken Sofia on the trip. She wasn't ready and he should have known it. Really, he *had* known it, hadn't he?

Three times they stopped so he could check his GPS compass and map against his memory of the map on the sat nav display the night they had driven up to the Helgelands' house. While he got his bearings, he would plant his poles at his sides for balance, lift up one ski at a time and bang it down and forward, to clear off any snow stuck to the underside. Then he got going again, finding his rhythm, choosing his route based on what little he could see from the soft residue of moon or starlight seeping through the cloud and reflecting off the snowbound land.

Now and then, he called to Sofia over his shoulder, to check she was OK and not cold, and she answered that she wasn't cold but he knew she was crying still.

'We'll be there soon,' he told her, but did not speak often because the wind snatched his words away, flinging them into the night, and the pulk was heavy and he needed his breath.

But he was strong. The wind against him was unequal to him, and he strode through the deepening snow, the pulk whispering along at his rear.

They'd been moving for over an hour when he began to fear he had made a mistake with the map or the compass, or that his memory of the sat nav had betrayed him, because there was no sign of the Helgelands' place. The shape of the mountains looming in the dark looked familiar. He thought he was skiing across the frozen lake around whose edge they had driven, but he couldn't see the house. Had seen no other habitation at all. And the fear grew in his belly like the ice forming beneath his skis.

*I could turn around*, he thought. *Go back to the tent and wait until morning*. But he knew their tracks were already being buried, and what if he couldn't find the tent? They couldn't stay out in a snowstorm.

He kept going. The snow stinging his face. The rhythmic gush of his own blood booming loud in his ears, relentless as a ticking clock.

Maybe the Helgelands had gone out and he couldn't see their house because they'd turned off all the lights. Or maybe he'd brought them to another mountain. Another frozen lake.

And then he saw it. In the far distance. Nestled at the foot of the mountain, swaddled in the Arctic night. The yellow glow of the windows and the movie-projector throw of light across the snow beyond them.

The home of Lars and Karine Helgeland.

# 5

KARINE AND LARS answered the door together, no doubt disquieted that someone should be out wandering at night and in a snowstorm. Their obvious surprise at seeing him and Sofia standing there was matched only by their eagerness to get them inside and warm.

As Erik closed the door, snow swirled into the house, as though the storm was reaching out a hand, making one last grab for him. Then it was gone and they were safe, and for a while he stood in the Helgelands' living room, watching Karine fuss over Sofia, and Lars opening up the woodburning stove to rebuild the dying fire. Adrenaline still fluttered in the muscles of his thighs and shivered in his heart, and he was afraid of what might have been.

Karine made them mugs of hot milk and honey, and Lars poured Erik a brandy and a small one for himself. He sat opposite Erik and asked where they had camped and what route they had planned to take on the tour.

'You did well to find us out here and in the dark,' Karine said, glancing up at him from where she sat beside Sofia, gently unwinding the dressing on the palm of her hand. She pressed a wad of cotton wool onto a bottle of antiseptic ointment and tipped the bottle upside down. 'This will sting a little, dear,' she said, then dabbed the cut, which to Erik's relief had stopped bleeding. Sofia winced, sucking air between her lips. 'How on earth did you do it?' Karine asked, taking a bottle of skin glue from the first aid box and giving it a shake.

Sofia looked at Erik. 'On a knife,' she said. 'Trying to split wood for the fire.'

Lars shook his head in silent self-reproach, acknowledging his culpability to Erik. But Erik owed the Helgelands his own apology for his behaviour over dinner two nights ago, and said so. 'I was out of line the other night,' he told them, wrapping his hands around the mug of hot milk and locking eyes with Lars.

'Don't even think of it,' Lars said, batting his confession away.

They drank. 'We're old-fashioned people up here in the mountains,' Lars said. 'We don't much care for change. But sometimes we have to accept it.' He shrugged. 'What else can we do?'

Erik thought about that. He nodded. 'We keep moving forward,' he said, looking over at Sofia. Thinking of all the tears his family had shed over the last ten months.

'There we go.' Karine lifted Sofia's hand towards the table lamp to examine her work. 'I'll wrap it again, but not too thick like your *far* did it.' She lifted an eyebrow at Erik. 'Was he trying to wrap you up like an Egyptian mummy?'

Karine prepared the spare room for them, and Erik thanked her and said he wouldn't call Elise now because it was late and she would be asleep. She would only worry about Sofia for the rest of the night if he told her what had happened.

'Good idea,' Lars agreed. 'Call in the morning, then I'll give you a ride back to your camp on the snowmobile to fetch the rest of your things. When you're ready and Sofia's feeling up to it, you can set off home again.' He sipped his brandy.

'Unless, of course, you decide to carry on with your trip,' Karine said, coming back into the room and perching on the arm of the couch next to Sofia.

Sofia looked at him hopefully. He gave the slightest shake of his head, forewarning her that that was not going to happen, and seeing this, Karine squeezed her good hand in sympathy.

'Thank you both for your hospitality,' Erik said. He had finished the milk and the brandy, and now he stood. Nodded to Lars. 'We've kept you up long enough.' He glanced at the clock in the kitchen. Eleven p.m. Not late really, but probably later than the Helgelands liked to stay up.

Lars stood without argument. 'Well . . .' He clapped his big hands together like some formal signal of the closing of proceedings. 'Please, treat our home as your own,' he said, bending to the stove to draw the air vents across, dampening the flames within, while Karine gathered up the mugs and glasses and took them through to the kitchen.

'Goodnight, Mrs Helgeland,' Sofia said.

Karine nodded at her good manners. 'You sleep well now, Sofia, and we'll have a nice breakfast in the morning.'

\*

He was woken by the high-pitched growl of engines, like a swarm of angry bees out there in the night. It took him a moment to remember where he was. Sofia lay fast asleep next to him, so he eased out from beneath the blankets and went over to the window, the old floorboards creaking with every step. Moving the curtain aside, he saw snowmobiles approaching the house, chewing up the snow, their LED headlight beams slashing the night, now and then flooding the house and his room with light as the machines crossed the Helgelands' undulating, snow-blanketed meadow.

The motor sleds pulled up in front of the house in a neat line. Four men dismounted and trudged to the door, while beyond his bedroom he heard feet on the landing, then descending the stairs, as a fist hammered a five-beat tattoo on the front door.

He opened the bedroom door a crack and could hear men with thick accents talking to Lars downstairs. Karine was there too. He heard one of the men apologize to her for waking them up. Not police. Not with those accents. He tried to guess why four men would just ride up here in the night and bang on the Helgelands' door, but could come up with no answer. He looked back over his shoulder to check that Sofia was still sleeping, then opened the door wider and stepped out onto the landing, slow and quiet, not wanting to be seen in his underwear and T-shirt, but also ... not wanting to be seen.

He stood on the landing to watch and listen. Sheltered in the shadow. Peering between the banister rails, he felt like the child he had once been, spying on the guests at the Christmas parties his parents had held at their home. Amongst the group he recognized the tall man from town who had helped him repack his cans of beer. Stood beside him, sweeping a red NYC beanie off his head to reveal his short white hair, was the one who had made him spill the shopping in the first place. He didn't recognize the other two, but one of them asked Lars for a drink, to put some heat inside them after the ride up here, and Lars fetched a bottle of vodka from the cocktail cabinet.

'What are you doing here at my house at this hour?' Lars asked the men, moving warily amongst them as he poured each a glass. 'This is not the way things are done. If Novotroitsk Nickel has something to say to us, they can do it at the town meetings.'

'Or on the Facebook page,' Karine put in, tightening the belt on her dressing gown, then folding her arms over her bosom. She had planted herself between the kitchen and the living room and stood there like a mountain.

The tall man thanked Lars for the drink. 'This is no more than a courtesy call,' he assured them. 'We would have been here earlier. Some trouble with one of the sleds.' He tipped his head towards the window as he drank. 'You don't expect that from a Japanese machine.' He shrugged. 'They're probably made in America.' He drank again. 'We want to reassure you, and all the good people around here, that Novotroitsk Nickel takes your concerns seriously.' He looked from Lars to Karine. 'The company is determined to do nothing that will upset you or harm this . . . beautiful land.'

The tall man lifted his glass to Lars and Karine in turn and downed the contents. The other three men had already drunk theirs and begun helping themselves from Lars's bottle.

'The company just wants you to dial down the protests.'

The tall man smiled and pinched his thumb and forefinger together. 'A little.' It wasn't just the scar running through his lips that made his smile unsettling.

'Novotroitsk Nickel knows the impact reopening the mine will have on the environment,' Karine said, 'and on the grazing land. We won't turn a blind eye.'

'You misunderstand me, Mrs Helgeland,' the tall man said. He put the empty glass down and reached inside his jacket. 'We would like to make a small contribution to your cause. A . . . *gesture* of goodwill.'

He held out an envelope which was fat enough to suggest it contained a considerable amount of cash. 'To help the Sami people who have been mistreated in both our countries for so many years.'

He saw Karine shake her head at her husband, but Lars took the envelope and Erik let the breath he hadn't realized he was holding escape, relieved that Lars did not refuse the offering. He could practically smell the violence coming off these men like vodka fumes. He took a step back from the banister, into darker shadow, but did not leave.

'I don't think we can make the next couple of protests anyway,' Lars told the tall man. 'I have enough to do around here.' He looked at Karine. 'It would be a good time to start work on the barn.' He turned back to the tall man. 'The roof beams are rotten. Need replacing.'

The tall man nodded. 'Honest work, Mr Helgeland,' he said. Behind him, the other three men were making themselves at home. The one with the white hair was by the window, going through the contents of the wooden box on the sill: the horn needle case, the leather purse with tin thread embroidery, examining each object as if it were something from another time. Another world. His companion, a shorter, bull-necked man, was poking an iron into the fire.

He couldn't see the fourth man.

The tall man turned to Karine, his head leaning to one side as if he could see something in her which needed exploring, and it gave Erik a very bad feeling. 'What about you, Mrs Helgeland?' the man said. 'Will you be too busy for all this . . . protesting? Like your husband?'

Karine locked eyes with the man. Gave no response.

The tall man picked up a carriage clock from the mantle and held it against his ear for a moment, seeming to appreciate the quiet *tick, tick* of the second hand. 'You know, we have a saying where I come from,' he said. '*Volki syty – ovtsy tsely*. It means, the wolves are fed and the sheep . . . are safe.' He put the clock back and smiled at Karine. 'Think carefully now, Mrs Helgeland. For the sake of the sheep.'

Karine looked at her husband. There was steel in her eyes, and Erik felt a tightening in his guts. He crept gingerly back to the bedroom and knelt by the bed, put his hand on Sofia's head.

'Sofia, wake up,' he whispered. She stirred and gave a quiet murmur. He kissed her cheek. 'Wake up, Lillemor,' he said, and she opened her eyes, confused for a moment, as if she didn't know where she was or how she had got there. He ushered her out of bed and pressed a finger to his lips, then fetched her clothes from the chair at the foot of the bed and gave them to her. 'Hurry,' he hissed.

'What is it, Pappa?' she whispered, her eyes wide as she pulled her thermal base layer on over her head.

'Shhh. Quickly,' he said, climbing into his own layers. Then they both heard Karine Helgeland's raised voice telling the men downstairs to get out, and there was something in her tone that made Sofia move faster, made her pull on her shell trousers like they were flameproof and a fire was coming.

Erik edged back to the door and out onto the landing, pressing himself into the gloom of the wall, looking down onto the living area.

'We will not betray our people,' Karine told the tall man.

'Karine,' Lars growled, then showed the tall man his palms. 'My wife is proud,' he said, 'that's all. We don't want any trouble.'

The tall man considered those words for a moment, then turned and walked over to the window. He stood with his back to them all, looking out across the snow. 'Your husband accepted my money, Mrs Helgeland,' he said, his breath fogging the glass. 'Where I come from, it is considered bad manners to return a gift.'

'I don't care where you come from,' Karine said, then lifted her chin at Lars. 'Give him back his money,' she told him, gesturing at the tall man's back. Lars shook his head, and Karine bared her teeth and pointed at the tall man, who was still gazing into the silent night surrounding them. 'There is no agreement between us, may my ancestors witness it. Now get out of my house.'

Erik wondered at the resolution in her voice, the certainty, the bravery.

The white-haired man stepped towards her and Erik saw the pistol in his hand, which he shoved beneath Karine's chin, forcing it upwards.

'Stupid fucking woman,' the man sneered.

Lars lunged at the man with his big hands, but the man twisted, fast as a snake, and whipped the pistol across Lars's temple. It happened both impossibly fast and in slow motion. Lars's legs buckled and he fell sideways, his head striking the hearth with a sickening crack of bone.

'Shit, Konstantin!' the bull-necked man said.

Karine screamed. Erik's blood froze. His limbs became numb weights, even as his heart thumped against his breastbone.

'You idiot,' the tall man said to his colleague with the pistol, striding over to Lars's unmoving body.

'Chill out, big brother,' the white-haired man said, shoving his pistol back into the belted waistband of his trousers as the tall man crouched and pressed two fingers against Lars's neck. Five seconds. Ten seconds. He rolled Lars over, revealing the pool of blood spreading beneath the man's cracked skull. Growled something filthy in Russian.

'What have you done?' Karine asked the tall man, her voice small but her eyes bulging. She lifted her hands, pressing them to the sides of her face. 'What have you done?' Louder now. With venom.

Erik's body came back to him and he moved as quietly as he could back to the bedroom. He passed Sofia, who stood petrified by the bed, undid the window catch and slid it slowly up. Snow and wind swirled into the room like the cold breath of a demon.

'Hurry,' he said, grabbing Sofia's hat and pushing it onto her head, then helping her up onto the window ledge.

'Pappa!' she hissed.

'Shh! I'll lower you down,' he whispered.

Squatting on the sill, she turned back towards the room and Erik took both of her hands in his own.

Downstairs there was a clatter of furniture and Karine

screamed again. He heard one of the men yell at her to run. That they would give her a five-minute head start.

'Ready?' Erik asked Sofia.

'But, Pappa . . .' she gasped.

'We have to go,' he said. 'Just hold tight.' So she did, and she slipped her feet over the edge. He braced, then leant forward, lowering her down against the outside planks of the house.

Then the Helgelands' front door slammed open and he saw Karine run out into the snow, her nightgown flying behind her, slippered feet plunging through the moon-washed drifts.

'Don't let go! Not yet!' he told Sofia, whose cheek was pressed against the wall of the house. Because the tall man walked out into the night, as casually as if he were stepping out for a smoke, and went to one of the snowmobiles, where he pulled a hunting rifle from a scabbard and screwed on the suppressor.

'Don't move, Lillemor,' he said, looking up to see the other three men come out onto the snow. They were laughing. Konstantin was carrying the vodka bottle. Another had brought the glasses.

'I can't hold on, Pappa.' Her eyes were desperate. Round with fear.

'I've got you,' he hissed into the biting wind. 'Just keep still.'

His back was screaming at him and he gritted his teeth against the pain as he watched the tall man draw the bolt to chamber a round. Push the bolt forward and lift the rifle. Plant the stock into his right shoulder, put the scope to his eye. The whole manoeuvre performed with the smooth efficiency of perfect muscle memory.

Karine Helgeland had managed seventy to eighty metres across the snow, but the treeline was still another twenty metres away. She didn't make it. The bullet took her in the back and she dropped face first into the snow as the bull-whip sound of the shot split the night.

'Don't move,' Erik begged Sofia, and lowered his head to hide his face as the tall man turned back towards the house. Back towards them. Then he slung the rifle over his shoulder and trudged back into the bloom of the electric light.

The second Erik heard the door shut, he breathed again.

'Was that . . . a gun?' The whites of her eyes looking up at him were luminous.

'I'm going to swing you out and let go.'

'No, Pappa,' she said.

'It's OK. I'll be right behind you. Ready? One . . . two . . . three.'

He braced and swung her as best he could and she dropped into the drifts below. He grabbed her rucksack and threw it after her, then threw his own and climbed out of the window, lowering himself until he was hanging from the ledge. Glancing down to check that he wouldn't be landing on her, he pushed himself off and hit with a *crump*.

But the store was on the other side of the house and the curtains at every window were open. Because the Helgelands loved those mountain views. Because there was nobody around to look in.

'Stay behind me and stay low,' he told Sofia as she thrust her arms through the shoulder straps and clipped the ruck-sack on.

'What's happening, Pappa?' She was crouching beside

55

him, looking out towards where Karine's body lay unmoving. Still as a rock. 'Did they shoot Mrs Helgeland?'

'We have to go. It's OK but we have to go.' His whole body was shaking but he kept the tremor from his voice.

'I'm scared,' she said.

He grabbed her shoulders and pulled her close so that all she could see was his eyes. 'I'm here, Sofia. With you. It's going to be OK. If we go *now*.'

She nodded, uncertain and afraid but willing to trust him.

He set off along the side of the house and she followed, both of them keeping low, close enough to the wall that he could smell the tar-based oil in the planks. When they came to the big living-room window, they crawled on their hands and knees, and he saw from the shadow on the snow that someone was standing at the window, looking out.

He stopped and Sofia stopped too. He dared not breathe for fear they would see the rising vapour of his breath. And he looked at the four snowmobiles lined up by the front door and wondered if the men had left the keys in them. But if they hadn't, and the two of them were seen from the porch window . . . The risk was too great.

The shadow retreated across the snow and so they crawled on, and once clear of any windows, they stood and plunged towards the store beside the house. He told Sofia to wait and watch the house while he eased the door open and slipped inside. Lars's snowmobile sat there, bright and red like a beacon, but he couldn't find the key for the ignition and so he fetched his and Sofia's skis and dragged the pulk outside.

'Can you ski?' he asked her, gesturing at her right hand. At least she had managed to get her mitten over the dressing Karine had put on.

'Yes,' she said.

They clipped into their skis and he put on the pulk harness, and imagined one of the men in the house noticing the four mugs on the kitchen sideboard. Or the two brandy glasses. Or one of them going upstairs and seeing the unmade bed in the spare room. The open window.

'We'll have to go fast,' he said. 'As fast as you can.'

Sofia nodded.

He lifted his ski pole and pointed it towards the woods. 'We'll get to the trees,' he said. 'Don't look back at the house. Don't look at anything but the trees, OK?'

'That's Mrs Helgeland, isn't it?' she asked. Staring across the snow. He could see she was trembling. Breathing too fast. A hair away from full-on, limb-freezing panic.

'I said look at the trees,' he snapped. She tore her eyes from Karine's body and stared towards the woods instead. 'Ready?'

'Yes,' she said.

'Go!' They kicked off, the hiss of their skis too loud. They raced across the snow, and he felt like a mouse making a run for it beneath the owl's perch. Then he heard a shout behind them. From inside the house. He risked a glance over his shoulder and saw a man appear at the open guest-room window through which they had made their escape.

'Hey, you! Stop!' the man yelled, then turned and let rip a torrent of what sounded like Russian to the others in the house.

'Faster!' Erik barked at Sofia, and he caught a glimpse of Karine Helgeland as they skied past her. Of her dark hair. Her grey cotton nightgown rippling in the wind. Her blood staining the snow.

When they reached the fir trees, he told Sofia to keep on going. Turning back one last time, he saw the tall man stride back out into the snow, and for a heart-clenching moment their eyes locked across the distance, through the dark.

He turned back to the trees and saw Sofia skiing between them, her arms and legs striding out. Perfection and power, as she raced away.

'Go, Sofia!' he shouted, as behind him the snowmobiles growled into life and the beams of their headlights stabbed amongst the trees around him. 'Go!' he yelled again.

And he skied after her.

Light flooded the woods, obliterating the night, making in its place an unnatural day, revealing naked fir trunks and snow-laden boughs and everything that should have lain hidden in darkness.

A bullet *thunked* into a tree beside him, sending a bright chip flying as the *whip crack* of that bullet breaking the sound barrier followed.

'Down! Get down!' he shouted, and ahead of him Sofia dropped sideways into the snow, but he couldn't because of the pulk, so he crouched, hauling breath into his lungs, his right arm wrapped around a slender tree for balance.

*Don't move*, he willed Sofia. Not daring to call out to her again. *Please. Don't move.*

The four men had ridden their snowmobiles to the edge of the wood, the vehicles idling now, as if all the power of their Yamaha engines was being used to pour that deluge of cold white light into the night. Erik didn't move a muscle, because there were trees behind him and he squatted in their shadow, the light surging into the woods on either side. Sofia was about forty ski strides away. He could see some of her blue rucksack sticking out over the top of a drift. A sliver of her green jacket. Not lit by the headlights of the snowmobiles, but not fully in darkness either. She lay at the edge of the light bloom, as if trapped between two worlds. A soul in purgatory, awaiting some final judgement.

*Stay still*, he told her in his mind, hoping the men beyond the trees back there couldn't see what he was seeing. And she *was* still. So still that for a sudden, heart-stopping second he feared that she had been shot.

No. There was movement. Or rather, it was the absence of complete stillness. The slightest rise and fall of the rucksack as she breathed. Barely noticeable, like a trick of the eye, a moving image generated by his own desperate will.

But he dared not call out to her in case they heard him over the sled engines. Then the petrol rumble of the machines lessened and the wash of light amongst the trees dimmed, so that much of the wood fell in darkness again. He could hear the men shouting to one another. He stood, painfully slowly, keeping within a slender finger of shadow still, but leaning his left shoulder against a fir trunk and peering back the way he had come.

In the glare of the lights he saw two of the men fetching skis and equipment from their sleds. One of them walked in front of his companion's Yamaha, and his shadow was hurled deep into the woods, like some misshapen giant out to get them – a *stallo* of Sami legend perhaps. A disembodied presence amongst the trees.

Then the two snowmobiles still idling growled into life and turned side on, one tearing off one way, the other heading in the opposite direction around the edge of the woods, their engines screaming with the thrill of the chase.

*Now!*

Erik bent forward, lifting his heels off the bindings, stiffening his arms and shoulders and planting the poles in the snow just beyond the toe of his boots before applying his weight, then his abdominal muscles, then his back muscles to the poles and pulling himself forward.

'Get up, Sofia!' he yelled, bending, planting the poles and pulling, feeling the lateral muscles stretch in his back, then swinging the poles forward again. 'Go!'

She got up on her skis and, like him, began double-poling between the trees.

'Faster!' he called. 'Don't stop! Don't you stop, no matter what!'

A tree two metres ahead threw splinters and a loud crack made Erik pull his head into his shoulders, though he knew he was reacting to the sound after the bullet had passed. Had it been on target, he wouldn't have heard a thing, and Sofia would now be alone in the night.

But Sofia was fast, sometimes double-poling, sometimes striding, weaving between the firs like a breeze, and he couldn't catch her. Harder for him because of the pulk. Not because of the weight; it wasn't heavy. But because he had to choose a path wide enough for the pulk to pass through after him. Yet he didn't consciously think about it, just let his brain and body decide for him in a thousand split-second decisions – an act of lightning-speed choreography in which he did not interfere other than to let himself move.

The drone of the snowmobiles was fading, the beams of their headlights far away, glimpsed only now and then as they circumnavigated the woods, their drivers looking to cut off their quarry, or perhaps seeking an easier way in, to where the trees thinned and they could ride between them.

But he couldn't worry about the motor sleds now. The two men on skis coming after them were his concern. Whoever they were, he knew they would kill him and Sofia without hesitation, and that thought lit a fire in his belly and beneath his skis, and he poled through the dim dark, his blood in spate, the relentless cadence of his breath like a mantra given up to some higher power. *Help us. Help us. Help us.*

Brittle lower branches clawed at him, snapping against his shoulders and thighs.

He couldn't see her much of the time. It was too dark and she was too far ahead, and he couldn't follow in her tracks because of the pulk. He thought he should undo the straps and leave the pulk behind, but he didn't. And whenever he caught a glimpse of her rucksack, or of the parallel furrows she had made just moments before, it was as if each sighting was a shot of oxygen in his blood, fuelling his cardiovascular system and his muscles, flooding his thumping heart with impossible strength.

He didn't know how close their pursuers were, as he couldn't risk stopping to peer into the dark woods behind him, but he had never been so afraid. Never before felt like some hunted, helpless animal.

But then, as though some fickle deity had decided to give the prey a chance, he and Sofia were given something else: true darkness. It came upon the wood and fell amongst the trees. He looked up, seeing no moon through the gaps in the fir canopy. No stars. Not even the cloud that concealed them. In front of him and all around, just the suggestion of trees. Moments before, the snow had possessed a faint luminosity, a gentle blueish glow. But that otherworldly radiance had left it now, and even the pulk three metres behind him lay hidden in the murk, and he could just make out the poles leading off to an indistinct shape on the snow.

Often, he lost almost all forward momentum, and in places the snow was so deep that he sank down into it and was reduced to a thigh-burning trudging walk that made a mockery of his skis and stole the breath from his lungs. But if that was his experience, then surely it was his pursuers' too, and maybe they would give up the chase. Maybe the will to survive was stronger than the will to destroy. He hoped this was true. He also knew that Sofia was light and agile, and even if the snow was up to two metres deep in places, he was sure she would glide upon its surface and put more ground between herself and the Helgelands' murderers.

And yet, as much as he willed her to go on, he couldn't bear the thought of her alone in this darkness. He would no more consider that possibility than allow it to happen, and so he fought on, striding or plunging through the snow for a long time, seeing more than before, his eyes adapting to this deeper dark, the moon not yet reappeared to spill its light amongst the trees.

Then he heard it. Like the sound of someone ripping the top off a soda can. He came to a stop, planting his poles beside him, looking this way and that because he had not been able to place the direction of the sound. He wanted to hold his breath so as to hear better, but he was winded and his lungs needed more air, not less. Then the sound came again and he snapped his head around to peer into the gloom to his right. But he could see nothing. Just subtle shades of black trees against grey ground. All of it somehow the more discomfiting now he was no longer occupied with the physical action of skiing. Standing there in the night, with the wind plucking at the boughs above him, with the killers somewhere behind, he felt the darkness closing in. Became aware of a dizziness swirling behind his eyes. The spreading panic of being blind and knowing that you cannot see what is trying to harm you.

'Sofia?' He hissed her name but said no more because he had no clue if the men hunting them were a thousand metres behind or fifty.

'Pappa. I'm here, Pappa.'

He skied over to her, unclipped his bindings and undid the pulk harness and plunged through the snow, throwing his arms around her and pulling her into him.

'Pappa,' she said, her shoulders bouncing, her chest heaving. She wasn't so much breathing as gasping, a fast staccato of half inhalations which he knew was short-changing her lungs of oxygen. He held her tighter still, as if by constricting her, by stopping the spasms, he might help her find the way back. 'They killed them, didn't they? I saw her. She was dead, Pappa. I saw her!'

'Shh, Lillemor, it's OK. I'm here. We're OK.'

He held her against his chest and even through the layers of their clothing he could feel her heart thumping like a trapped bird.

She pulled away before he was ready to let go.

'Are they coming?' she asked. Not looking into the darkness behind them, but into his eyes, as though only he could give her the answer she needed. 'Are they coming, Pappa?'

she said again. Even in the dark he could see her round eyes glisten with tears. Her mittened hands were shaking in his.

He hated that he couldn't give her the answer she wanted.

'I don't know,' he said. 'I think they might be. We need to go.'

Now she looked back the way they had come, and so did he.

'We need to find somewhere safe,' he said.

He unslung his rucksack and undid the straps to open the top lid. Thrust his hand inside. Withdrew his hand and went in through the side access, then patted the side pockets. He swore under his breath. Unclipped the water bottle and handed it to Sofia.

'Drink,' he said. She took the bottle with trembling hands but downed several mouthfuls without spilling any, then handed it back, and he took a mouthful.

He didn't want to ask her the next question but he had no choice.

'Did you grab the phones before we left?' he said.

Her teeth bit into her bottom lip. 'They were on the chair, I think,' she said. She drew in a deep but stuttering breath.

He lifted his chin to indicate the rucksack on her back.

'You sure you didn't pack them?'

She shook her head. 'Sorry, Pappa.'

'It's not your fault,' he said, pulling off his glove and thumbing the tears from her cheeks. 'It's my fault. I should have brought them.'

'I think I left a towel on top of them,' she said. 'That's why we didn't notice them.'

'No, you didn't. They were right there. I should have seen them. But we had to get out. It's more important that we got away, right?'

64

'But they're coming?' she said.

'I think we have to go.' He threw his rucksack over his shoulder. 'We'll find somewhere safe to hide until morning.' He grabbed for her hands again. 'Can you ski?'

She nodded.

'You're not too tired?'

'I'm fine.'

'What about your hand?'

She lifted her mittened hand and looked at it. 'It stings a bit,' she said.

He pulled the mitten off. There was fresh blood on the bandage. He nodded and held the mitten open and she pushed her hand back inside. They would deal with it later.

'Let's go,' he said, and was about to turn and go back to the pulk when she gasped, seeing something, and ducked, pointing off into the woods, her other hand pressed against her mouth as though she might scream.

He turned and saw it right away. A red light. Hard to tell how close because the light didn't throw any beam or illuminate the woods. At first he thought it was flashing, then realized the man holding it was moving amongst the trees. Not holding it, wearing it. A headlamp. The red LED moving around as the man looked this way and that. Searching for them.

His blood ran cold in his veins and he hurried to the pulk and put on the harness, then his backpack. Hissing at Sofia, he grabbed his sticks and pointed in the direction they had been heading before. She didn't move for several seconds, but just stood there on her skis, staring at him.

*Go,* he mouthed at her, not knowing if she could see the word on his lips. *Go,* he mouthed again, and she planted both poles and bent and pushed off into the darkness. He looked behind him. The red light was getting closer. He could tell that much. But at least he knew where this man was. There was another man in the woods with them. Where was he? Had he fallen behind? Maybe. Or maybe, unlike his companion, he wasn't using a headtorch, which meant they wouldn't see him, which meant he might be even closer. Might be almost upon them. Might be lifting his rifle and watching Erik through a night scope right now.

He kicked off, transferring his weight from the pushing ski to the gliding ski, feeling the power in his hips as he raced after Sofia, the pulk rasping behind him.

He thought of his cellphone, still sitting with Sofia's back there on the chair in the Helgelands' spare room. But no amount of thinking could undo what was done, could teleport those objects into his moving backpack. Maybe if Sofia hadn't left her towel on the chair, covering them, he would have thought to pack them before they climbed out of the window and dropped into the snow. Then again, in his fear and panic he would perhaps have forgotten them anyway. And at least if they were not in plain sight, there was a chance that Lars's and Karine's killers hadn't seen them either. Because what if they had? What if one of those men had Erik's phone right now and was thumbing through his contacts and messages, his most dialled numbers and his photos? What if they already knew where he lived? No. They'd had no time to search the room, he decided. The guy had shouted from the window and seconds later he and his buddies were running out into the snow and starting up their sleds.

*Don't think about it – just ski*, he told himself.

He glanced over his shoulder. No red light now, which probably meant the man had switched it off to avoid being seen.

*Just ski. Ski and don't stop.*

He knew that the military used red flashlights during night-time operations because they didn't affect your night vision as much as white light and were less visible to others. Were these men Russian ex-military? Whoever they were, he knew they would have little difficulty in following his tracks or Sofia's. They might stay ahead of their pursuers a while longer, for another two or three kilometres perhaps. But Sofia was a child. She would tire. And when she did, he would not be able to protect her.

# 6

ERIK COULD FEEL the wind on his right cheek. And the snow in that wind. It numbed his face, slanting down in the darkness. Never-ending veils plunging down and down, as if whoever had created the world had decided to wipe it clean and start again. He and Sofia skied on through the half-vanished world, and the men with guns skied after them.

But Sofia was slowing. Her gliding ski didn't travel so far now. She planted her poles with less conviction than before, and she hadn't been using the double-poling technique for a kilometre or more. He had hoped she was conserving energy, putting in less effort, just for a while. Taking an active rest. But he knew she was not. Knew her young legs must be drained by now. Her triceps and biceps fatigued, her lungs scalding, her heart beating itself empty. They had skied the whole day before making camp, and she had slept no more than three hours at the Helgelands'.

The fear in him twisted and writhed, changing into

something else. A metamorphosis taking place in his rushing blood. The dread mutating into an anger that filled his chest and his lungs.

'I can't, Pappa,' she called to him, striding, planting her poles. Striding again.

He had caught up with her and was skiing beside her now, the two of them always facing forward, weaving their way between the trees.

'Yes, you can.' Their skis hushed along together, side by side, almost silent as they skimmed across the hardpack snow.

'I'm tired,' she said. 'My arms.'

'You can do it,' he said. 'You're strong.'

She didn't answer.

On they went through the darkness. Kick and glide, kick and glide. The blood gushing in his ears. His breath deep within its own groove, an unrelenting rhythm that put him in mind of an old Charlton Heston movie where the sweat-glistening galley slaves pulled their oars in time with the beating drum. Some of those slaves fell dead from their benches, he recalled. But they didn't have this girl beside them.

*I would ski for ever*, he thought. *I would ski to the edge of the world for her.*

The ground was rising. A gentle slope but getting steeper. Leading to a pine-covered ridge.

'I can't,' Sofia said.

'Yes, you can. I'm with you. Just keep going.'

He told her to go faster. To create some momentum so they could glide up the rising ground. More effort now but rather that than slogging up to the ridge, herringboning all the way.

'That's it,' he said, because she had picked up the pace, and his heart swelled with pride. 'Keep going.'

A bird startled from its roost, beating up and away like a spirit departing the flesh, causing snow to trickle down between the fir boughs ahead.

They glided up the slope, defying gravity, skis and wax, technique, skill, strength and intuitive balance combining in a moment of perfection, and then they were atop the ridge. Sofia kept going, but he stopped and looked over his shoulder. Could see no red light through the grey vapour of his own hot breath.

He caught up with her and their strides synchronized again, and it seemed that Sofia had tapped into a reserve of strength because her skiing was fluid once more. Her strides long. Her gliding skis whispering unknown things to the land that slept beneath the snow.

And he could see her better now. Could make out individual trees at a distance and their boughs with their white burdens. The cloud in the west was thinning, allowing more moonlight into the world, like blood seeping through bandages. Ahead to the north-east, the high-pitched gnarl of a snowmobile percolated into the silence, and he feared he was running them into a trap. But he did not know what else to do, because the two men behind them were on their trail and to stop was to die.

And yet. What if they could get the man off his snowmobile? What if they could take the machine for themselves and get away?

He cursed beneath his breath and shook his head. It was impossible. He swore again, angry for letting his imagination run wild, for conjuring eventualities far beyond what was achievable. He pushed the thought away, concentrating instead on his form, ensuring his skiing was efficient, that Sofia's was too.

Still, if they kept on this course, sooner or later they would run into one of the snowmobiles prowling the northern edges of the forest. It wasn't hard to picture being caught in the blinding wash of illumination from the vehicle's head-lamps, being robbed of his vision as his pupils constricted to keep out the light. The panic, and Sofia screaming, and him reaching out for her as, somewhere beyond the white glare, the man on the snowmobile raised his rifle and squeezed the trigger.

Maybe they should cut west and double back. Try to get around the two men tracking them and race back to the Helgelands' house. But he couldn't see how. Chances were, they would run right into one of the men. Or else, seeing his and Sofia's tracks turning back on themselves, their hunters would communicate with the two on the snowmobiles, who would ride back around the woods, and he and Sofia would find themselves in the same situation. Because surely their pursuers were in contact via phones or walkie-talkies?

*So keep going*, he thought, and then he said the words out loud. For himself and for Sofia too.

And yet. What if he *could* get hold of one of the snow-mobiles? Was there a chance he could do it? And did they really stand a chance of surviving if he couldn't? If their only hope was to try out-skiing men and machines and get to town or some other safe place?

This time he did not push the idea away.

'We have to try something, Lillemor,' he said, a little while later. They were both breathing hard, vapour trailing from their mouths and noses and freezing on the air. 'We have to try to get one of their sleds.'

'No, Pappa!' she said. Planting her poles, kicking and gliding. Not looking at him but at the darkness ahead.

'We have to try,' he said. 'We can't keep this up.'

They skied between two trees, whose shoulder-height branches gave way, spilling their burdens of snow before the pulk.

'You said we'll be OK, so long as we keep skiing,' she said. She had picked up her pace as if to prove herself to him, but she had already proven herself a hundredfold and it hurt his heart to see it. He didn't want to kill her hope, but knew she couldn't go on like this. 'Let's just keep going, Pappa,' she said. 'Just . . . keep going.'

'Listen, Sofia,' he said. Snow was finding its way through the upper boughs and swirling around them, and the wind was seeking amongst the firs, freezing their tracks behind them. 'If we can steal one of their sleds, we'll get away. They won't catch us.'

She didn't answer.

They skied through the dark woods, the grating whine of the engines growing louder behind them.

'Will you help me?' he asked her.

Still she was silent.

They skied on.

After a while, she said, 'OK, Pappa.'

He was afraid. His heart was racing in his chest, as if to warn him with its beating because it had no other language. *Not this. Not this. Not this*, it said.

He had taken off his gloves to better hold the rope. His

hands were shaking. Even in the dark he could see the trembling in them and so he clenched and unclenched his fists over and over, silently telling his hands that they had always served him well and that he needed them now.

He was aware suddenly of his full bladder. After a moment's hesitation, he fumbled with his jacket and over-trousers, pulled down his inner layers and urinated onto the snow, exhaling in relief. Just as the single beam from a snowmobile's headlight shafted through the woods like the fierce-eyed glare of a cyclops searching for those who would steal his sheep. Desperately, he squeezed out the final drops and tucked himself away.

He laid the rope on the snow and looked back amongst the trees where he had left the pulk. Clipping back into his skies he moved out between the birch trees and up the gentle slope, then stopped and stuck his poles into the snow. He watched and waited as the light grew brighter.

Every instinct told him to hide. To find cover amongst the trees before the white light sweeping through the woods fell upon him and blinded him. Before the man riding the machine saw him. Before he put Sofia at such terrible risk, because what he was doing now felt like he was offering her up as some sort of sacrifice, and it sickened his stomach. But he had made his decision and would not go back on it now.

'Over here,' he said to the motor sled and its probing light. 'Right here, you son of a bitch.'

For a terrible second he thought the machine had somehow heard him, that it was more than steel and carbon, plastic and Kevlar. A living, sentient being that shared its rider's cruel intent. Because it turned and growled, its wheels like massive gears, their teeth powering the tracks and driving it forwards. Towards him.

*Run!* his mind screamed.

His muscles bunched, ready to explode into movement, but he fought against their insistence and remained still, waiting on the brow of the small slope. Because he needed to be sure.

'Here I am,' he said, peering through the fog of his own breath. Wanting the man kneeling on the sled to see him, but also not wanting it. 'Here I am, you bastard.'

The snowmobile was heading towards him now. Maybe coincidence. Maybe not. The shaft of light raced along the snow, strobing through the trees, and he stood there.

*Not yet.*

On came the sled, skis sliding, tracks biting into the snow, engine wailing.

*Not yet.*

Then it was coming up the rise and suddenly the white light flooded him, and for a moment he was like a deer mesmerized in the headlights and his breath was a pall of silver smoke around his face.

*Now!*

Erik lifted his left ski over and round, then his right ski, and now, with his back to the snowmobile, its beam throwing his shadow up onto the white-cocooned trees ahead of him, he flew, double-poling back down the slope.

He was cast in shadow again and his eyes were useless, pupils still pin-prick small from the glare of the sled light, and so he skied blind, but straight, hoping his tracks were deep and conspicuous. Hoping the man on the sled would see them.

His vision adjusted just in time to be sure of where he was. He stopped and unclipped from his bindings, picked up the skis and hurled them towards the pulk. Clutching his poles, he ran then, plunging through the deep snow, back towards where the ground began to rise and where he had chosen to make his stand.

'Oh God!' he said. 'Oh God, no!' Because he couldn't find the rope. He was on his knees, sweeping his bare hands across the snow, feeling for the rope that wasn't there. 'Please!' he begged, panic rising from his stomach.

Then his fingers brushed against something. The rope. He grabbed it, peering through the dark towards the snow-sheathed spruce three metres away, to whose trunk he had tied the other end as the motor sled roared down the slope, eating up his illuminated tracks.

He waited a heartbeat longer, then pulled the rope taut, throwing his end twice round the stub of a broken branch and leaning back, the rope snarled around his forearms for better or worse.

He felt the impact run through the tree and the rope like a passing train, and the rider was catapulted backwards off the sled, and the sled screamed and lunged into a fir with a splintering crunch.

Erik grabbed his poles and lumbered, stumbling, half-falling, like some rabid yeti or moon-mad mountain troll, towards the snowmobile, lodged inert amongst the lower boughs of the fir.

'Pappa!' Sofia cried. He twisted and saw the dark figure moving against the grey backcloth of snow. The sled's rider was on his knees, pulling at his helmet, his yelling suddenly clear and startling as he wrenched the helmet off and threw it aside. White hair. Eyes bulging with fury and hate in a pinched face. Konstantin.

'Get back!' Erik warned Sofia, who stood frozen, almost within reach of the man who rose on unsteady legs, bellowing in Russian like a man cursing God and all the saints. Erik dived at him, taking him down, and felt the whoosh of the man's breath in his face. Smelt the vodka in it.

'Pappa!' Sofia cried again.

The man bucked beneath him and scythed an elbow across his temple, sending myriad white starbursts through the black void of his sight. He felt the man roll over and half saw him scuttle away on hands and knees, breathing hard. And Erik reached out, snatched up one of the ski poles, got to his feet and stumbled after him. He swung the pole down, lashing it across the back of the Russian's head, yet the man twisted back like a snake and threw himself up at his thighs, grappling him, tackling him down onto the snow.

The terror was all in him, cold as fjord water in his blood and in the marrow of his leg bones and in the folded coils of his intestines, because if this man killed him, he would kill Sofia next. But the fear was like a bolt of electricity too, animating him with terrible speed, and he broke the man's hold, scrambling backwards, still holding the pole. He climbed to his feet, took two plunging steps and gripping the pole in both hands he drove it down into the man's neck, roaring like some primitive being.

For a fraction of a second, the basket near the tip of the pole caught on the Russian's collarbone, but Erik contracted his abdominal muscles and drove it down and down, and felt something hot whip his face and knew it was blood, spraying geyser-like from the man's mouth because the pole was in his lung. But Erik held on, and the man impaled before him began to convulse, his teeth chattering in his skull, one of his arms flapping madly, the other limp as a broken wing.

He let go of the pole and grabbed the man by the neck with both hands and squeezed, and they both fell, but he kept throttling the neck, feeling the gristle of the man's windpipe beneath his bare thumbs.

'They're coming, Pappa!' Sofia said, but he did not dare let go. He had started to kill the man and he couldn't stop now, because if he did, the man might rise up and kill him and then Sofia. He knew too that it would be more abhorrent to leave the act half done, to have created a broken, blood-spewing monstrosity there in the snow. A pitiful abomination trapped between life and death. So he squeezed with all his worth until he felt the cartilaginous tube give, his thumbs pushing so deep he thought they must break the skin and meet his fingers on the back of the man's neck. He heard a gurgling, then a soft exhalation, the sigh of a body letting go of a life that had lasted decades.

Caught in the dead man's glare – his eyes less sharp with aggression and threat now – he realized that Sofia was calling him again and again. With great effort, he pulled the ski pole out of the man and for a moment held it before him in the dark, watching the steam rise from the aluminium. Then he turned and lumbered through the snow to where the Yamaha sat half tipped over against the trunk of the fir.

'It's broken, Pappa,' Sofia told him. She was right. The sled's left ski had been sheared off with the impact, rendering the vehicle useless.

The high-pitched wail of the other snowmobile was loud,

its headlight beam slashing through the woods not a hundred metres beyond the body of the dead Russian.

'We've got to go,' he told Sofia, hurrying back to where he had left his skis and the pulk.

But she didn't move. Erik sensed her staring at him as he fastened on the harness and threw on his backpack. He could feel her eyes on him and felt a thickness in his throat too. Tasted a sourness that made him want to spit. Tasted shame. He was disgusted at what he had done and all the more because his little girl had seen him do it.

He trudged over to her and took her by the shoulders with those same hands that moments ago had strangled a man to death.

'We have to go,' he said again. He glanced up at the light and noise coming towards them, then back into the dark forest behind, because he knew the men on skis were also coming. He could feel Sofia trembling in his hands and gave her a gentle shake. 'We have to go, Sofia,' he said. 'Understand?'

'They killed Mr Helgeland too, didn't they?'

His mind played back the moment when Lars had gone down, his head hitting the stone. 'Yes,' he said.

Sofia seemed to catch her breath. Her eyes fell away from his and she looked down at the snow.

'So we had to do it,' he told her. 'You see that, don't you?'

She *did* see. He could tell, even in the dark and in her silence.

'We have to go now,' he said. She nodded.

He clipped into his bindings and skied back to the broken motor sled. From the scabbard fastened alongside the seat, he withdrew the Russian's rifle. He went over to the dead man and patted him down, finding a handful of cartridges in the chest pocket of his fur-lined parka. He thrust them into his own pocket.

'Go, Lillemor,' he said, pointing to the north with the bloodstained pole – which was bent, he noticed. 'Go.'

Sofia ghosted off amongst the trees. He looked over his shoulder once more, then set off after her.

They skied all night. Now and then they saw by the suffused moonlight the landscape through which they moved. The great snow-shrouded firs standing like giants frozen long ago by some enchantment in a war between ancient races. The soft blue radiance of the mantle over which they moved. Rocky overhangs fringed with massive icicles sharp as the canines of vampires, or else ice gathered on rock faces in vast sheets as if suspended in mid-cascade, like a converse lava flow from some polar eruption.

When Sofia could ski no further, they rested a while in the lee of a rock on the edge of a frozen lake. He gave her a chocolate bar and took the little gas stove and melted some snow for water. Then he pulled her against him and held her tight. He feared they had little time to rest, but when she fell asleep he did not wake her.

Luck had been with them in the forest. They had heard the engine behind them, followed by shouting, faint in the distance, and knew that their hunters had found the wrecked sled and their dead comrade. And he had been sure that the other snowmobile would take off after their trail and run them down like exhausted animals. But Sofia had given everything she had, and they emerged from the trees into the open, which might have been a death sentence in daylight but was their salvation in the dark. Because the snow which had drifted on the wind beneath the dense canopy of trees was a full-on blizzard out here beneath the sky. Their tracks were filling up behind them and would all but vanish mere minutes after their making.

It had made it harder to ski at times, when some hill or other obstacle meant they had to turn into a wind which was whipping snow into their faces, but he told her about the tracks. He said that someone up there in the grey swirling dark must be on their side, even though he didn't believe in such things.

In truth, he believed they were alone and that neither the trees nor the cold sky nor the silent looming mountains, nor any omnipresent deity conjured by man had any concern for them one way or another. They could live or they could pass from the world, and nothing else about this night would change so much as by the width of a hair on his little girl's head.

He held her tight and counted her long breaths, one after another, telling himself that he would wake her after another fifty. Then another fifty. And another. But then he closed his own eyes and when he woke with a start, one of those falling dreams, he cursed himself for drifting asleep, woke Sofia and told her they had to move again.

'I'm tired,' she said.

'I know. Me too,' he said.

She looked into his face. He could smell the chocolate on her breath. 'Maybe they're not chasing us any more,' she said. 'Maybe they've given up because they can't follow our trail.'

He shook his head and thumbed some snow off the rim of her hat. 'We can't risk it.' If the thought of having taken another man's life sickened him, knowing that man was the brother of the tall man was like a blade of ice in his guts.

She frowned. 'But where will we go?'

They couldn't turn for home and Elise. He wouldn't risk leading the Helgelands' killers there. Same for any other isolated cabins they might come across. He knew what would happen if the men hunting them turned up at the door before any help they had summoned over the phone could arrive.

'We'll go north,' he told her. 'Across the glacier.' He looked up, squinting against the falling snow that was sweeping around the rock against which they rested and would bury them if they stayed too long. 'If this blizzard keeps up, it'll cover our tracks. They'll have to give up. They can't chase us for ever.' He hoped that was true.

One after another she pulled open the cuffs of her mittens and huffed hot breath into them. She frowned at him again. 'What about Mrs Helgeland's brother? The reindeer herder. Hánas, I think.' She lifted her chin towards the driving snow. 'Mrs Helgeland said he's out there somewhere beyond the glacier. Maybe we can find him.'

'How?' he asked.

She thought about it, then said, 'They can see his light sometimes. All the way from their home. If we find him, he can call for help. Or help us hide.'

'It'll be light before we get across the glacier,' he said. 'Even if we saw his lamp now, which has to be impossible in this, we'd lose it again before we got to higher ground.'

She fell quiet again and he felt her body give in to shivering, as if the hope had been warmth that had gone out of her.

After a quiet two minutes he realized what he'd done.

'How big is his herd?' he asked her. She looked up at him. 'How many reindeer does this Hánas have?'

Her eyebrows met the rim of her polar bear hat. 'Mr Helgeland said only tourists ask how many reindeer a herder has. It's rude. Like asking someone how much money they have.'

'But it must be a lot,' he said. Maybe not hundreds, if Hánas was alone up there. But probably at least fifty animals? Maybe a hundred? He didn't know if reindeer made much noise. He didn't imagine they were like sheep, talking to each other all day. Still, surely no herd of animals would be completely silent either.

'So we look for reindeer?' she asked.

'We look for anything,' he said. 'Smoke, a light, anything.'

She looked north, biting her lip, then turned back to him. 'We will be OK?' she asked him. And this time he didn't want the hope to leave her like an outward breath.

He nodded. 'We'll be OK,' he said.

They crossed the frozen lake, the wind hurling stinging snow against their left cheeks and half blinding them, then climbed a steep hill, stopping now and then to catch their breath and drink from their bottles and look back for signs of their pursuers. Then they came amongst fir trees again and were glad for the shelter, but he knew they could not tarry there.

It crossed his mind that the last snowmobile must run out of fuel sooner or later. But they might have spare fuel, maybe fuel cans from the two sleds they had left at the Helgelands'. And besides, the two men on skis were out there somewhere too, and so they must keep going. Northward in the wind-flayed dark. Ever further from home.

They came out of the trees and relished a long descent down which they skied with little effort, just poling now and again for balance and to reassure themselves in the gloom. At any other time they would have grinned until the cold air hurt their teeth. Sofia would have shouted *egg!* and bent forward, tucking in to reduce wind drag, her poles under her arms and sticking out behind her as she sped past him.

When the ground levelled out he saw they were in a narrow valley, the uplands on either side like dark serrated blades cutting into the grey clouds, spilling their innards upon the world. Snow upon snow.

The wind howled across the pass, so that he feared they wouldn't hear the motor sled amongst it. Sofia had thought the same thing, he knew, as she was looking back the way they had come. He told her they would see the light of the sled and that she should keep her eyes on the untrodden path ahead, though he kept looking over his shoulder into the swirling chaos.

'We'll rest again soon,' he told her.

He knew she needed to eat. They both did. What was the point in pulling the pulk all this way if they couldn't stop to make use of the things in it? As he skied, his head staged a silent debate. Part of him dared hope that those who had set off after them had given up the chase, the trail lost to the dark and the new snowfall and the snow that the wind blew in drifts like waves across the white-mantled ground. The other part of him knew that the men were still coming. Knew it with absolute certainty. This voice buried the other beneath its cold and quiet knowing, and so on they went, past the endurance of the body into that of the mind.

For maybe an hour, neither he nor Sofia spoke, each lost

in their own movement, two automatons out there, synchro-nized and ceaseless. Crossing land where countless glaciers had grown and melted over a million years, advancing and retreating, each successive pass over the bedrock like one of his own carpentry planes down a length of timber, grinding away the rock bit by bit.

He knew their own strength, of body and mind, was being eroded too.

But then Sofia saw the red light.

'There, Pappa,' she said, stopping and lifting her pole to point with it.

He looked, but saw nothing.

'It's gone now,' she said.

He leant towards her to be heard over the wind's moan-ing. 'Are you sure, Lillemor?' he asked, a sick feeling spreading in his guts. Because Sofia hadn't pointed behind them but rather ahead, where the looming mass of moun-tain along the valley's western side came to an end before the opening to the glacier. 'You're sure you saw a red light?'

Even in the pre-dawn dark he could see the strange blue–grey brilliance of the glacial ice at the head of the valley.

'Yes, I'm sure,' she said, looking out to where she had seen it. 'Just for a second, then it was gone.'

He wanted her to be wrong. Even if it meant she was so tired that her eyes or her tormented mind was playing tricks, conjuring sights that did not exist in reality.

'How did he get ahead of us?' she asked.

'I don't know,' he said. That wasn't the important ques-tion now. As heartbreaking as it was to know that after all the effort, all the numbing hours of skiing through the bliz-zard, they still had not escaped those hunting them, the

question troubling Erik was why the man had risked alert-
ing them to his presence by using the head torch. Not to
follow their tracks, seeing as he was a kilometre or so in
front of them. To see where he was going? Because he was
struggling in the blizzard? Erik didn't think so. Clearly the
man hadn't struggled to overtake them, and if they could ski
without a torch then so could he. Which left only one answer.
He had used the light to signal to one of his companions.

'I promise I saw it, Pappa,' Sofia insisted.

'I believe you,' he said. He lifted his hat off his right ear
and turned that side to the south, shielding it from the wind
with his gloved hands. He closed his eyes and tried to shut
out the blizzard, listening for the mechanical moan of the
remaining snowmobile. But all he heard was the storm, the
frenzy of it out there in the world, for they were protected
somewhat down in the valley as the westerly hurled its
wrath across the mountains.

'What shall we do?' Sofia asked him.

He peered through the whirling snow, fearing that the
motor sled was close, that the man driving it had turned off
the headlight for stealth.

'We have the rifle,' he said. He unhitched the pulk harness and fetched the rifle, kept dry with their sleeping bags
and other kit, then put his backpack in the pulk. He held
the rifle up to her, meaning to reassure her. 'We have this,'
he told her, patting the wooden stock, then lifting the scope
to his eye. He could see little through it. She looked at the
rifle with a kind of horror, the way any child would who
had seen a woman lying dead in the snow in her nightdress with a bullet hole in her back, the wound steaming in
the cold.

Taking his eye from the scope, Erik saw the fear in his daughter's face. 'I'll only use it if I have to.'

He pulled the bolt back and brought the rifle up to his eye to look down the breech. Peeling off his right-hand glove with his teeth, he poked his little finger down into the breech to make sure there was no round in there already. Empty. Still gripping the glove between his teeth, he took one of the shells from his coat pocket and pushed it down into the magazine, feeling that there was no room for another, which meant the magazine was full, though he didn't know how many rounds it took.

He thought back to the handful of occasions he had handled similar rifles, during his military conscription and more recently, in his thirties, when invited on elk-hunting trips. He recalled the thrill of stalking through the wet and dripping forest at dawn. The distant barking of the unleashed dogs. The atavistic vibe that had permeated amongst them like a spell, as it had bound hunters for fifteen thousand years, since men first gathered with firebrands and branches to separate mammoths from the herd and steer them into traps.

Not that he had ever brought down an elk. They had mostly proved elusive, and the one he'd got close to had been rump-on with no clear shot, so he hadn't pulled the trigger.

'We have it if we need it,' he said, raising his voice above the wind and pushing the bolt forward, hearing the bolt head stripping a round from the magazine and into the chamber. Then he thumbed the safety, slung the rifle over his shoulder, put his glove back on and fastened the clips of the pulk harness.

'Let's go,' he said, changing direction slightly to take them away from where Sofia had seen the red light on the western side of the valley. Still heading for the glacier, they would ski up to it from the east side, hoping they could get past the man on skis before he could cut them off.

But what if they couldn't? What if Sofia was too tired? What if the man had night-vision goggles as well as the red head torch, and was even now watching them in monochrome, seeing the world in shades of green? How could they escape then?

He had the sickening feeling that these men were making a sadistic game out of it. One of them skiing ahead to lie in wait while the other two pushed him and Sofia into the trap.

Like the mammoths.

'Keep going,' he said to himself, the words escaping on a wisp of white fog. 'Make it to the glacier and disappear up there.' Find somewhere to shelter. Hide until these bastards gave up the chase. It was all they could do. 'Just damn well ski,' he murmured into the night.

Then he heard the engine.

# 7

'I CAN'T, PAPPA,' Sofia called over her shoulder. 'I can't keep it up.'

'Yes, you can,' he called back. 'I'm right with you. Just keep going. We're nearly there. Just another few hundred metres, that's all,' he lied. 'You can do it.'

'My legs are jelly,' she called. 'I'm going to fall.'

It was getting light now. The cloud beyond the eastern ridge glowed a pale pink, though shadow clung to the valley still, slinking there like some ill-willed animal hoping to go unnoticed until night came again.

'You won't fall,' he said, though he thought she might.

Twenty, thirty more strength-sapping metres passed before an idea came to him. 'Stop, Sofia, wait.' He took her poles and tied the strap of one to the basket of the other, looking back into the dark as he worked. Then, using a carabiner, he clipped the strap of this second pole to the back of the pulk. The spare pulk ropes would have been better, he knew, but he had used them to kill a man in the night and they were gone now.

'I just need you to hold on,' he told her, giving her the basket end of the first pole. 'I'll do the rest.'

'But you're already pulling the pulk,' she said. She wasn't crying but she was scared and exhausted and her face was a mask of anguish. 'It'll be too heavy. You can't pull us both.' Even so, she gripped the pole tightly in her mittened hands.

'Just don't let go,' he told her. 'We'll see how it is. If I can't pull you, we'll leave the pulk.'

'But we need it,' she said.

'We can take out the most important bits and put them in my backpack, OK? But let's try first.'

She nodded. 'OK.'

'Hold on.'

'I will.'

He set off once more. It took a little while to work up any momentum, and it was hard work pulling the pulk and Sofia too, but he knew he could do it.

'OK?' he called over his shoulder.

'Yes,' she shouted back, hanging onto the pole, keeping her own skis close together, running on the snow smoothed over by the pulk.

They continued in this way for what he guessed might be a kilometre. He knew for sure now that the man on the snowmobile was driving without the headlamp on, because it was close now, the engine's high-pitched snarl cutting through the keening wind, though he couldn't see the vehicle itself. He guessed it was performing slow diagonal passes across the valley, because the sound came and went. This gave him hope. It told him that the driver was fearful of Erik's rifle. That the man was unwilling to make himself a target by following their ski tracks with his light on, because he knew Erik could take up a position and fire at the lit-up vehicle.

*So just keep going,* he told himself. *Get up onto the glacier and lose them in the storm.*

'There, Pappa! The light!' Sofia yelled.

'I saw it,' he replied. A flash of red. And close. Two hundred metres away. Maybe closer. There and then gone.

He did not stop. He was breathing hard through his mouth, sucking the freezing air into his lungs. His heart thumping against his breastbone, urgent and dogged, a metronome keeping the pace, and he would not slow.

On the higher ground at the head of the valley, the snow was flooded with blue from the glacial ice beneath. They were going to make it. The other skier wouldn't see them before they had passed him, or rather passed the place where they had seen the flash of red light. Then he and Sofia would climb up onto the glacier and, up there in the open, in the maw of the storm, their tracks would disappear and they would either find shelter or make their own.

As he thought this, his legs feeding hungrily on that hope, something tugged at his shoulder and he looked down and saw a tear in his jacket, unbalancing and nearly falling as the rifle shot rang out, a stark, abrupt sound amongst the near-constant wail of the wind.

Sofia called out and he looked behind him to check she hadn't been hit.

'We can't stop,' he told her and lengthened his stride, putting more into each kick and glide. 'Get down, Sofia,' he called. 'Stay low.' He risked another look and saw she was squatting behind the pulk. He could just see a sliver of her pale face and her eyes peering into the dark as she clung to the pole.

He glanced at his shoulder, at the rent in the fabric, and some part of his mind recalled stories of people being shot and feeling no pain, at first. Then he saw a muzzle flash in the dark and felt the bullet whipcrack the air beside his face, and he flinched and ducked, every instinct telling him to make himself small, to cower in the dark. To call out to the shooter and beg for mercy. To do whatever the man wanted, so long as he promised not to hurt Sofia. But he knew there would be no mercy and so, even as his skis slowed to a stop, he shoved his poles down between the pulk harness and his hip, pulled off his gloves, unslung the rifle and brought it up to his shoulder.

He thumbed the safety off and peered through the telescopic sights. But he could not see the man.

'Stay down, Sofia,' he shouted, now looking through the scope, now taking his head away and letting his eyes sift the dark, now going back to the scope. Panic flooded him.

*Where are you?*

He knew the man would fire again any second, but he couldn't see him.

*Please!*

Where was he? Erik's hands were shaking. He was trying to breathe in and out through his nose, to gain control over his racing heart and trembling flesh. He took a lungful of air and held it, fearful that the fog of his hot breath was visible in the gloom.

*Please! Let me see the bastard.*

He dropped to one knee, keeping the butt of the rifle in his right shoulder, its barrel pointing roughly to where he had seen the momentary bloom of orange fire. It was hard to keep his eyes open under the cascade of snowflakes spewing into his face. Hard to see, let alone find his target and make the shot.

Then another muzzle flash and he was showered with ice shrapnel, the round having hit the snow three metres in front of him and driving deep.

He moved the barrel across and pulled the trigger, the Remington Model 700 kicking like a mule, then he hauled back the bolt and pushed it forward again, slamming another shell into the chamber. Cursing himself for how aggressively he had pulled the trigger, instead of squeezing it. Most likely he'd jerked the rifle and spoilt the shot, though all he'd had to aim at was the memory of that split-second burst of flame out there in the night.

'Pappa,' Sofia hissed behind him.

'Shh, Lillemor,' he said.

'But, Pappa, it's coming.'

Then he heard it and knew that the Russian on the motor sled had seen the flashes from the muzzles of their rifles and was coming to the aid of his comrade.

'Kill him, Pappa,' Sofia said. 'Please!'

'Stay down,' he growled. Bare hands already hurting from the cold. Eyes sifting the dark shapes in the landscape. The humpbacked, snow-covered mounds. The tops of tall scrub and stunted birch poking up through the mantle, thin silhouettes bristling in the wind. He thought he saw something move. Maybe a trick of the swirling snow. Maybe not.

'Come on,' he growled under his breath, trying to remember his firearms training from his twelve months as a conscript in the army. A long time ago.

*Steady. Aim. Breathe. Fire.* He squeezed the trigger. The rifle recoiled into the layers of clothes and the flesh and bone of his shoulder, the report shockingly loud because the Remington was not fitted with a suppressor.

He shuffled to the side, making himself smaller, knowing he had again given away his position. Then a flash, and the space in the world which he had occupied three seconds previously buzzed, the round already long gone.

*If you hear the shot, you're still alive.*

Blood beat in his ears, an aqueous gush within which the sounds of gunfire rang still, like tinnitus. He worked the bolt and chambered another round but he did not fire.

*Where are you, you fucking bastard?*

The wind mourned, and he squinted his eyes against the squalling snow. He was shaking with fear for Sofia. Shaking with fury and hatred too, for the men who were doing this to her. Again, he wanted to call out to the man he could not see, to tell him they could do what they wanted to him. Shoot him in the face. Flay the skin from his body while he yet lived. Anything, so long as they let Sofia live. But he knew they would not, and the unfairness of that put a rage in him like nothing he had ever known.

His left hand, gripping the forestock, and his right-hand trigger finger were growing numb now, but he didn't squeeze his finger back because he dared not shoot and miss again. Yet he knew every second he delayed was an invitation for the other man to shoot and kill him. His body seemed to shrink inside his clothes, as if it expected the next bullet to rip into flesh and bone and internal organs. A carnage of white-hot agony and failure.

'He's coming, Pappa,' Sofia called.

He glanced over his shoulder in the direction of the engine's four-stroke growl and saw nothing but snow churning in the dark. Then the headlight lit, its beam flooding across the snow. Erik snapped his head back around and returned his eye to the scope, in time to see the man with the rifle throw a hand up against the glare from his colleague's machine. Erik yanked on the trigger. No time to squeeze. The man's head exploded in a spray of skull, brain and blood, the whole show lit up like a one-man play in a deserted theatre. Then Erik spun round, pivoting on his knee in the deepening snow as he cocked the rifle, pulled the weapon into his shoulder and fired at the light. Reloaded and fired again. The motor sled swerved, ascended an unseen mound, then tilted and flew six, maybe eight metres, its engine screaming, before coming down on its side with a crump of metal and fibreglass.

Erik pulled back the bolt, pushed it forward and pulled the trigger again. Nothing happened but for a dry click, and he knew the magazine was empty.

'Sofia, let's go!' he yelled.

She stood, untying her poles from each other and unclipping them from the carabiner on the pulk.

'I can pull you,' he told her.

'It's OK, I can ski,' she said. 'Are they dead?' She was looking over her shoulder.

Some seventy metres away, the motor sled lay on its side, its headlamp still casting its glare over the snow. He couldn't see the driver.

'I don't know. One of them is,' he said, strapping on the pulk harness. 'We have to go.'

She nodded and planted her poles, then pushed off, taking

up the diagonal stride through the deep snow. He slung the rifle over his shoulder. He knew he'd not been hit, that the bullet had just grazed his jacket, but pulled at the material to inspect the damage nonetheless.

'I'll catch you up,' he called.

'Pappa!' she shouted over her shoulder.

'It's OK. I just need to check something. Go on – I'll catch up.'

She headed off into the dark.

'Jesus,' he said under his breath as he skied up to the dead man. The man's mother would not have recognized him. The face and most of the skull were gone, and Erik tried not to look at the steaming wet ruin of what remained. Even so, he knew from the man's build that he was the broad-shouldered, bull-necked man who had been poking an iron into the Helgelands' fireplace before Konstantin had knocked Lars down and broken his skull.

He leant over, balancing on his skis, keeping his face half turned away as he patted down the pockets on the man's fur-lined parka. He could smell the blood and offal stink of wet brain mush and felt the bile squeeze up from his stomach into his throat. He felt something – a phone? – in one of the big side pockets of the dead man's jacket.

'Pappa!' Sofia called. He turned to see her faint outline in the dark, where she had stopped to wait for him.

He looked back at the motor sled lying on its side. No sign of movement over there.

'Please, Pappa. Come on!' Sofia shouted.

He pulled the object from the coat pocket. Not a phone. A walkie-talkie. He shoved it into his own pocket and straightened up. The guy must've had some spare ammo somewhere. No time to look for it now. And where was his damn rifle? There. Six feet away, half buried in snow.

'Pappa, come!' Sofia called.

'Let's go,' he said. And together they set off towards the head of the valley, ears straining for the crack of gunfire behind them.

They climbed in the dawn. Up the snow-covered ice and between the two peaks at the head of the valley. It was hard going but adrenaline electrified his blood, and they were climbing out of the shadow of the valley and into the light. That pale light drew them on as if with the promise of salvation, as if they were children fleeing the monsters that lurk in the night.

He didn't want to think about what had happened back there in the valley. But a momentary image had been captured in the sudden wash of light from the snowmobile, like a chemical record on photographic film, and he could not rid himself of it. The skier's head exploding with the impact of the bullet. Bits of skull and brain flying everywhere. It was a repulsive sight, even in the replay of his mind's eye, and yet it thrilled him too. Aroused some savageness in him, which he realized he didn't want to entirely subdue. The man had been trying to kill them. He would have pointed his rifle at Sofia and snuffed out her life with no more thought than if he was extinguishing the flame of a candle. Well, now he was dead. He was nothing. Just a lump of flesh in the snow. *Good.*

Once they were up on the glacier, they found it hard to see through the sting of the snow blowing across the open plain. If he had to say, he'd put visibility at around a hundred metres, give or take. The wind was bitterly cold. It wailed from the west and seemed to him sentient and, worse, maleficent, in a way he had never thought of it before. It numbed his chin and froze the sweat where his hat met his forehead. It found a way through his gloves to his fingers, seemed to creep through his boots and socks to his toes, and he feared it seeking its way through the billions of pores in the Gore-Tex fabric of his jacket and overtrousers. Erik knew that whatever he was feeling, Sofia would be feeling it too, though he was glad she had mittens because they would be warmer than gloves.

'Look, Sofia!' he called, pointing behind them to the tracks they had made. They were filling with snow. Vanishing before his eyes.

'Do you think they're still coming after us?' she asked him, squinting against the snow. He could see her exhaustion, knew that fear alone kept her on her skis. There were dark circles under her eyes, like bruises. She was clenching and unclenching her hands on the poles and he knew she was beginning to really feel the cold.

'There's still one on skis,' he told her, thumbing the last rounds into the Remington's magazine. 'I don't know about the other one.'

'You shot him,' she said, turning to look at him, the hope in her tired eyes clutching at his heart.

'Maybe,' he said. He was reluctant to allow her too much hope.

She looked back again at the way they had come and at their fading tracks. Then she turned her face to the north and looked into the white-out, which told them as much about their future as a fortune-teller's crystal ball wreathed in dry ice.

'Can you go a little further?' he asked her, slinging the rifle. 'Just until we find a good place to make a snow hole?' She frowned, but at least it wasn't a no. 'I have the shovel. We can make something good. Cosy and warm.' It was becoming hard to speak because his jawbones were growing numb and he could feel the words slurring from his mouth like snow tumbling off a roof. 'We'll make some hot food and you can sleep for a while.'

She gave him a pained stare. She was shivering and her mittened hands were restless, two small avatars of her internal anxiety, opening and closing around the poles.

He lifted one of his own poles and pointed ahead. 'Just a little further,' he said, 'then we'll rest. I promise.'

She nodded.

They skied for another hour, if you could call it skiing. More like walking on skis. At times they leant into the wind and it felt as if they were making little progress. Other times, to avoid a crevasse or knoll, they walked eastward, and if they held their arms and poles out wide, making sails of their bodies, the wind almost pushed them along.

He called ahead to Sofia, telling her to stop because he had seen something. A white shape in the white world. He skied a little way off their intended course and was relieved to see that his eyes had not fooled him. There was a rise in the ground, perhaps over a bluff or large rock beneath the ice, so that when the great weight of glacial ice had ground over it, the ice had split, a lip rising eight metres or more above the plain.

He went back to fetch Sofia and together they skied around the ridge. They both knew this was the place where they would rest, protected from the worst of the wind and driving snow and, they hoped, invisible in the white-out. He glanced at his watch. It had been just over nine hours since they had fled from the Helgelands' place. Nine exhausting, fear-soaked hours. Blood-soaked hours. He unclipped from the pulk and from his skis, fetched the shovel and began to dig.

He cut into the wall of pack snow, while she helped by pulling out the wedges and throwing them out of the way. They worked in silence. Both too exhausted to waste breath on words. Putting in this last great effort in exchange for the coming reward. Now and then, he stopped to catch his wind and listen, and twice he walked back around the ridge to peer into the snowstorm to reassure himself that their tracks were being covered.

He didn't know if he was doing the right thing by stopping to let Sofia rest. But he didn't think she could go on the way they had. Better to take the chance and lay low now, while this blizzard reduced visibility, than get caught later out in the open when they were both dead on their skis. And so he dug.

It took a long time and, once it was done, they stood back to admire their work. Their breath fogged around them and still they didn't speak but looked at what they had made as if it were their lives' greatest achievement. The cave was a T-shape cut into the snow face. The central chamber would collect the cold air, while on either side, the arms of the T would be their sleeping platforms.

They climbed inside and worked on the ceiling, making it curved and as smooth as they could get it, flattening any little peaks that would have dripped icy water on them from above. Then Sofia went back out and returned with a ski pole, which Erik poked upwards, excavating into the roof until they could both see weak daylight through the hole he'd created.

'We'll have to keep pushing it through,' he told her, his voice dead and muffled inside the little cave.

'Because of the carbon monoxide,' she said. 'But we can light a candle in here?'

'We can light a candle,' he said.

She smiled then and it seemed like a small miracle.

They took what they needed into the snowhole, including the rifle, and put their backpacks in the cold well and then he pulled the pulk up to the entrance and threw a thin layer of snow over it. Behind this, at the threshold, he set up the stove and filled a pan with snow. When the water was boiling, he placed into it two foil pouches containing pre-cooked meals. One was chilli con carne, the other spicy vegetable rigatoni. Sofia chose the rigatoni, and eight minutes later they were wolfing down their food.

Next they heated two pouches of chocolate pudding and he watched the girl eat, each mouthful a boon of precious calories. Afterwards he made hot chocolate, which he poured into cups, giving one to Sofia. She clutched it in both hands, blowing the sweet smell of the steam towards him. Her eyes had a faraway look, and he worried that she was remembering how the man's head had disintegrated. He masked a shudder and hoped it was just that she was exhausted. When she had finished her hot chocolate, he took the cup from her and cleaned it out with snow, then tucked her sleeping bag around her. They would sleep fully clothed for warmth and in case they had to leave in a hurry. They wouldn't even get into their bags, because if they heard an engine or the sound of a bolt-action rifle chambering a round, every second would count. 'You need to sleep now, Lillemor,' he said.

She frowned, looking so like her mother. 'But what if they find us?' she said, turning her tired eyes from him to the entrance of the snow cave, beyond which the blizzard flailed in the new day.

'I'll keep watch,' he told her, taking a candle and pushing it down into the snow in a little alcove he had made in the wall.

'But you need to sleep too, Pappa.'

He shook his head as he struck the match and held the flame to the candle wick. 'I'm fine, Lillemor. I'll sleep later.' He poked the match into the snow, then leant across and kissed her forehead, gently pushing her down onto the ground mat shielding her from the cold sleeping platform.

For a moment they both watched the flame.

'If it starts flickering, it means there's not enough oxygen in here,' she said.

He smiled. 'I'll keep an eye on it.'

She lay her head back and looked up at the glistening ceiling.

'Go to sleep,' he said.

'I'll watch the air hole to make sure it doesn't get blocked,' she said.

Less than five minutes later she was fast asleep.

He took the spare snow blocks he had cut earlier and bricked up the entrance, then lay on his side, the rifle beside him, watching the candle and watching the girl.

He did not sleep.

A sound startled him and he pushed himself up and grabbed the rifle, pointing the barrel at the entrance of the cave. Then

101

he heard it again and realized it was the sound of static interference and a man's voice, coming from the walkie-talkie in his pocket.

He took it out. Looked at Sofia. She was still fast asleep. The static hissed again and he snatched off his woollen hat to smother the transceiver, whilst putting it against his ear and turning away from Sofia.

'I know you can hear me.'

His heart kicked in his chest. It was the tall man. He knew it with absolute certainty. It was the man who had strolled out into the night and shot Mrs Helgeland in the back. He recognized his voice. He had spoken with the man that day in town, when both Karine and Lars had been very much alive.

He lowered the walkie-talkie and looked at it in his hand, and it hissed again, startling him.

'I know you have my comrade's radio,' the disembodied voice said. Then silence. But the push-to-talk button at the other end was still depressed, and he could almost feel the tall man on the other end of it. Waiting. Thinking.

'I know you can hear me,' the voice said. 'And that's good because I need you to know something.'

He almost pressed the talk button himself. He wanted to beg the man to leave them alone. To leave Sofia alone. But he also felt it was better to say nothing. That speaking would make him suddenly visible to the man, the way the Eye of Sauron would turn upon the world in the direction of Frodo whenever Frodo was stupid enough to put on the ring.

'Tell me, is the girl listening?'

He smothered the receiver and looked over at Sofia. She was still asleep, but he pressed his hat harder around the instrument and kept watching her.

'No. Maybe you've dug a little hole in the snow, like two little foxes. Maybe the girl is asleep right now, looking . . . so peaceful. Maybe she thinks you're going to protect her.'

Erik's heart was going like a jackhammer. He was struck with the possibility that the tall man was somehow here. Now. Standing beyond the entrance to their snowhole. He shuffled over and peered through a crack and saw only snow sweeping down, swirling in the world beyond their hideout.

'I need you to know that I'm going to kill you,' said the voice. 'There is nothing you can do to change it. I think you already know that. But perhaps some part of you dares to think that your daughter . . . She is your daughter?'

Erik clamped his teeth together. There was a short sharp hiss of static, followed by the squawk of the talk button being pressed. 'Yes, I think she is. Perhaps part of you thinks she's going to be OK. I need you to know that I'm going to kill her too.'

His finger and thumb went to the knob on top of the transceiver. He wanted to turn the radio off but couldn't.

'Because maybe it turns out that I kill you first. And if that's how it plays out, I want you to know that I am going to kill your girl.'

Watching Sofia's sleeping face, he turned the switch and buried the transceiver in his jacket, like a man guilty of theft or worse, and then watched Sofia for a long time.

He hated waking her. He wanted her to sleep and sleep. But he knew they had to keep moving, and so he stood in the cold well and put his mouth against her ear and whispered her name over and over, until at last she opened her eyes.

'I was dreaming of Emilie,' she said, groggy with sleep.

His lost daughter's name kicked him in the gut, as it always did.

'Was it a good dream?' he asked, handing her a mug of water which he had held over the candle flame to take the chill off it.

She cocked her head, her gaze fixed on the candle, which had burned down to the nub.

'We were skiing together,' she said. 'And she kept telling me to ski faster, but I couldn't.' She drank until the mug was empty, then lay there on her side, staring at the mug as if the last dregs of her dream were in the bottom of it. Like tea leaves.

'You've skied better than I could ever have imagined,' he told her.

'But you had to pull me,' she said, not looking at him.

'Only for a little while,' he said.

'And now we have to set off again.'

'Yes.'

'To find the reindeer and Mrs Helgeland's brother.'

'Yes, if we can,' he said. He didn't tell her about the voice he had heard over the transceiver. Maybe later. Maybe never.

He started packing up the last of their things; the mugs, the candle and the ski pole he'd used to keep the air vent free of snow, and put them with the stove and his ground mat at the end of his sleeping platform. Then Sofia said she needed to go to the toilet and so he turned his back while she squatted and urinated in the cold well.

'If it's very yellow, you should drink some more water,' he said, but she told him it was fine. He pushed the snow bricks away from the entrance and crawled, stiff and aching, out into the day, like some creature emerging from winter's womb.

He stood slowly, cautiously, listening and watching. Behind him, Sofia crouched anxiously at the mouth of the den.

'It's OK. There's no one around,' he said. 'It's safe – come on.'

She scampered out and together they stood amidst the falling snow, Sofia crossing her arms and thumping her shoulders to get some warmth into her flesh. Erik stretched, wincing at the stiffness in his joints and the soreness in his muscles.

'How long was I asleep?' she asked.

'Three hours. Just over,' he said.

'And you stayed awake the whole time?'

'I'm not tired,' he said. 'Get your skis on.'

She picked up her skis, dropped one in front of her, then turned the other over and looked at its underside. 'You waxed them,' she said.

'A little. Not very well,' he said. 'I heated it over the candle to soften it. But it should help.'

She threw it down next to the other, then used her poles for balance while she put them on.

'Do you think Mamma knows something's wrong?' she asked him.

He was down on one knee, fastening up his backpack, but stopped and looked up at the white sky, feeling the snow on his face and eyelashes. Still a lot of snow coming down, but the wind had died somewhat and he could see more than before they'd taken refuge.

'I think she must,' he said, standing. Feeling a half dozen aches and pains in his body.

'She'll be wondering why we haven't called,' Sofia said.

'She knows weather like this can wipe out the phone

signal,' he said, 'and there's next to no signal up here to begin with.' He put the backpack in the pulk and fastened the cover tightly, then slung the rifle over his shoulder, put on the pulk harness and clipped into his skis. 'But I think she'll be more worried about the blizzard itself. About us being out in it.' He watched her tightening the hip belt of her rucksack and considered whether or not to risk getting her hopes up. He decided that hope was a good thing, because it might keep her going. 'I think it's likely there are people looking for us right now,' he said.

Clearly the idea came as a surprise to her, as she immediately looked east and south, her eyes scanning the landscape, sifting through the falling snow as if she half expected to see a mountain search and rescue party skiing across the glacier.

'Let's get going,' he said and he kicked off, leading the way to set a trail for her, the newly fallen snow flying before his skis.

The food and rest had done them both good. Erik was tired still. Woozy. A feeling like jetlag, but with his muscles at least now fuelled by energy from the meat, rice, and chocolate pudding. A thousand calories doing their thing. Sofia seemed renewed too, and they set a good pace across the glacier, though it was hard going with so much fresh snow to plough through.

After an hour of steady progress, he asked if she was all right and she said she was.

'How are the skis?' he asked.

'Better,' she replied.

'Gripping better?'

'Yes.'

'And sliding better when you kick forward?'

'I think so,' she called back.

After another ten minutes he said, 'You're not talking much.'

She didn't reply.

'Is it because you're a teenager now?' he said, immediately regretting trying to be funny. Hardly the time for dad jokes. But her silence worried him. He wondered if she was thinking of Karine Helgeland lying dead in the snow. Worse still, that she was thinking of what he had done to that man. What would it do to a daughter, seeing her father murder someone? Witnessing her pappa's desperate terror and savagery as he drove a ski pole down into another man's insides? Or blew a person's head apart with a rifle?

He could barely think about it himself. It made him feel ashamed.

'We'll be OK,' he said.

Seven strides later, Sofia said, 'How do you know?'

Then he saw the cabin at the northern edge of the glacier.

# 8

ERIK FOUND IT on their map. It was a DNT hut, like the one they had planned to stay in on the second night of the Long Ski. This one, though, was a no-service cabin, which meant it wouldn't be stocked with the usual provisions of tinned goods, coffee, tea, crispbread and powdered soup packets.

Coming off the glacier, they had climbed up through a stand of tall snowbound firs and now stood looking up at the log hut which sat at the top of the slope before them. There was less snow coming down now and he thought it might stop altogether, but it was colder than before. The air scant and thin and sharp as broken glass in his lungs.

'What is it, Pappa?' Sofia said. He could feel her eyes on him.

'I'm just looking,' he said.

'Do you think he might be in there? The one on skis?'

The cold was working its way into him. He could feel his body trying and failing to repel it. Could feel a tremor taking hold in his flesh, seeking deeper down towards his bones and the marrow within.

'I don't think so. But I don't know if we should go in,' he said. 'Maybe we should keep going.'

He looked at her. She pulled her fleece neck warmer up over the lower part of her face, so that only her eyes were looking out at him, glistening in the freezing air and brimming with worry. He could see how much she wanted to go inside the cabin, and how hard she was trying not to say it.

'You're too cold,' he said.

Sofia nodded.

He clapped his own hands together, the sound muffled by the gloves. 'Me too,' he said, looking back up at the hut. Around it, the snow drifts were so deep it seemed the whole place was slowly being swallowed, like an offering from humanity being claimed by the land or some god of the cold northern mountains.

He pulled off a glove and cupped his numb chin and lower face in his hand, trying to impart some warmth. He couldn't feel his own touch. 'Let's take a closer look, OK?'

'OK,' she said, the word muted by the fleece covering her mouth.

He put the glove back on and they climbed the slope, Sofia keeping in his tracks. As they neared the top, he told her to stay amongst the trees on the brow of the rise. He unclipped his skis, fetched his snowshoes from the pulk and put them on.

He inspected the house again. The windows were dark. There was no smoke rising from the chimney. But still he stood there, his breath fogging the thin air, watching as if waiting for some sixth sense to kick in and tell him if there was a beating heart within those four timber walls. He couldn't rule out the possibility that the tall man was waiting inside, having guessed that he and Sofia wouldn't be able to resist the temptation of warmth and shelter.

He glanced back at Sofia and nodded once. She nodded back, so he unslung the rifle from his shoulder, took off the safety and worked the bolt, stripping a round from the magazine into the chamber. He took off his gloves and shoved them into his coat pockets, hoping his fingers wouldn't go numb. Then he thumbed the safety back on and walked around to the east side, past the woodpile and up the five steps to the covered deck, making no noise but for the soft *crump* of the snow beneath the aluminium snowshoes.

He stopped beneath the eaves and studied the ground around his feet. There was evidence of other tracks leading to and all around the cabin, beyond the encroaching drifts. Not fresh tracks like the ones he was making, but places where the snow was less deep because it had been trodden down with boots or skis. He trudged around to one of the windows and looked in, putting a hand against the glass to shield his eyes. It was dark inside. He saw a table and six chairs, all neatly stowed. The galley kitchen and a kettle, and some tin containers on the sideboard. No sign of occupancy. He walked around to another window and saw an unlit bedroom with two bunkbeds, neat and undisturbed, awaiting tired members of the Norwegian Trekking Association. He couldn't circle the entire building, because the drifts had swept down from the higher ground and piled up against the back wall, so that he would have to clamber up the snowbank to look through the window there.

Sensing no immediate danger, he went back to the front

door and, holding the rifle into his shoulder with one hand, reached towards the door handle with the other. Even these days DNT huts were sometimes left unlocked, but he didn't dare hope that this one would be. Yet when he turned the handle, the door opened softly inwards. No creak of hinges. No call of welcome from within. No gunshot. Just a feeling like a sigh of a threshold being broken and inert air disturbed.

He lifted his left hand to support the rifle, then stepped inside, sweeping the barrel left and right, his finger kissing the cold metal of the trigger. Still covering the small entrance hall and the main living room beyond with the Remington, he dropped to one knee and, with one hand, unfastened each of the snowshoes. He stepped out of them and walked into the living room and dining area, and glanced into the kitchen. The floor seemed dry everywhere. A good sign. Not a guarantee. He took a moment to steady his breathing. Three bedrooms still to check. He nudged open the door to the first one with the barrel of his rifle. Bending to look under one of the two sets of bunk beds, he held his breath, wondering if he'd have time to see anyone in the shadows beneath. Before being shot in the face. He couldn't picture the tall man lying under a bed on the off-chance that Erik and Sofia would turn up . . . but still, this was stupid.

At the second bedroom, he gingerly unlatched the door, then lowered himself to the floor, lying on his side. Remington in both hands, he kicked the door open and pulled the stock against his shoulder, ready to fire, as the room revealed itself. Nobody would expect him at floor level and he could see beneath the bunks inside. Nothing.

The final bedroom waited with its door ajar. He used the same method as with the second, mouth dry and heart

111

thumping in his chest all but audible. This door creaked a warning. But there was nobody inside to hear it.

Letting out the breath he had been holding, he closed his eyes and knocked his forehead once against the wooden floor, then clambered to his feet and went back outside to fetch Sofia. Ten minutes later, he was sitting at the kitchen table and she on the sofa, their boots off, rubbing the life back into their cold feet and groaning with pleasure.

'Can we make a fire?' she asked him. Kindling had been left in a neat pile beside the stove, along with a box of matches. A single match had been laid across the open box, ready for anyone who arrived with numb fingers. On the pine floor next to the stove was a bucket full of split birch logs and a folded old newspaper for tinder.

'I don't think so,' he said. 'The smoke would give us away.'

She nodded, looking more embarrassed for not having thought of that than disappointed about the fire.

'We can't stay long,' he said.

'I know,' she said.

He looked down at his toes, waggling them with the joy of being free of his boots. His nose was less thankful. He knew he would stink if he took off all his layers.

'Can we make some hot food?' she asked.

He glanced up at the nearest window. 'If we're quick,' he said. 'And if we keep a look-out.'

There was no running water. No electricity. And it was hard looking at those logs by the stove, knowing they couldn't get a roaring fire going. But it was a comfort all the same, having four sturdy walls and a roof around them. To be out of the wind and snow. To use a toilet and to be able to take off their hats and gloves.

He carried the kettle outside and while he was out there, took the walkie-talkie from his pocket and went up and down the channels, pausing a moment on each one in case he overheard someone talking. It could happen sometimes, he knew, if the other person was within range, because there were only so many available channels. Stepping on other traffic he'd heard it called, when you joined another conversation. Bad etiquette. God, but he would jump on that traffic if he found it. He would tell whoever it was that men were trying to kill him and his daughter. That they had already killed Lars and Karine Helgeland.

But there were no friendly voices. Twenty-two channels and nothing but white noise on any of them. Like the inanimate vocalization of the storm itself. White noise in a white world.

Not that he was surprised. Who else would be out here in this?

He put the transceiver away, then filled the kettle with snow and brought it inside, where he set up the camping stove on the living-room floor. As the water came to the boil, he made his daughter a hot chocolate and himself a cup of coffee with a jar of Nescafé some previous visitor had left in the kitchen cupboard. Sofia boiled up two of their food pouches while he stood by the window, drinking his coffee and looking south towards the tall firs beyond which lay the glacier.

'Look at me cooking us a full breakfast,' Sofia said, eyes tired but smiling. She gestured at the pan over the hissing blue flame. 'Beans, sausages, bacon and omelette for two, coming right up.'

He smiled back at her. 'We'll tell Mamma when we get home that you can do all the cooking from now on, OK?'

She nodded. 'So long as it comes in a foil pouch,' she said, then pinched the fingers and thumb of one hand together and kissed them like an Italian chef.

He laughed then, in spite of everything, and turned reluctantly back to watch the snow coming down beyond the window. When the food was ready, they ate quickly, shoving their spoons down into the steaming pouches and cramming the hot sausage and beans into their mouths, wincing at the heat and sucking air in between their teeth to cool the food.

He lifted the last of the coffee to his lips. 'Another few minutes and we'd better set off again,' he said into the cup. 'But first I need to look at your hand.'

Sofia was on her knees, packing away the stove and the little gas canister into his rucksack, but she held her hand up for him to see. 'The bandage is stuck to the dried blood. I don't want to take it off in case it starts bleeding again.'

He thought about that. 'We'll leave it for now,' he said. They had no fresh bandages anyway. Better to keep it clean.

'Why can't he just let us go?' she asked, looking up at him.

'Because we know that he and his men killed Mr and Mrs Helgeland,' he said. 'So he wants to make sure we can never tell anyone.' He tipped the last drops of coffee into the sink. *And because I killed two of them*, he thought. *Maybe three. And one of them was his brother.* 'Also, I think I've upset him.'

He regretted his grim smile immediately. Sofia was too young, probably too traumatized, to appreciate that sort of dark humour. She looked up at him with round eyes, and he felt dirty to his very marrow for what those eyes had seen him do. It sickened him. But Sofia was alive, and there was no depravity, no corruption of his humanity, no wickedness he would not partake of to keep her safe.

'I don't know who these people are,' he said, 'but I do know they have something to do with the copper mine the Helgelands were speaking out against.'

There were tears in Sofia's eyes now. 'How could they do it?' she asked. She looked genuinely confused. 'How could they just kill people like that?'

He didn't know how to answer her, but knew she needed him to say something.

'Some people have no light in their souls, Lillemor,' he said.

She mulled this over, and he thought about himself and wondered if *he* had any light in his own soul. *You are my light*, he thought, looking at her, but didn't say it.

Then Sofia stood, pulling tight the drawstring of the rucksack and fastening the lid. And as he watched her, he knew he loved her far beyond his ability to express it or even grasp the extent of it in his own mind. She was his heart walking around outside his body.

'Pappa,' she said, hefting his rucksack in both hands and waddling it over to him. Her face seemed to clench in on itself, the small muscles in her cheeks tightening like hard little knots. 'Are we going to die?'

Her words hit him like a freight train. And yet he bit back the impulsive reply that sprang to his lips. The question had taken courage and he would not patronize her. Not any more. He took the pack from her and set it down on the floor beside them. Gripping Sofia by the shoulder, he tilted her chin with his other hand and gazed deep into her eyes. 'We're not going to die,' he said, 'because we never give up. No matter what.' He thumbed a tear from her cheek. 'No. Matter. What,' he said again, giving each word its own space and weight.

She watched his eyes, frowning, her teeth pulling at her bottom lip, which was dry and cracked from wind and cold. 'If it was Emilie here . . . instead of me . . . you'd have a better chance,' she said. 'She was such a good skier.'

'Sofia,' he said, and shook his head. 'Emilie was a great skier but so are you. And you're *so* brave. I couldn't have got this far without you. I mean it.'

The crease between her brows deepened. 'I wish she was here with us, Pappa,' she said. He saw a tiny speck of bright blood well on her lip. 'I know that's selfish of me. Because if she was here now, she'd be scared like I am. She might be killed. But . . .'

She looked away, leaving her words hanging there between them. Suddenly Erik was no longer in a DNT hut in the Lyngen Alps, but in a climbing centre in south London on a grey Saturday morning. What was meant to be a holiday visiting his father had turned into a nightmare beyond imagining. He remembered being on his knees beside Emilie's broken body because she had fallen. Six metres. A fault with her safety harness. A survivable fall, but as they say, it's not the falling that kills you. In his mind he was there, stroking Emilie's face and telling her she was going to be OK, even though he knew she was not.

'I'm sorry, Pappa,' Sofia said, and now she reached out and brushed a tear from his own cheek. 'I shouldn't have talked about her now.'

He reached out and blotted the blood on her lip with his knuckle. 'Yes, you should,' he told her, squeezing the words past the lump in his throat. 'It's good to talk about those we love, even if they're no longer with us.'

'Because in a way, they *are* still with us,' she said, as much a question as not.

'Yes,' he said. Then the two of them were quiet for a moment, giving the words and the memories time to settle.

'Now,' he said, and bent, grabbing the straps of his backpack, 'we really should—'

She stepped back from him, eyes wide, her mouth open as though she was trying to scream but could not.

'What is it?' he asked, his stomach lurching, and he twisted around to follow her gaze, which was fixed on something – or someone – beyond the window glass.

'Pappa,' she whispered.

'Down,' he said, pulling her down beside him, cold terror flooding his bowels.

He reached up and took the rifle off the countertop. Gestured at Sofia's rucksack which she had left on a chair by the table. 'Go,' he hissed, because Sofia was still staring up at the window, unwilling or unable to move. 'Go,' he said again, with a gentle push. She looked at him with bulging eyes, then crawled on hands and knees and took her backpack, wrapping her arms around it in a frightened embrace.

The tall man had been emerging from the treeline, his rifle raised as he came up the slope on foot towards the hut.

'We've got to get out.' His blood thrashing in his ears, Erik pointed to the door, which he knew could not yet be visible to the man outside. He eased Sofia's hat and jacket down from the hook and gave them to her, before hurrying on his own gear. A nod from him and Sofia opened the door.

They moved through it at a crouch and out onto the deck, and he looked off towards the firs beneath whose low-slung branches he had hidden the pulk and their skis. Reading his thoughts, Sofia moved, but he grabbed hold of her. No time. By now the tall man would have crested the rise. At any moment, he would come around the side of the hut and see them running for the trees. He would fix them in the scope of his rifle, first him, then the girl. The crosshairs on their backs. Two easy shots. Then he would bury them deep in the snow back down on the glacier where their tombs would remain frozen until the inexorably warming world revealed them to folk who saw only rotting mummies and not the people they had once been.

'Down there,' he hissed, and they dropped over the edge of the deck and slid underneath it, feet first, squeezing themselves and their packs between the wooden structure and the cold rock beneath. A desperate scramble. His guts churning with fear, his hands clenching around the rifle like a man thrown overboard clinging to a piece of driftwood.

'Pappa,' she whispered beside him, the whites of her eyes bright in the shadow.

'Shhh.' He pressed two fingers against her lips, their breath fogging in the dark space, which smelled of the nearby log pile and of the lichen on the rock and the spruce deck over their heads.

Then the *crump* of a booted foot on the first step. And another.

Sofia moved towards the light and he reached out to stop her but then he saw it. Her pink woollen hat, lying where it had fallen, just beyond the entrance to their hiding place. Sofia's hand shot out, grabbed the hat and pulled it into the darkness, and the two of them waited, holding their breath, terrified that the man had seen.

*Crump. Crump.* When the tall man mounted the steps, he took three paces, the planks creaking beneath his weight, then he stopped. He was standing right above their heads. Erik looked at Sofia. A trickle of snow fell through a small gap onto her upturned face.

*Crump . . . Crump.*

He gently thumbed the Remington's safety and pointed the barrel up to the crack in the boards where the snow had drizzled in, settling his finger on the cold trigger. He had three rounds left. One in the chamber, two in the magazine. He could squeeze the trigger and the round from the Remington 700 would maybe tear through the wood and drive up into the man's groin and kill him, or at least incapacitate him. But equally, the round might deflect. Could miss altogether. And then what? The tall man would kill them like rats in a bucket.

He let the tension from his finger transfer to the trigger, taking in the millimetres of slack until the trigger stopped moving. Any more force and the rifle would fire.

*Crump, crump, crump.* The man moved away from them, towards the door of the hut, waited ten seconds, let himself in.

*Not yet*, he told himself. *Not yet.* Let him get inside properly. Maybe go into one of the bedrooms. Kneel down to check under the bed.

He counted to five in his head.

*Now!* He shoved their backpacks out through the gap, then scrambled after them, wriggling out from under the deck. Then he turned and reached back to pull Sofia out. They put on their packs and he mouthed *go!* at her, pointing off towards the firs, and she ran through the deep snow while he turned back to face the hut and brought the rifle up to his shoulder, training the sights on the windows, each in turn. Walking backwards. Sinking up to the knee with each awkward step.

He could hear Sofia behind him, dragging the pulk out from the trees, but he kept his eye to the rifle scope. He thought he saw movement through the kitchen window and held his breath, but he held his fire too and kept moving away. He would only shoot if he could rest the crosshairs on the man's body. Below the throat and above the navel. Centre mass. With any luck a fatal shot.

And yet, for all he knew, he might at that very moment be filling the scope of the other man's weapon. Was the tall man standing back in the shadow beyond one of the windows, his finger on the trigger? Taking a breath and letting it slowly out between his lips. Seconds from firing.

The thought prickled the skin up and down his body. *Just keep moving.*

'Hurry, Pappa!' Sofia hissed, and now he turned and saw that she had his skis and the pulk ready for him. Finally turning his back on the hut, he put on the harness, slung the rifle over one shoulder and went to clip into his skis. The right ski went on easily enough but he could not clip into the left.

'Shit!' he growled. There was snow wedged into the binding and snow stuck in the toe end of his left boot.

'Quick, Pappa!' Sofia said.

He unclipped from his right ski, picked up the left and banged it against a tree, then burrowed a thumb into the binding to clear the last of the snow. Then he dropped the ski and kicked the tree with the snow-wedged boot to free up the little metal bar at the front.

'OK,' he said, clipping back into his skis.

'Your gloves, Pappa,' Sofia said, looking at his hands gripping the poles.

They were still in the house, hanging on the knob of a kitchen cupboard to dry. He ground his teeth. 'Doesn't matter. Go,' he said, and they pushed off into the woods, snow spilling from the lower branches as they forced their way amongst the firs.

They skied uphill for over two hours, through woods that were frozen in time and steeped in solitude. No sign that anyone had been there before. No tracks of animals, no movement or sound of birds. No trace of life beyond their own pluming breath and beating hearts. It was a silent, heavy, shadowy place and reminded him of a book he had read to the girls when they were small. About a place called Narnia. A land of ice and snow, where it was always winter but never Christmas.

Sofia looked strong. *She's showing me that she can ski just as well as Emilie*, he thought. But then he knew that wasn't it at all. She was showing Emilie how she could ski.

*Because in a way she's still with us.*

They followed the contours of the land, avoiding the steepest climbs and skirting the edges of small valleys, and when they emerged from the forest onto the lower slope of a wind-scoured hill, they stopped to catch their breath and look back the way they had come.

'Your hands, Pappa,' said Sofia.

He thrust his poles into the snow, cupped his hands in front of his mouth and huffed hot breath into them. Then he crossed his arms and buried his hands in his armpits. 'They're OK,' he told her. But they were not OK. He knew his own hands better than most people knew theirs. His livelihood depended on them. They were his tools, and any craftsman knows you look after your tools or you pay the price. Almost all feeling had fled from his hands not long after leaving the hut. He had hardly been able to grip the poles and would have lost them were it not for the straps around his wrists.

'Let me see,' Sofia said, skiing over to him.

'I'm fine,' he said.

'Let me see, Pappa,' she insisted, and held her own hands out to him.

He placed his hands in hers. They were deathly white against the dark blue of her mittens.

'Can you feel this?' She was squeezing his hands and rubbing them with her good thumb.

He shook his head. All he could feel was a throbbing in the flesh and a sensation of pins and needles. He looked up at the darkening sky and the snow coming down.

'Maybe you could take my ring off,' he said, looking at the silver wedding band on the fourth finger of his right hand. 'In case my fingers swell.'

She twisted the ring off and put it in the chest pocket of his jacket.

'But don't tell Mamma I took it off,' he said, forcing a smile.

She took off her rucksack and opened it and dug around until she found her spare socks. Then she pulled her mittens off with her teeth and stuck them on her pole handles and asked for his hands again. He gave her his right one first and she pushed one of the socks onto it, tucking it beneath his jacket sleeve and mid-layer but over his thermal base layer, until it reached almost to his elbow. Then she felt for the joint at the base of his thumb and when she had it, she pinched the wool over it and kept it pinched as she pulled the sock off.

She took out her Swiss Army knife and started with the little scissors. They snagged against the material, so she pulled the main blade out and set to work cutting off the piece she was holding between her finger and thumb. Then she repeated the whole process with his left hand and the other sock, and when she had finished he held up both hands with their new sock mittens and smiled.

'What? It's better than nothing,' she said defensively.

'I love them,' he said. 'They'll all be wearing them soon.'

She smiled back at him and they set off, the moment's levity easing the route ahead. But it wasn't long before the weather worsened and the clouds descended again, as if the storm itself, having lost sight of them when they were sheltering in the DNT hut, had been searching for them ever since. The storm swooped down, turning the once-white world a monotonous grey. After that came heavier snow. It enveloped them as if they were skiing into an impenetrable wall of static, the random fuzzy pattern on an old analogue TV when no transmission signal was received. He could see barely five metres ahead, which made it slow-going because they had to be careful and read the ground. Any downward gradient now might lead to a sudden drop, so they all but crept down any such slope, whereas before they had seized the opportunity of speed and momentum.

He made Sofia ski behind him and the pulk. He didn't like that he couldn't see her, or that she would be the one the tall man saw first if he caught up with them. But it was up to him to lead the way. And he decided it was better that he broke through the new snow first and gave her some sort of track to ski in. Perhaps he could even shelter her in his wake, take the brunt of the wind – which was growing in its malevolence. The surface of the snow ahead was creeping towards him in whorls and eddies. Before long, it came at him in freezing veils and he had to almost shut his eyes to keep from being blinded, and hold his lips pressed tightly together, or else the snow would seek to drive into his throat and lungs and stop his breath.

*I should have taken the shot back at the hut*, he told himself. But he hadn't, and now he feared the two of them would freeze to death out here. Or stumble off a cliff edge and break on the rocks far below. And wouldn't that be some dark twist of fate? Enough to make anyone believe a family could be cursed.

Now and then they stopped to check the GPS compass on his watch. He had taken it off his wrist and put it in his pocket so he wouldn't have to remove his new mitten to get to it. But his hands now lacked the dexterity even to fetch it from his pocket, so he gave the watch to Sofia and told her to check that they were heading north-west. They could not see the mountains around them, or the trees, and with the very surface moving beneath their skis, there was nothing to fix his eyes upon. Each time they stopped, the snow silted into their tracks, so it was impossible to tell which way they had come from. The compass and the driving wind were their only indicators of direction. And the wind couldn't be trusted. Even when he thought they'd been skiing in a straight line, the wind on their left side, covering them in a layer of ice and snow, he would feel it swoop down on him from ahead. Erik wondered if it was being channelled by valleys that he couldn't see.

'We need to find shelter before it gets dark,' Sofia called to him, her voice frail and far-flung, like a small bird caught in a tornado.

'We keep going,' he yelled back to her. She was right, though. They couldn't stay out in this. And surely it would only get worse the higher they went. But look what had happened the last time they had stopped. His decision to rest had almost cost them their lives.

'We keep going,' he yelled again, this time giving the words to the storm. A declaration of his defiance. Of *their* defiance. Even though he knew he was no match for this. But the girl. She had to endure. He would not concede any other possibility.

He wasn't a religious man. Elise would probably say he was not a spiritual man either. And yet he'd not completely closed his mind to the idea of there being something more. Something beyond the human experience. Science couldn't explain everything, and while he didn't believe in some benevolent power hiding behind the curtain, he couldn't help but think, or at least hope, that not everything was random, every biological life a feeble and brief ember amidst the chaos. He couldn't help but hope that chaos, having snuffed out Emilie, would not now snuff out Sofia too. He would not let it. Not while he had breath. Not even if his heart stopped beating.

These were the nonsensical thoughts that swirled somewhere in his mind as he pushed on through this shifting, unsound world.

Each time they came to an incline and looked up, the

slope vanished into the swirling mists above their heads and they didn't know if they would be climbing ten metres or a hundred. But up they went, herringboning or side-stepping up the steepest parts, Sofia turning her face from the blasts, he struggling with the pulk.

By four o'clock it had been dark for almost an hour. He couldn't grasp his poles at all now and so would push down with his wrists onto the tops of the grips, which lessened his propulsion but was better than letting the poles hang on their straps and drag through the snow. He feared they were going too slowly, and knew Sofia must be freezing, because he was freezing. Their muscles weren't generating enough heat. But it was too dangerous to ski faster when they could barely see where they were going.

*Just keep going. Because he's out there. He's out there somewhere and he won't hesitate like you did. He'll take the shot.*

They came up onto a plateau and some instinct drew them together, and for a while they stood holding each other in the storm. Holding on to each other and breathing hard, and he pressed his mouth against the layer of ice on her hat and said they were going to be OK. But when he lifted his eyes to look around, the world was ill-defined. Diffuse and unreal. Not properly formed, like some heavenly body far, far from the sun, composed of gases and debris. A failed star.

He could feel her body trembling with cold and didn't know what to do.

'I'm so tired, Pappa,' she said, her head heavy against his chest. He held her tighter still, trying to wrap himself around her to shield her from the wind and the stinging ice, and thought that maybe they should take the shovel and dig a hole right where they stood. Nothing fancy, just a hole deep enough that they could lie down out of the wind and sleep. But he knew he wasn't thinking straight. His brain was dulled by tiredness and cold. It wasn't useless yet, like his hands, but he no longer trusted it completely. He knew that people suffering from exposure and the onset of hypothermia often felt a euphoric urge to sleep. But if they lay down, there was a strong chance they would never get up again.

He rubbed his arms up and down Sofia's body. He was so frightened for her.

'What's your name?' he asked her.

'What?'

'Just tell me, what's your name?'

'Sofia Frida Amdahl,' she said wearily.

'How old are you?'

'Pappa? What are you doing?'

'How old?' he shouted.

'Thirteen,' she said, louder now because she had realized what he was doing.

'What did you get for your birthday?'

She pulled her neck warmer down so he could hear her better.

'A Fjällräven backpack. It's blue. Some headphones. The new Stephen King book.'

'What else?'

She was quiet for a moment, then said, 'A green hoodie. A Bluetooth speaker.'

The wind couldn't scatter her words because they were trapped in the pocket of protected space between their two bodies.

'Anything else?' he asked.

'This stupid pink hat,' she said.

He smiled in spite of everything. 'You said you liked it.'

'I lied,' she said.

'At least you're not wearing socks on your hands,' he said.

'I thought you liked them,' she said.

'I lied.'

Her speech wasn't slurred. Her mind still sharp.

'Let's go,' he said.

The ground beneath his skis fell away and even as he tumbled down, he yelled to Sofia to warn her. Then he was moving faster and faster and couldn't breathe as the snow roared around him and he flailed helplessly against it. Then silence.

It was pitch-black and still. And so peaceful. He didn't feel cold or afraid. Quite the opposite: he felt safe. Protected. As if some part of his mind recalled a memory of the womb. He thought he could sleep at last. Just sleep and let everything fade away.

Or . . . was he already dead?

No, he decided he wasn't dead. Because something was tugging at the corner of his mind, like a fish hook caught in a mackerel's lip.

A sound now, distant and vague, somewhere beyond that strange tranquillity. Like the low rasping voice of a raven.

*Why would a raven be here?* he thought.

He was sure his eyes were open, and yet they were blind. He tasted blood and felt its warmth and the salty sting of it in his eye.

That faraway sound again. Why could they not leave him

in peace? He needed to rest. Just for a while. He closed his eyes and felt himself drifting, unmooring from himself.

He was vaguely aware of the slow, even rhythm of his breathing.

Then . . . nothing.

His bones and organs jumped inside him, like a hypnic jerk in someone who's beginning to fall asleep and believes, for a split second, that they're falling.

*Sofia.*

He gasped. Not enough air. He tried to lift his arms but couldn't. It was as if he was encased in concrete, and now there was no tiredness, no serenity, only blind, heart-pounding panic.

'Sofia!' he yelled. A dead sound. 'Sofia!' He remembered falling, his skis and legs being swept away as the ground disappeared beneath him. Had Sofia fallen too? She'd been right behind him. Was she buried somewhere nearby? 'Sofia!' He tried to kick out. Tried to thrust his hands into the pack snow all around him. He felt the blood running from his lip into his eye and didn't know how this could be, but then he knew. He was upside down. He had no other way of telling which way was up and which way was down, but the blood told him. And maybe the pressure in his head, now that he thought about it, pushing against the inside of his skull and the back of his eyes.

He stopped struggling and listened. He knew he didn't have much time before he used up what oxygen there was, so he held his breath and stayed still, and then he heard her calling him. He heard her shouting 'Pappa', and knew she must be utterly terrified. She was alone in the dark and so he started fighting again. Grinding his useless hands into the snow, trying to create space in which to move. He no longer cared about conserving his air. He raged. And he heard the rhythmic bite of a shovel in snow and knew she was digging.

'Here – I'm here!' he yelled, the sound of his own voice strangely muted, as if the air around him was not air but water.

The digging stopped and so he yelled out to her again. Then the shovel bit once more, closer now, maybe somewhere above his left shoulder. Down came the shovel, again and again, and he managed to bring his arms closer to his body and began to burrow up through the snow towards her.

'Hold on, Pappa,' Sofia said, her voice muted and far away, though she was no more than half a metre ahead.

His skis were off and so he pointed his feet and stabbed the toe ends of his boots upward, chipping away at the compacted snow.

For a while, the two of them worked in silence and eventually he felt a rush of cold air flood down upon him.

'I see you,' she said, her voice clearer, and she dug even faster now.

'I'm OK,' he said. 'I'm OK,' he said again, this time to himself.

'Hold on, nearly there,' she said.

Much of the weight upon him gone now, he found he was able to move, and he twisted around, half swimming, half crawling up through the loose, broken snow towards her, gasping, like some undead fiend escaping the grave.

Sofia fell to her knees and threw herself at him, embracing him for a moment before standing and trying to pull him up onto his feet.

'What happened?' he asked, standing unsteadily, drawing the freezing air into his lungs.

'You fell from up there,' she said, pointing upward with the shovel. 'There's a ledge and there was a lip of snow overhanging it. Like we sometimes get on the roof at home.'

He could just about make out the edge of the drop in the darkness, because the wind was sweeping freezing clouds of snow over it.

'I must have brought a load down on top of me too,' he said, running the back of his hands over his body, doing an inventory of his limbs and bones to make sure nothing was broken.

Sofia pointed at his face. 'You're bleeding.'

He cuffed his lip and eye. 'It's nothing. Think I hit myself with my pole on the way down. I'll never call you clumsy again.' His hearing wasn't right and it made him feel unbalanced.

She stepped into the heap of snow and helped him, brushing the loose debris off his jacket and head. 'Stand still,' she said. 'You've got snow in your ear.' He grimaced as she stuck her little finger in his right ear and dug out the icy plug. 'That's better,' she said, stepping back.

He dragged himself to his feet and realized he was still harnessed to the pulk, which lay on the surface nearby. Lucky it had not been buried with him, or Sofia would not have been able to use the shovel to dig him out.

He reached out for the shovel now. 'Need to find my skis,' he croaked.

'Your hands,' she said.

He looked at his hands, at the snow sticking to the wool of the sock mittens she had made for him. He tried to clench

131

his hands into fists but could not, and knew she was right and that he would be unable to grip the shovel. So, he had to watch while she dug again. It didn't take her long. She found his skis and the pole that had gone astray and cleared the snow from his bindings.

'You're cold, Pappa,' she said.

'I'll be fine,' he said. But he was shivering. He'd been still for too long and now he was out in the open again, his body temperature was dropping fast. 'We need to keep climbing,' he said, fumbling with the poles until he had looped the straps over his hands. He lifted his feet one at a time, banging the toe end of each of his boots with the pole to knock ice away from the little bar that inserted into the bindings. Then he clipped into his skis while Sofia straightened out the pulk behind him. The other pole was bent now too, though not enough to cause a problem.

He looked up into the dark at the snow swirling out over the edge from where he had fallen. He could have twisted a knee or broken a leg had the skis not come off. Could have broken his neck. Sofia could have been alone now because he hadn't seen the drop. The thought turned his stomach.

*You're alive. You're fine*, he told himself.

'Ready?' he asked her. But how could she be ready? How could anyone be ready for this?

'Yes,' she said. 'You?'

'Yes.' He swallowed hard. He thumped one hand upon the other and it seemed to him that the flesh itself had frozen, as he could feel the vibration of the impact in his wrist and forearm but nothing at all in either hand.

'I'm ready, Pappa,' she said again.

He nodded. He pushed his right ski forward and then his left. His body felt heavy and so did his mind, but he was moving again, his skis furrowing the snow. His wrists forcing the poles down with each step. The wind moaned in the night like a soul in torment, trapped in some dark and dreadful plane between life and death.

# 9

AT SOME POINT in the early evening, they came across a rock sticking out of the snow. As they began to skirt around it, Erik told her to stop. They were dead on their feet. They needed food and water and so he had Sofia take the avalanche probe and poke it into the snow at the base of the rock. She did this all the way around until, on the eastern side, the seven-foot aluminium pole sank almost up to the hand grip, telling them that the rock had an overhang.

She took the shovel and dug out the snow, piling it up on the edge of the trench as he told her to. Then he dragged the pulk behind the wall of snow she had made, and the two of them clambered down into the hole behind the pulk and the embankment, out of the wind, sheltered by the overhanging rock.

Beyond their den, out there in the dark, snow drove in gusts, swirling around their rock like white jinns summoned by some sorcerer to do his bidding. As if they were searching for the man and the girl and were working themselves into a fury.

He crossed his arms over his chest and held himself and she did the same. 'Is this good?' he asked her. She said that it was, and she moved closer to him, until their bodies pressed against each other and he could feel her, each breath in and out.

After a while she said, 'What if he finds us, Pappa?'

'We won't stay long,' he told her. The clouds of their breath were mixing, a silver pall spreading in the gloom. 'But I need to get my hands working again.'

She was hunched down into herself and very still, but her eyes moved beneath the folded rim of her hat, taking in the rock above their heads and the night beyond their little refuge.

'It's warm here,' she said.

He smiled. 'I think it's cosy. Maybe we should buy it.'

She almost laughed, and he pulled her against him, felt the warmth of her breath.

For a moment they sat there in the hole, safe from the storm and the night and the man who was out there somewhere.

Then she pulled away from him and her eyes met his in the dark.

'Can we use the stove?' she asked.

He looked at her face and saw the hope there, and he couldn't bear to disappoint her.

'Yes, we can use the stove,' he said.

She crawled out and fetched what they needed, and in twenty minutes they were spooning hot food into their mouths and drinking hot water flavoured orange with soluble energy tablets.

The fog of their breath mixed with the steam and the aroma of pasta and meatballs in tomato and garlic sauce. An incongruous but comforting smell that belied their situation.

'Do you think he has any food?' she asked, meaning the man hunting them.

He hadn't thought about it. 'I don't think so. Why would he?' he said. 'He couldn't have known he'd be chasing us all this way from the Helgelands' place.'

'Then he'll be hungry,' she said.

'He will.'

'And weak. Maybe weaker than us.'

'Maybe weaker than us,' he said, though he didn't think that was true somehow.

'I was thinking, Pappa,' she said, then frowned and blew on the spoonful of hot pasta, 'maybe Mamma won't have called for mountain rescue.' She shovelled the pasta into her mouth. 'She'll expect us to be snugged up in one of the DNT huts,' she said, eating with her mouth open to let out the heat, 'waiting for the weather to improve.' She shook her head. 'And as you said, phones don't work up here, so she won't be expecting a call.' She turned her frown on him then. 'You said what you said to make me feel better. Didn't you?'

He considered how to answer, in the end deciding she had earned the truth.

'Yes,' he admitted. 'I didn't want you to give up.'

She flinched. 'Do you think I would give up?'

He knew what she was really asking him: *Do you think Emilie would give up if she were here instead of me?*

'No,' he said. 'I don't think you would ever give up.' And he meant it.

She watched him, weighing his words in the silence between them as the storm frenzied around the rock that was their sanctuary.

'Give me your hand,' she said. He did as he was told, and she asked if they could run the stove again, just to help warm him, but he said they couldn't afford to waste what little gas they had, and so she began to knead his right hand with her own.

'Can you feel this?' she asked.

He knew his face had already told her the answer. 'Not really,' he said.

'Not really, or not at all?'

'Not at all,' he admitted.

She swore under her breath. He didn't chastize her for it, just watched her hands manipulating his.

'Just five minutes with the stove. I could heat another mug of water and press your hands around it,' she suggested.

It was tempting but he shook his head. 'I think it's worse if you warm up and then freeze again,' he said. 'And anyway, we can't stay here much longer.'

She took off her own mittens so she could better work into the flesh of his palm and each of his fingers.

'No, Sofia,' he said, worried that her own hands would get too cold.

'Just for a minute,' she said. 'It's cosy in here, remember?'

'Just for a minute then.'

He let her work as best she could with her own bandaged hand, and when she had massaged both his hands, said he had some feeling back in them. Then he shoved them inside his jacket, beneath his arms, and they sat for a long while.

It was truly a respite from the pain and effort, and the thought of leaving the rock was almost too much. The silence between them felt to him like a spell suspending time and cloaking them from the physical world, and he knew she felt something similar – that if one of them spoke, it would break the enchantment and the sand timer would run again, and the tall man would resume his hunt for them. The longer the silence stretched, the more they feared to break it, and at some point they both fell asleep.

He dreamt of the figure in the broad-brimmed hat. He and Sofia were in a forest at night. They were lost, he couldn't find his skis, and he realized he had no boots either, just the socks on his feet as they tried to move through the snow. But he couldn't move. He was stuck, as though the snow around his feet had frozen, locking him in place, while Sofia continued on without him. Deeper into the forest she went and he called to her but she couldn't hear him. Even before he saw the figure, he felt its presence, like a weight in his chest.

He yelled at Sofia to stop, to wait for him, but she kept on going, moving further ahead, towards the figure who was coming forward to meet her.

He yelled again for her to stop. He yelled at the man to stay away from her, but no sound broke the space between them. As he struggled, the man came closer, and Erik saw he was dressed in black, or grey perhaps, which explained why he was hard to make out amongst the shadowy trees in the claustrophobic darkness. He saw the glint of an eye amongst the gloom, a baleful ember glowing beneath the hat which was pulled down low, and he screamed and pulled one foot free of the ice, desperate to get to Sofia before the other man did. Then the other foot came free and he was running now, plunging through the snow, and his shoeless feet didn't feel the cold. He was running, his breathing ragged, his soundless cries painful in his throat, and yet each pace took him no nearer.

'Pappa.'

He woke and could see from Sofia's wide, staring eyes that she was afraid, and for a cold heartbeat he feared that the tall man had found them. 'You wouldn't wake up, Pappa,' she said, a tremble in her lip, and he knew that was what had scared her.

'Just tired, Lillemor,' he said, scrubbing the sleep from his face, then pulling his hands away in confused horror because there was no sensation in them, just of something cold against his cheeks. In that moment of waking, he had forgotten that his hands were numb. 'I was deep in a dream,' he told her.

Her brows drew together. 'The one about the strange man?' she asked.

His stomach lurched. How could she know about that?

'Mamma told me,' Sofia said, reading the surprise on his face. She picked up his right hand and began to massage it. 'She said you sometimes have scary dreams about a man whose face you can't see. She said it started after Emilie died.'

'It's nothing,' he said. He tamped down the irritation – no, anger – that Elise would have shared this.

'But who do you think it is?' she asked.

'It's just a dream, Sofia. It doesn't mean anything. Dreams are your mind's way of clearing out all the rubbish while you're asleep.' He tapped two fingers of his left hand against his head. 'All the bits and pieces you've picked up without even knowing. Your mind tries to stitch them together into something. That's why they don't usually make any sense.'

'I know *you* say that.' She looked angrily into the dark. 'When I have a nightmare, you always say it's just a silly dream, but there's more to it. Sometimes at least.' He watched her working on his hand, thinking how strange it was that he could barely feel her touch.

After a while he said, 'What do you think dreams are then?'

She screwed up her face and shrugged. 'I don't know. I think they can be trying to tell us something.'

'Ah,' he said, and nodded. 'Well, the night we came up to the mountain, I dreamed I was eating a pizza. And then I needed to pee but couldn't find a toilet anywhere.' He smiled in spite of his aches and pains. 'That's some deep shit.'

Sofia tutted. 'Pappa,' she said, lightly slapping his hand before putting it down onto his lap and picking up his left one. 'Not that kind of dream. The other sort. Like the one you keep having. I think it's trying to tell you something.' She turned his hand over and pressed her thumbs into his palm. 'Maybe the man needs you to know something?'

'The man?' he said, though he knew who she meant.

'The one whose face you can't see.' She brought his hand up to her face and huffed warm breath onto it. 'Maybe he wants to tell you something about Emilie.' She said this in a quiet voice, head down but eyes looking up at him from beneath her brow.

He looked away. *But it's you who's there in the dream every time*, he thought.

'Maybe it's something to do with the accident,' she went

on. 'And the man whose face you never see is a representation of your own conscience. A personification of some kind.'

'Good word,' he said.

She scowled.

He nodded. 'I'm sorry. It's just that you sound like your *mor*. I don't need you getting involved with my stupid dreams too.'

She let go of his hand, folded her arms and slumped back against her rucksack, looking hurt. Looking angry. Maybe she wanted to talk about Emilie. Maybe that was why she had brought up his recurring dream. But now was not the time. They had enough to worry about. What good would it do either of them to bring the weight of it all down upon themselves? That avalanche of grief.

'We've been here too long,' he said. 'It's my fault. I shouldn't have slept.'

'But what about your hands?' she asked.

'I'll keep moving them as much as I can.' He looked down at them. 'When we find Mrs Helgeland's brother, he'll be able to help. If anyone knows what to do about cold hands, it'll be a reindeer herder who spends the winters out here.'

Sofia nodded and pulled her backpack around in front of her. 'I'll help you loop the poles over your hands.'

'It's mostly uphill now. I'm better using my legs. They're strong.' He smiled at her. 'Not as strong as yours, but strong enough.'

She smiled back and twisted and thumped a mittened hand against the boulder. 'Thank you, rock,' she said with a formal air. 'You have helped us and we are grateful. Maybe we'll come back and see you again one day.'

'The storm isn't so bad now,' he said, up on his knees and peering out. He didn't know if it was true, or he was just growing used to the wind and the snow. But he did know that for all the storm had taken out of them, they wouldn't have survived for so long without it.

They clambered from underneath the rock, pulled out the pulk and the rest of their kit, and wearily clipped into their skis. He saw the look of grim resignation on her face and wished more than anything that he could take this suffering from her. If there was a god, or some great arbiter to whom fell the task of tipping the scales in favour of those without sin or a catalogue of misdeeds, or even yet the years to have made mistakes and learned from them, then he would pray to that judge now. And if that didn't work, he would jump up and down and wave his arms and curse that loathsome power until his throat bled. Thus, by making himself known, the judgement would be made, the sentence carried out. His ruin for her salvation.

But there was no such power. There was just the mountains and the snow and the dark. And the man out there who was hunting them.

'Ready, Pappa? she asked him, banging her poles together to knock off the snow. *She* asked *him*.

'I'm ready,' he said.

Up they went, snow skimming across their path like a running sea, like spindrift racing across the grey scudding water of the fjord. Up between dark, looming crags, along narrow ravines whose normally jagged edges were rounded and bulbous with overhangs that terrified him. A cruel gust could dislodge one of those cornices and bring it down to bury them alive, their fate known only to themselves as they drew their final suffocating breaths and closed their eyes in the dark for the last time.

They moved as fast as they dared and were relieved whenever they found themselves on open ground. Eventually he was sure they had arrived on the plateau where Mrs Helgeland had told them her brother and his herd were located.

'So where are you, Hánas?' he said under his breath, turning his face into the wind and squinting against the whipping flakes as he scoured the darkening twilight for sign of the Sami or his animals, or perhaps a light from inside the man's tent. 'Keep your eyes peeled,' he told Sofia. 'I don't think we're far from where Hánas was the other night.'

'It's colder up here,' Sofia said, crossing her arms and beating her shoulders with her hands. Her face was pale in the gloom, her mouth spread in a closed-lipped grimace of discomfort.

He skied up to her and told her to stick her poles in the snow. 'Do what I do,' he said, then he started spinning his arms in circles, keeping them straight out and to the sides. Slow at first but getting faster, the circles getting bigger. 'It'll put heat in your shoulders, chest and upper back and push the blood into your hands,' he said, as she started swinging her own arms round and round. He hoped it would help his own hands too, and after fifteen repetitions he stopped the movement and reversed the circles. Sofia did the same.

'Do I look as silly as you?' he asked, feeling like some Neanderthal attempting to mimic the creatures of the sky. She rewarded him with a wan smile. When at last they finished, he felt the thrum of pins and needles in his hands, which was better than the previous dead numbness.

143

'Where now?' she asked, looking around. She unzipped his watch from her pocket and held it out, tilting it to catch what little light there was so they could both read the compass display.

He glanced at the watch, then turned his face to the east and, through the slanting snow, could just make out the peaks of the lower summits beyond the Strupbreen glacier. 'Karine's and Lars's house is down there somewhere,' he said, thinking how strange it was that he and Sofia were now up here alone in the dark when just two nights ago they had been safe and warm in that cosy cabin, drinking hot milk and honey in front of a blazing fire. And to think that Lars and Karine no longer existed. That they were gone.

It made him feel even colder.

'Let's keep going,' he said.

They pushed on and after another hour he was sure that the wind was lessening. But the result was thicker cloud, slung low above their heads, laden with snow and pressing down upon them and the world through which they struggled. The storm had less anger in it now but more hate. It was so cold that if they needed to rest, they dared not stop for long for fear of freezing where they stood. And with night coming, it was only going to get colder.

'Maybe we should have stayed at the rock,' Sofia called. She was skiing just behind him and the pulk, and it was slow-going because of the dark and their fear of ground they could not properly see.

'We'll find somewhere better than the rock,' he said over his shoulder, though he wasn't so sure. It was getting very dark and he felt a creeping fear in his gut that he had made the wrong decision, that climbing higher into the mountains in search of some elusive stranger was a fool's errand. For all he knew, Hánas might have known that a storm was coming and taken his herd down some other way to lower ground. Didn't the Sami possess a sixth sense for that sort of thing? Or was that just some racist bullshit? He'd read online that the Sami had more than one hundred and eighty words for snow and ice. Or was it tracks in the snow? Something like that. Either way, Mrs Helgeland's brother knew more about these conditions and these mountains than Erik did, which meant they needed to find him and very, very soon.

To his right, something swept past in the darkness, stopping his heart for a second. Just a bird. An owl out hunting hare.

'The rock was good,' he admitted, 'but we couldn't stay there.' He hoped there was still enough snow coming down to bury their tracks. Enough wind to silt them up. To erase their passing.

'Because the man would have found us?' Sofia said.

'If he saw the rock, he would have taken a look. Wouldn't you?' His mouth was stiff with cold. His speech felt clumsy, like he'd had one too many bourbons. 'If he looked, he'd have found us.'

They strode on, and he was starting to hate the pulk now. Starting to wonder if he could just take out the essentials and put them in his backpack and leave the pulk behind. Push it over a ledge and be rid of it.

'So what will we do,' Sofia asked, 'if we can't find Hánas?'

'We'll find him,' he said.

'And if we can't?'

'We'll find him,' he snapped.

She didn't speak again for a long time, and he felt bad for how he had spoken to her. She was afraid – of course she was. And she had every reason to doubt him. He had got them into this situation. She was his child and his charge. His role on this earth was to protect her until she grew stronger and wiser, and more capable than him. But look what he had brought her to.

They came amongst a forest of birch scrub, the miniature trees no thicker than his arm and growing close together so that they had to pick their way between them, which slowed their progress further. Now and then, the pulk caught on a trunk or on some tangle of rotten logs poking up through the snow, or else snagged on one of the many half-fallen trees or on the snow-laden branches that interlaced the forest. Each time, he cursed and growled, expending precious energy in getting free again. Several times he got stuck fast and had to wait while Sofia moved the pulk off whatever was obstructing it.

It snagged and caught again, and in frustration he reached out and grabbed hold of a tree to pull himself forward and free the pulk. But the birch crumbled and broke and he fell backwards into the snow. For maybe two minutes he just lay there in a tangle of skis and poles, twisted because of the harness, staring up at the dark cloud sliding across the dark sky. The tree had been dead for years but had stood there anyway. Maybe it could not accept that its time was over.

'Are you OK, Pappa?' she asked, looking down at him.

He knew that if he closed his eyes, he would sleep. And it would be bliss.

'Help me up, Lillemor,' he said, and she did, brushing the

snow off him when he was up on his skis again. 'That damned tree was—'

She clutched his arm and snapped her head around, looking behind her, and he put his hands on her shoulders and pressed her down into a crouch alongside him.

'Shhh,' he whispered, a soft, low breath. Not because she had spoken, but because she must not. They stared off into the darkling forest, gooseflesh running up his arms, the skin of his scalp tightening beneath his hat. He thought Sofia must hear his heart thumping.

Because someone was there. He had heard the same thing that had brought her head around fast enough to create its own breeze. A snapping of sticks. A small sound but incongruous in the relative quiet of this primeval forest of living and dead trees.

Slowly, so slowly, he slipped the rifle strap off his shoulder and brought the weapon round. When he found he couldn't close his hand around the forestock, he let it rest on his open palm while his other hand fumbled for the safety, then moved to the bolt handle. He could no longer take hold of the handle because his fingers wouldn't obey him, but he thought he could operate it using the side of his hand.

The wind was in his face, and he narrowed his eyes against it. In his peripheral vision he saw the whites of Sofia's eyes, saw her mouth say *Pappa!*, and felt her mittened hand clutching at his coat, yet he made no attempt to draw the bolt and chamber the round because he feared the *click clack* sound of it giving them away. If it wasn't already too late.

Still peering into the darkness, he pulled his face from the rifle and put his mouth against her ear.

'Get behind me,' he whispered. 'Do it now.'

She moved, slow as a glacier because she couldn't risk their skis tangling. And because she was almost rigid with terror. And he winced at the sound of her left ski running across his own. But when he felt her body pressed against his shoulder blades, he lifted the bolt and slowly slid it back, the sound smooth and metallic, then eased it forward, pushing a round into the chamber and cocking the rifle.

Another snap of a twig out there amongst the trees. He moved the rifle's muzzle from left to right, his muscles tight, pumped full of blood. His eyes sifting the still shapes of those stunted birches for the shape of a man, because he needed to pull the Remington's trigger and kill the tall man before *he* killed them.

And then he saw movement in the corner of his eye and swept the rifle across and fired, the muzzle blooming with red-orange light for a fraction of a second before the report, which shocked him with its loudness. Then he ducked and felt Sofia behind him do the same, the two of them expecting the tall man to fire back. But no shot came, and he heard a thumping, rumbling sound and the snapping and cracking of birch twigs, and wondered if his gunshot had started an avalanche and what they could hear was snow tumbling down a mountainside.

'Reindeer!' Sofia said. 'Look!' She was pointing with her ski pole.

He saw them then, or rather saw a mass of dark shapes in flight, vanishing amongst the trees like shadow spirits fleeing a dream. The rumble of their hooves in the snow faded and, ten seconds later, the only sound was his and the girl's breathing, fast with fear, and the wind moaning amongst the birch trees.

'Well, we found the herd,' he said, slinging the rifle across his back and reaching down to pick up his poles by threading his hands through the straps. The relief he felt was immense, though marred by unease and regret. He wished he'd not fired the rifle. The shot would have been heard two kilometres away, maybe more. He could only hope that wherever their pursuer was, the swirling wind had made it difficult for him to pinpoint the direction from where the shot had come.

'What do we do now?' Sofia asked him. She stood wide-eyed beside him, shivering in the cold. She looked so young, so fragile, and yet he knew that if he told her they needed to ski another five kilometres, she would thrust her poles down into the snow and kick off.

'We find Hánas,' he said. 'He must be close.' He tried to ball his hands into fists but they wouldn't comply, and he remembered that as a child he had tried to move objects across the kitchen with his mind. This was like that. He willed his fingers to curl, but willing mind did not make willing flesh.

'Maybe we should stay here,' she suggested. 'Maybe he heard the rifle and is coming to see who is shooting at his reindeer.'

That was a good point, he realized, and it was not lost on him that they might be in danger of being shot at by Hánas too, if he saw shapes out there in the dark and thought people were trying to poach his reindeer. Did people do that out here? Was reindeer poaching a thing?

'I think we should keep moving,' he said. 'Better to stay warm.'

They moved off in the direction the reindeer had run, and

came across the snow where the animals had churned the ground in their panicked flight. He thought about the one that had wandered off from the herd and hoped he'd not hit it. If he had, he hoped it was now dead, not out there suffering, bleeding out in the snow. He did not believe in karma but here and now, with everything against them, was no time to be wrong.

They came to a ridge and his first instinct was to turn around and find another way, rather than risk skiing down dangerous ground in the dark. But then a possibility occurred to him. He told Sofia to wait while he went on, another twenty or so cautious strides.

He edged to the crest of the ridge and looked down, breathing hard. He blinked a few times, because now that his hands had betrayed him, he didn't fully trust his eyes either. 'Thank Christ,' he said to himself, the words rising in a fog of hot breath. 'Thank fucking Christ.' Because there, no more than a hundred metres away, in the lee of a round hill and protected from the wind by a wall of drifted snow, was a tent, glowing softly in the dark.

# 10

'WHO ARE YOU?'

The voice stopped them in their tracks. Erik fumbled to bring his rifle to bear, knowing he would have been dead already if the man asking the question had wanted it.

'Are you Hánas?' he asked. He had twisted around as far as he was able in the harness with the sled poles and pulk behind him.

'How do you know my name?' the man asked. His accent was thick.

Erik brought his skis up and around, repositioning the pulk so that he was now facing the man. Sofia turned too, and they both stood there, breathing hard, wondering if what they were looking at was real. The figure standing just two ski-lengths away seemed to have come out of nowhere, as if the wind and the snow and the dark had coalesced to form him. A man made of Arctic night.

'Who are you?' the man asked again. He looked to be

wearing a long coat, probably of reindeer hide, and his face was mostly hidden by a hood. He held his hunting rifle down by his hip, though it was very much pointed at Erik. Beside him stood a black dog, hackles raised, lip hitched to show its teeth.

'My name is Erik Amdahl and this is my daughter Sofia.' He lifted his arm and gestured to the girl, whose pale face was wreathed by her breath. 'We've been looking for you.'

The herder took two steps towards them, his snowshoes giving him the appearance of floating above the drifts. Erik knew he and Sofia must have skied right past the man and his dog, barely metres away, yet they had not seen him.

'Why?' The herder jerked up the barrel of the rifle. His dog was growling, a low rolling gnarl made more ominous by the dark and the steam issuing from the sides of its mouth.

'There's a man out there somewhere,' Erik said, sweeping an arm towards the high ground behind them, the pole dangling by its strap from his wrist. 'He's trying to kill us.'

The Sami tilted his head as if he thought he must have misheard.

'Someone is trying to kill you?' he said. His dog gave two short sharp barks. The man growled something in a language it understood, and the dog looked up at him, then sat obediently. 'You said someone is trying to kill you?' the herder asked again. The eyes within the shadow of his hood held only suspicion.

'It's true,' Sofia said, sliding forward until she was beside her father. 'There were more, but now there's just him.'

Hánas looked from her to Erik, who lifted the Remington a touch, as if to answer the herder's unspoken question.

Then the herder looked up to the ridge. 'Was that his rifle shot I heard?'

'No, that was me,' Erik said. 'I thought I saw something. But it was your reindeer.'

'You shot one of my animals?' Hánas asked.

'I don't know. I couldn't see. Look, we need your help. My daughter's freezing. We need shelter.'

Hánas looked at Sofia, then back at him. 'Your hands,' he said. Of course he had seen the way Erik was holding the rifle. Not holding it so much as resting it on his open palms.

'Frostbite,' Erik said.

'You don't have proper gloves?'

'I lost them.'

Hánas looked back up to the ridge. 'Why are men trying to kill you?'

'Because we saw them murder some people,' Erik said, not wanting to say more. Not yet. 'Will you help us?'

Hánas lifted his rifle and scoped the higher ground. The weapon looked like an antique compared with Erik's. His dog stood again, alert. Listening.

'Please help us,' Sofia said.

The herder lowered his rifle and looked back at Erik. 'How do you know my name?'

Erik glanced at Sofia, who nodded. He said, 'My wife is working with your sister. Karine told us about you.'

Hánas stood there a long moment as the wind keened around them and snow swirled and eddied in the dark.

Now and then Erik caught the scent of woodsmoke on the air, coming from the tepee-like tent, and it was intoxicating. Sofia started to speak, asking again for the man's help, but Erik held up a hand to stop her. 'Wait, Lillemor,' he said, watching Hánas watching them.

'My sister,' the Sami herder said. 'Is she dead?'

A pause. Then Erik nodded. 'Yes. I'm sorry.' Truth was all he could give this man in return for his help. 'Lars too. The man who killed them is now hunting us.' He lifted the rifle towards the softly glowing tent up ahead. 'You don't want him to see that.'

Hánas glanced back at the tent, looked at Sofia, turned. He growled something at the dog and started tramping back through the snow, keeping to his own prints, which were already silting up, the dog walking beside him like a shadow.

'Come and get warm,' he called over his shoulder.

Rather than lose the heat of the fire by extinguishing it, Hánas hung some more skins around the inside of the tent. Before Erik got comfortable, he went outside again and walked off fifty paces and looked back at the tent. He was surprised to see that it was dark, as dark as any other stunted tree or rocky outcrop in this snowbound landscape amidst the mountains. No firelight showed on the *lávvu*'s waxed canvas sides. No light at all spilled out into the dark, and he reported this to Sofia and Hánas when he went back inside, though the man seemed not to hear him.

Sofia looked at Erik. He shrugged in reply to her unspoken question and looked back at the herder, who sat on a bolster of rolled fur, staring into the fire around which the three of them clustered. Four including the black dog, which lay beside its master, head resting on its forepaws as it looked up at Sofia with intelligent dark eyes.

After a while, Hánas pushed back his hood and Erik saw

he was younger than his sister. When Karine had talked of her brother, a man who rejected the modern world and lived as their ancestors had lived, insofar as he could, Erik had imagined an older, more careworn face. A man who had chosen a life of discomfort, like some medieval penitent in a hair shirt, or a devotee of self-flagellation. A grizzled misanthrope stubbornly suffering in some vain protest against the world. But that was not who Erik saw now. Hánas looked strong and vital. His wind-burned cheekbones were high and his eyes were knowing and narrow, as if from squinting against the blizzard, wind and snow glare. And from shutting out the world he wanted no part of. As if focusing only on that which was relevant to his existence and the well-being of his reindeer. He looked at ease. A man perfectly adapted to his environment in a way that someone like Erik could never truly understand. A study in Darwinism. Or something deeper. Something spiritual.

'How did they die?' the herder said. He pulled his black beard through one fist, his gaze in thrall to the fire.

'Men came to their house,' Erik said. 'Russians, I think.' He glanced at Sofia, who was holding her bare hands near the flames. He kept his own tucked under his arms because he knew he mustn't warm them too fast. 'Something to do with the copper mine,' he said. 'They were trying to bribe Lars and Karine into giving up with the protests.' He stopped speaking for a moment and worked his jaw. His speech was slurred. He felt as if his face had been frozen but was now melting and his words were running out like water. 'Lars took the money but—'

'My sister refused to be bought off,' Hánas said, pre-empting the rest of the explanation. He continued to eye the flames and it occurred to Erik that no man alive has ever grown tired of looking at fire.

'Pretty much,' he said. He and Sofia looked at each other. 'They didn't mean to kill Lars. One of them hit him and he fell. He hit his head on the fireplace. Karine ran, but . . .'

He left those words hanging and watched the fire working its way along a birch log, the thin white paper bark catching and crackling. He was so tired. He had a headache that felt like his skull was slowly shrinking, squeezing his brain. He felt nauseous. Like a kind of seasickness.

Hánas said something in his own language.

Erik looked at Sofia, but Hánas translated for them before they could ask.

'I dreamt of death,' he said. 'Two nights ago.' The way he was watching the flames, you might have thought he could hear whispers in their soft fluttering. 'That day, one of my animals was killed – a young female. She had become separated from the herd. Because of the storm.' He shrugged. 'A lynx killed her. A big one. There were claw marks on her flank and belly.' A birch log fell away from the flame, so he leant forward and used a stick to push it back in. 'I thought that was the cause of the dream. But it was because of what was happening to Karine.'

The log spat an ember onto the pelt-strewn floor. It glowed orange for a few seconds, then died.

'A lynx can kill one hundred reindeer in a year.' He shook his head. 'But everyone wants to protect the predators.'

Silence filled the tent, but for the crackle of the fire.

'I'm sorry,' Erik said. 'Karine and Lars were good people. Your sister was a brave woman.' It felt surreal to be talking about Lars and Karine in the past tense. This whole thing felt surreal. His thoughts were blurring. He thought he must be dehydrated, so he asked Sofia to take the water bottle from his backpack and put it near the fire to take the chill off.

'Let me see,' Hánas said, nodding at Sofia's bandaged hand. She looked at Erik and he nodded, so she shuffled closer to Hánas and let him take a look. He carefully unwound the bloodstained bandage, Sofia wincing when it tugged at the raw wound on the pad of flesh below her thumb.

'It's opened up a little, see?' he said. She nodded, and the herder stood and went outside and two minutes later came back with a handful of green moss. It was glistening as if he had just dug it up from beneath the snow, and he held it close to the fire to dry and then pressed it against the wound, using a fresh bandage from his own kit to bind it in place.

'There's iodine in the moss. It will keep the wound sterile.' Hánas nodded to say he was done, and Sofia thanked him and shuffled back.

Erik caught the man's eye and nodded his own thanks.

'We'll change the dressing later, but I think it will be fine,' Hánas said.

After a long silence, Sofia said, 'Your dreams. Do they tell you things? Warn you about things that might happen?'

Hánas considered this. 'Sometimes,' he said. 'I don't dream as often as I used to.'

Sofia half glanced at Erik. 'Father has a recurring dream. About a man in a big old-fashioned hat.' With a hand she described a circle around her head.

'Not now, Sofia,' Erik said.

'*Far* doesn't know who he is, but I think this strange man is trying to tell him something.'

157

'Enough, Sofia,' Erik warned.

She frowned but said no more.

'Hánas,' Erik said, watching the man.

Nothing in Hánas's face showed that he had heard. It was as if his mind had flown, leaving his body sitting there like an empty vessel.

'Hánas,' Erik said again, his tone sharper this time, because however much he pitied this man for his loss, Erik had Sofia to think about. She was all that mattered. 'We need to move soon.' Still nothing. 'Hánas, listen to me!' He lifted a hand which still wore one of Sofia's hiking socks. 'He's out there somewhere and if he finds us here, we're all dead. We won't even know it. Do you understand? He could be out there now. We need—'

'He's not out there,' Hánas cut in. 'Not close anyway. Čalmmo would tell us.'

The dog's eyes flicked towards its master at the mention of its name.

'I left the dead calf where I found it,' Hánas said, 'because something must have scared the lynx away. Last night, I waited with my rifle but it did not come back. I was heading out there again tonight when Čalmmo heard you.'

'Or smelled us,' Sofia suggested.

Hánas nodded at her. 'So the lynx will have a good meal if the meat is not frozen solid.' He looked at Erik. 'The man who comes to you in your dreams. Does he speak?'

'Forget about the stupid dream,' Erik said.

Hánas spoke to Čalmmo in Samisk, and the dog's pointed ears flicked and it lifted its head and looked to the entrance of the *lávvu*. Then it stood, tail wagging, and Hánas got up on his knees and unfastened the tent flap. '*Johtalit*,' he said, pulling the canvas back just enough that a few flakes of snow found their way in on a cold breath. '*Johtalit!*' he said again, and Čalmmo barked once, squeezed through the gap and was gone.

'He'll keep watch while you rest,' Hánas said, looking from him to Sofia. 'If this man comes, we will know.'

'You don't have a snowmobile?' Erik asked.

Hánas lifted his head and eyed Erik. 'Of course I do.' He gestured at the fire and the ancient-looking black kettle beside it, and the tent around them. 'You think just because I live like this, I go around on a sled pulled by reindeer like Santa Claus?'

Erik's head was swimming. His hands were starting to hurt. Really hurt. He felt as though he might vomit. He put a hand on the ground beside him to steady himself and had to stop himself from crying out with the pain.

'Pappa?' Sofia said.

'I'm fine, Lillemor,' he said. 'Just tired.'

'Even my grandmother drove a snowmobile into her eighties,' Hánas said, poking his stick into the fire again, moving errant fuel into the centre.

'We can go now then, if it'll take the three of us,' Erik said, his heart racing at the prospect of them climbing onto this man's machine and tracking back down towards town.

'It's not here,' the herder said. He'd taken a leather pouch from a knapsack and now he poured some of the contents into his palm, weighing it carefully. It looked like pieces of dried apricot. Or maybe orange peel.

'It broke,' the Sami went on. 'The spindle that runs through the front of the trailing arm and connects to the ski.' He broke the stick he was holding. 'Snapped,' he said, and tossed both pieces into the fire. 'So my cousin came up here last week and took it back to town to get fixed. I don't need it.' He pulled the lid off the soot-encrusted kettle and dropped the dry mixture into the water, then placed the kettle in the fire. 'Not until I have to move the herd on to look for new grazing. They stay close together in winter, and there's plenty of food under the snow. Reindeer think with the nose, not the eyes. They go with the wind.' He picked up a wooden spoon and pointed with it. 'But anyway, I have dry food for them.'

Erik didn't give a damn about the reindeer. He was just trying to think what the hell they were going to do now.

'Can you help my pappa's hands?' Sofia asked Hánas. She knelt up and took Erik's hands in hers, as Hánas poked the spoon into the kettle and stirred the brew, releasing an earthy aroma into the tent. Erik cursed under his breath as Sofia gently pulled off his sock gloves. He winced at the look of what lay beneath, as much as at the pain. The skin on the back of his hands was mottled and the stinging flesh was swollen and inflamed.

'They look bad, Pappa,' she said.

'I know.' His vision was blurry but he saw that the ends of his fingers, from the knuckles to the tips themselves, were a blue-grey. Dead-looking.

'What about a phone?' Erik asked.

Hánas nodded. 'I have one, of course. But it's no good out here. Now, drink this.' Hánas was pouring tea into a gourd. He gave it to Sofia to hold because Erik couldn't hold it himself.

'What is it?' Erik asked. The tent walls around them were being pushed and pulled by the wind, which was seeking in vain for a way in.

'Medicine,' the herder said, their eyes locking for a moment. 'It will help with the pain.' Then he poured himself a cup and sat back on his bolster and closed his eyes, inhaling the steam.

Sofia pulled a face. 'It smells horrid.'

'It tastes as it smells,' Hánas admitted.

Erik nodded at Sofia, who brought the gourd to his lips. He breathed in the steam and recoiled, and Sofia lifted her eyebrows as if to say *told you*. Then he blew into the cup to cool the tea and slurped at it. It wasn't as bad as he'd expected. Musty. It tasted like the forest floor smelled in autumn after rain. But it was hot. He felt its warmth spreading in his chest and stomach, and knew it would help with the dehydration, so he kept blowing and sipping. And then he thought he should ask why Hánas needed medicine too. The man looked as fit and healthy as his dog. But before he could ask, the reindeer herder finished his own infusion and stood, pulling his hood over his head and moving to the entrance of the *lávvu*.

'Where are you going?' Erik asked him.

Stooping by the tent flap, Hánas turned and threw him a look. 'To speak with my sister,' he said.

Erik glanced at Sofia, who looked as confused as he felt, then glanced back at Hánas as the man slipped out into the night.

Sofia struggled with the zip on the chest pocket of her jacket, her teeth digging into her bottom lip as she concentrated on the task. Sometimes she looked so like her mother, it made him smile. No point in offering to help her with the zipper, given the state of his hands. But then she got it, the thing

161

coming unstuck, and she reached inside and pulled out a piece of paper, unfolding it carefully. There was printed text on one side, but he caught a glimpse of Elise's efficient cursive handwriting on the other.

'Mamma put it in my pocket before we set off,' she reminded him, glancing up before starting to read the letter. A tear escaped from the corner of her eye and rolled down her cheek before she could swipe it away.

'It's OK,' he said.

Hánas was outside somewhere, so they were alone.

She nodded. 'I know.' She cuffed her eye again, then held the note out to him. 'Want to read it?'

Erik shook his head. 'It's your letter.'

She looked down at the letter and read it again. 'She says we must look after each other.'

He nodded. 'And we will. We have,' he said.

Outside, the wind moaned in the night. At the same moment the flame in the fire flared, as though in answer to the wind's lament, and for a second or two he saw a face in the flames. Then it was gone, but he wondered who it had been.

The warmth of the tea was creeping through his limbs. Erik looked down at his hands and could see the heat spreading through the veins – threads of red and purple growing before his eyes, a network of filaments carrying an electric current from his wrists, through his palms and up into each finger.

'And,' Sofia said, 'she says we should talk. Really talk, about anything and everything.' She looked up at him, eyebrows raised. Her expression seemed to betray a combination of emotions. Guilt. Sadness. Hope?

'We'll have plenty of time to talk when we get home,' he said. 'All of us.'

She gave a slight nod and took a deep breath, then folded the letter over and tucked it back in her coat pocket.

'We'll be OK,' Erik said.

'I know,' she said. But he didn't think she believed it.

His eyelids were heavy. He felt as if he were drifting, but did not want to sleep. Even if Hánas's dog was out there keeping watch. He didn't want to leave Sofia awake on her own. Where was Hánas, anyway? He'd been out there a while now.

He looked towards the entrance of the tent.

'What do you think he's doing out there?' Sofia asked.

'I don't know.' Maybe a blast of cold fresh air would clear his mind. 'Wait here,' he said. He stood and pulled his hood up over his woollen hat, left the fire and walked out into the darkness. He paused a moment, drawing the cold air into his lungs and letting his eyes adjust. He felt snowflakes on his face, thought he could hear the soft whisper of them landing on the white mantle spread upon the earth. Other than that, silence. As if he were the last person alive in the whole world. Ahead, he could make out the distant ridge. To his right, the treeline. To his left and at his back, mountains rising into the cloud like ancient, unfinished sculptures. As though the artist who had created the world never got to complete his work.

Then he saw a human shape breaking the near horizon, a figure kneeling on the boundary between earth and sky. It was Hánas.

Some innate sense warned him against calling out, and so he walked towards the man, finding it easier than it should

163

have been, as though the land had at last accepted him as a creature of the snow and granted him passage. He found the reindeer herder kneeling there in the deep snow, facing the north. The eyes within his fur-lined hood were closed.

'Hánas.' The man did not answer. 'Hánas, what's going on?' He looked asleep. Was he meditating? 'Hánas, come back to the tent.'

The man did not move. And not moving out there, in these temperatures, was a problem, so Erik touched him on the shoulder and said his name again. 'It's too cold to be out here.' He glanced back at the tent. He saw a sliver of fire-light where he'd not fully fastened the entrance. 'I can't leave Sofia alone. I'm going back.'

Something caught his eye and his heart kicked in his chest. He looked up at the trees, ice water running in his veins instead of blood, because he had not brought the rifle.

There was a man walking through the snow. It took him a few seconds to be sure that the man wasn't coming towards him but walking away, towards the pine woods. Then he saw the other figure too. Someone smaller.

*No!* It was Sofia. Erik couldn't see her face but he knew it was her. Twelve years ago he had watched her take her first steps and had followed behind her ever since. He would know her shape in the dark, her gait, her mannerisms, even with no eyes to see.

'Sofia!' His breath plumed silver in the gloom. 'Sofia, wait!'

She half turned and he saw the pale crescent moon of her face, and yelled at her to run, and now he was running towards her. Unbound by the snow. Unfettered of his previous exhaustion, he swept across the snow like an owl swooping from a branch to take a hare on the run.

The tall man was taking Sofia! He would take her into the woods and he would kill her, and the certainty of this almost stopped his heart. It was a horror beyond his mind's ability to accept. And so he ran. He would throw himself at the son of a bitch, and the bullets ripping into his own flesh would not kill him before he had ripped and clawed the life from the man with a savagery that the world had never witnessed.

'Sofia!' He roared it. 'No!' She looked back at him once more, then she and the man slipped amongst the trees and he could no longer see them. *No!*

But the snow could not hinder him. He flew towards the wood. Towards death. Then he was amongst the pines himself and he found them.

'Pappa,' Sofia said. She stood there, waiting for him, her eyes round in the dark.

The man turned, his clothes sweeping with the movement, black as a raven's wing. The rim of his broad hat cast his face in shadow, though the patch over his right eye was still visible. Shades of black in the absence of light. Erik felt himself gasp on the frigid air. Felt his head turning this way and that as his brain refused to acknowledge what his eyes were seeing.

'No, this is not happening.' He reached out to Sofia. 'Lillemor.'

She shook her head. 'Come with us, Pappa,' she said.

He turned to the one-eyed man and pointed at him. 'Stay away from her. Who the hell are you?' The man was holding a staff in his left hand. A gnarled and timeworn stick. Like something he imagined Moses carrying. Or Gandalf.

'I have been known by many names,' the man said in a

deep and tired voice. 'Deceiver. Seducer. One-Eyed.' His good eye seemed to blaze at that last name. He held the staff out wide. 'Frenzied One. All-Father.' He turned and looked at Sofia. 'Journeyer.'

Erik's mind was unmoored. It seemed to be floating away into the dark, like a Chinese lantern. Yet he looked down at his feet and saw they were firmly planted in the snow.

'Am I dreaming now?' he asked.

Neither the one-eyed man nor Sofia answered him.

'I said, am I dreaming?'

'Come, Pappa,' his daughter said, holding out her hand.

He took it, and the three of them walked deeper into the woods.

No one spoke in the darkness. But he felt Sofia's hand in his own and that was of great comfort to him. They pushed through the brittle branches, between the snow-encumbered boughs, and came to a clearing where a fire burned and a figure sat on a mossy tree stump beside it. Somehow there was moonlight here, as though it had gathered in this clearing like water left in a rock pool by the falling tide, so that by its silver glow he could see the face of the girl intent on the flickering flames.

He tried to speak but could not. He mouthed her name, though. He felt the shape of it on his lips and could not breathe. Her presence washed over him, flooding him with a raw and terrible anguish. A pain like no other. Every fibre of his soul in that moment straining beyond its limits. Ripping. He could not bear it.

*Emilie.*

She looked up at him with eyes that were deep wells of

sorrow. They held a grief too profound for her young face, a grief that mirrored his own.

'Pappa,' she said.

'Em—Emilie,' he managed at last. A strangled utterance.

Emilie stood and turned towards them, and Sofia stepped up and threw her arms around her sister. 'We've missed you so much,' Sofia told her. 'Oh God, I'm lost without you, Em.'

The girls let go of one another and stepped back, and Emilie regarded her younger sister as though it had been a lifetime since she had seen her, not a year. And the sight of them together again was almost too much for Erik to take.

'I'm sorry I left,' Emilie said.

Sofia wiped the tears from her eyes. 'I miss you.'

'I miss you too, little sis,' Emilie said.

Then Sofia turned to Erik, watching him with glistening eyes. A silent invitation to speak. He took a step forward, slowly, because he feared that any sudden movement and Emilie would vanish. As if she were some freak play of the moonlight that could only be seen from a certain distance and angle.

'I'm sorry,' he said, his voice breaking. 'My girl – my precious girl ... I'm so sorry.' He was weeping now, his breathing ragged, the squirming mass of pain and guilt rising from his stomach, the great muscle of his heart pumping it upwards, like foul water from a well, up and up, filling him. Rising into his throat so that he couldn't breathe or talk but only cry. He staggered, feeling his legs would give way, but then Emilie was there, holding him, and he put his arms around her and held her tight, and she held him.

'It wasn't your fault, Pappa,' she said. 'Don't cry.'

Those words robbed him of any last vestige of self-control

and he sobbed. His chest was bucking on waves of loss, his lungs hyperventilating. He felt dizzy. His fingers and toes were fizzing. 'I'm sorry,' he told her again.

'It's OK, Pappa. It wasn't your fault. But I'm gone. You have to look after Sofia now.'

'I know,' he said.

'You have to run.'

'I know,' he said.

'You have to let me go now, Pappa. There's no time.'

'No.'

'You must.'

He clung to her. 'I can't.'

'I love you.'

'Please,' he begged. He would hold her there and not let go.

'I love you, Pappa,' she said.

'I love you. So much,' he said.

Somehow she stepped back, even though he still felt the substance of her in his arms. They looked into each other's eyes for a long moment.

Her eyes widened. 'Run,' she said.

Then the moonlight faded to darkness and he was standing there alone in the snow.

# 11

HE OPENED HIS eyes. He was breathing fast and for a moment didn't know where he was.

'It's OK, Pappa,' Sofia said. 'We're safe with Hánas.'

They were in the tent. He knew that now. He could smell something that made his stomach growl and the copper light of the fire danced with shadow across the skins and canvas around them. And for a while he lay there, because the dream . . . or whatever it had been, clung to him still, heavy and raw and full of emotion. He didn't want to sit up yet because they would see it in his face.

Hánas was stirring a pot of steaming food over the fire. 'We are having pasta and reindeer ragu,' he said, taking a bowl and spooning the food into it. 'It will give you energy.' He passed the bowl to Sofia, who thanked him and sat back again on crossed legs. He filled another bowl each for Erik and himself, then went outside to scrub the pan with snow, saying that if he didn't do it straight away the residue would stick to the bottom and he'd be tasting reindeer in his *rømmegrøt*.

'You were crying, Pappa. In your sleep,' Sofia said when they were alone.

He sat up, coming back to himself, though he wasn't ready for the dream to leave him completely. Not yet.

He looked at her. 'I saw Emilie,' he said. 'It was so real.' He felt choked, as he had in the dream.

Sofia didn't seem surprised. 'Did she ... did she say anything?'

'She said she misses you.' He shook his head. 'It was so real.'

Sofia was quiet for a bit. She sat there, staring at the bowl of steaming pasta.

'I held her,' he said, lifting his arms and trying to make fists with his nearly useless hands. 'I held her and I could feel her. Smell her.' He shook his head then and clenched his teeth. Sofia didn't need to hear this. She didn't need to be party to whatever psychosis his grief had stirred up.

'Did you see the man again?' she asked.

He looked at her. He knew who she meant. He nodded.

Hánas came in, holding the clean cooking pot and sweeping the hood off his head.

Sofia looked up at the herder. 'He saw the one-eyed man,' she said, her own eyes wide, then turned back to Erik. 'Hánas said you would find him.'

Erik glanced up at the Sami, who nodded. 'I hope you learned what you needed to know,' Hánas said.

There was a taste in Erik's mouth and he remembered the infusion Hánas had given him. 'What was in that tea?' he asked.

Hánas sat down and began to eat. 'A type of mushroom,' he said. 'And something to help you sleep.' He waved his spoon through the air. 'Nothing strong,' he added through a mouthful. He dug into the pasta and meat sauce and blew on it. 'I needed to speak with my sister. You—' he fed a spoonful into his mouth and started chewing, steam coming from between his lips as he spoke '—you needed to speak with the one-eyed man.'

Erik could still feel the mushrooms in his blood. A strange intoxication. 'I didn't speak with him,' he said.

Hánas shrugged, spooning in another mouthful. 'But you learned what he wanted of you. Or . . . something about him at least.'

Erik said nothing.

'Who could this man be in my *far*'s dreams?' Sofia asked Hánas.

Hánas scratched his cheek. 'Odin is depicted this way. One blind eye. A hat with a wide brim.'

'The god?' Sofia asked. 'The old Viking god?'

Erik pictured Anthony Hopkins as Odin in those crazy Marvel movies.

'I thought your gods were different,' Sofia said. 'Don't the Sami believe everything has a soul?' She frowned. 'That's what we learned at school. And that these souls represent things from the world around you.' She swept her bandaged hand through the air. 'Like the wind and birds and trees. Even stones and rocks.'

Hánas looked at her, lifted an eyebrow. 'Ours are not the only gods, Sofia,' he said.

'So . . . the god . . . Odin . . . that's who my *far* is seeing in his dreams?'

Hánas pursed his lips, but before he could answer, Erik looked up at Sofia. 'That's enough,' he told her. Then he looked at Hánas. 'You drugged me,' he accused him. His mind was foggy and he felt nauseous. Angry.

'I helped you,' the reindeer herder said, lifting his hand and splaying the fingers. 'How are they?'

Erik looked at his hands. The tips of the fingers were still grey, those three fingers on his right hand looking like they belonged to a corpse, but the pain was gone for now at least. 'They don't hurt,' he admitted.

Hánas nodded. 'I have some mittens you can use.'

The dream was fading now. Erik still felt it like a physical presence, but its grip on him was loosening with each minute he was back in the real world. Then a wrench of panic announced itself in the pit of his stomach. 'How long was I asleep?' he asked Sofia.

She took the watch from her pocket. 'It's just after five a.m.,' she said. 'So . . . three hours.'

'Shit,' he hissed. 'We have to go.'

'You need to eat first.' Hánas pointed to the bowl of stew, which Erik hadn't touched yet because of the nausea. And the dream. And how seeing Emilie again, holding her as if she were alive, had twisted him all up inside.

'It's good, Pappa,' Sofia said through a hot mouthful.

'But we need to move,' he said.

Hánas gestured to Erik's bowl with his spoon. 'As soon as you have eaten. You need your strength. And Čalmmo would have warned us if someone was out there.'

'I can help you.' Sofia moved towards him, but Erik lifted a hand and shook his head.

'I can do it,' he said, sliding his hands underneath the bowl to lift it, then balancing it on the flat of his left palm and picking up the spoon in his right as best he could, using his thumb as a clamp because he still had the use of it. He began to eat, only now realizing how hungry he was and how wonderful it was to feel that meat and pasta and hot sauce going into him. Fresh meat, not some pre-cooked food in a pouch with a shelf life of three years.

'Your hands must be getting better,' Sofia said hopefully.

'I think so,' he said, doing his best to get the pasta into his mouth while she was watching. He knew his hands were no better, but he didn't want her to know. He tried to concentrate on the task. To push the dream away. But it would not leave him. *She* would not leave him. Or rather, *he* was not ready to leave her. It had felt so real. Holding her. The image of her was vivid in his mind, even more so when he closed his eyes, as if the moon in that clearing had exposed the dream's patterns of light and dark onto the backs of his eyelids like a photograph.

'Do you want to talk about it?' Sofia's voice was cautious, exploratory.

He shook his head. There was no way he was going to sit there and talk about it, that the man he'd dreamt about a hundred times since Emilie died was Odin, chief of the Norse gods. Elise would have him sectioned and maybe she'd be right to. 'It was just a dream,' he said, turning cold eyes on Hánas. 'Or a trip,' he added, resentment welling inside him. 'What were you thinking? What if I'd done something stupid? Lost control? What if I was high or unconscious, and the man out there trying to kill us had turned up?'

'Pappa,' Sofia said, a worried scowl tightening her face.

'I did not give you enough for that,' Hánas said, putting down his empty bowl and spoon.

'How could you know?'

Hánas shrugged. 'You are a big man.' He leant over and picked up Sofia's bowl. 'And the tea was weak.'

Erik shook his head and continued eating. He was angry with the reindeer herder for all the reasons he'd said, and yet it was hard to regret what had happened, because he believed that some part of his being had been with Emilie again. Whether it was an effect of the magic mushrooms, or of his exhaustion and the trauma of what he'd endured, or just a coincidence. Just a dream. His subconscious mind sifting through images, ideas and emotions that his conscious mind tried to seal behind a locked door. He had seen and held his daughter again and she had said things he had needed to hear. He didn't believe in an afterlife. When you were gone, you were gone. But this had felt so real, and for all the anguish of it, he needed to cling to it for a while.

He looked at Sofia, wondering if he should say the words that wanted to be said.

She felt his gaze upon her and lifted her chin. 'What is it?'

He hesitated. But if he didn't say something now, she would worry about what he wasn't telling her. 'Emilie told us to run,' he said.

She looked at him and seemed to shiver inside her clothes. 'Is he coming?'

He took a breath. 'I think we should go.'

He looked at Hánas, who was watching him intently.

'Then we go,' the reindeer herder said.

Erik nodded. 'Your rifle,' he said, gesturing at the weapon lying on the furs beside Hánas. 'It looks old. What is it?'

Hánas picked up the rifle and worked the bolt, and Erik saw that the bolt handle had been bent to accommodate the scope, which looked sophisticated and new, incongruous on the antique weapon.

'A Mosin-Nagant sniper. Made in nineteen thirty-nine. My grandfather took it from the hands of a dead Russian on the shores of Lake Omega in forty-one. He was fighting with the Finns, who were trying to retake the territories lost in the Winter War.'

'What does it shoot?' Erik asked.

Hánas lifted one dark eyebrow as he picked a tuft of reindeer hair from where it had caught in the rear sling slot on the buttstock. 'Russian seven point six two. You can still buy it in crates. You peel the lid off the tins and get a whiff of vodka and kasha.' He patted the Mosin's magazine. 'Same size bullet, different cartridge length.'

'No good for this then,' Erik said, placing a hand on the stock of the Remington. He was down to two rounds and had been hoping to get some ammo from Hánas, although looking at the man's rifle he'd suspected the worst.

'No,' Hánas confirmed.

'So where will we go?'

Sofia had packed her rucksack again and was now busy pulling the straps down tight and fastening them. He was awash with sadness and pride at her courage.

'East for two kilometres, a climb, then south for three. Three and a half,' Hánas said. 'There's a ravine. A shortcut leading down to the glacier. If you didn't know it was there, you wouldn't see it.'

'Is it safe?' asked Erik.

'I don't use it in spring,' Hánas said. 'Risk of avalanche is too great. But this time of year? At night? This temperature?' The herder nodded. 'It's safe. If you can ski.'

Erik looked at Sofia. At her clenched jaw. Her serious eyes.

'We can ski,' she said.

*An understatement if ever there was*, he thought.

Hánas nodded. 'Then let's go.'

The herder's skis looked as old as the Russian rifle, but he moved on them as well as anyone they had ever seen. He carried a small pack, onto which he strapped a pair of red Evo snowshoes and over which he slung the Mosin-Nagant rifle. He set off at a brisk pace but they were able to keep up.

Erik thought it must stop snowing soon, and it crossed his mind that he would have to clear the cabin roof again when they got back. He knew this was an odd thought under the circumstances, but it kept his mind occupied. He couldn't decide if picturing himself up on the roof with the snow shovel was a positive visualization, something which might even help manifest its own fulfilment, or tempting fate. In the end he decided their fate was up to them. If he could ignore the pain that was starting to fill his hands again, if they could keep going and push through their exhaustion, and if Hánas could guide them through the mountains, taking them on routes that the tall man wouldn't know, then they would live.

But Sofia was tired. Her young legs had given so much already. Her muscles were spent and he thought that her mind might be close behind. The stress of seeing the Helgelands murdered. The terror of fleeing their home in the night and the bullets whipping amongst the trees. Then the breath-stealing cold, the icy wind seeking through the seams of their clothes, biting the exposed skin on their faces and seeping into bones. And even now, knowing that *he* was coming. The tall man. The one with the eyes that seemed to look through you. The man they both knew would not give up but would keep on coming, as though guided by more than faint tracks in the snow or sheer luck and persistence. Rather he seemed guided by some ancient predator's instinct – innate senses bred out of other men across tens of thousands of years, but not out of him.

'Everyone OK?' Hánas said, his voice shredding in the wind. He led at the front, then Sofia, then Erik and the pulk, in which he had stowed Sofia's rucksack.

'Yes,' Sofia replied, head down into the wind. Pushing on.

Čalmmo bounded alongside his master, no doubt confused as to what was going on and why they were leaving the reindeer unguarded.

'Erik?' Hánas called.

'All good,' Erik shouted back. Which was not true. His muscles were screaming. In his stomach, his shoulders, his triceps, lower back and thighs. His feet ached inside his boots, which he had not taken off since the DNT hut. Worst of all, but for his hands, were his knees. They were a problem now. It seemed that the muscles stabilizing the knee joints, enabling them to bend and straighten, were fatigued, and their last reserves of energy were flooding into the ligaments to compensate. The ligaments were consequently working too hard without support from the muscles. In the end they would fail and tear, and he would be unable to go on.

An hour after leaving Hánas's tent, they came onto a plateau where visibility was so bad he could barely make out the herder in front of Sofia, even though they were skiing close enough in each other's tracks that now and then one of them clipped the backs of the skis of the person in front. Snow from the sky and snow from the ground was flying into their faces, caustic like cinders from a fire, so that they all but closed their eyes against it, relying on Hánas to be their pathfinder.

'You want to stop for a bit?' the Sami asked them. He lifted his pole and pointed it toward a mound to their right, which was visible only because of the way the snow swirled around it. 'We could shelter there for a short while.'

'What do you think, Lillemor?' Erik said.

'Not yet, Pappa,' she said.

So he told Hánas they would keep going.

'We have to climb now,' Hánas said. 'Two kilometres. A little more.'

'I can do it, Pappa,' Sofia said.

He wanted to let her rest but knew they must keep going because they had stayed too long in the tent. And because his other girl, his wonderful girl who was no longer alive, had told him to run.

And so they climbed. Bent-backed and weary. Trudging up and up like three mountain trolls, the last of their kind, returning to their secret lair to lie down and sleep and never wake. Done with the world because it was done with them. His skis no longer felt like high-tech equipment designed to glide over the snow. They felt like an encumbrance. Like two crude planks tied to his numbing feet. He thought about taking them off and carrying them over his shoulder or putting them in the pulk and relying on his snowshoes, but knew that was a bad idea. And so he kept his gaze fixed on the girl in front of him, on her legs as they kicked forward in turn, on her arms as she planted the poles, and he willed her to keep going. One step at a time. Because if she kept going then so would he, for he would never leave her, even though nature decreed that he must.

They climbed and Hánas's dog bounded around them, seemingly inexhaustible, exercising his herding instincts by running up and down the line, making sure the three of them stayed close together, and after another hour the ground levelled off again and he told Sofia to get in the pulk.

'I don't want to, *Far*,' she said.

'What happened to Pappa?' he said, forcing a smile.

She shook her head. 'I can ski.' She said it loud enough for Hánas, who had stopped up ahead, to hear.

'No. You're exhausted,' he said. Her hat was covered in little lumps of ice, stuck to the wool, and snow had settled on the top. Her face was bone-white but for the dark patches beneath her eyes. 'Let me pull you for a bit.'

'I'll do it,' Hánas said, skiing back to them.

*You have to look after Sofia now.* Emilie's words were still in his head. Had crystallized like ice inside his skull. 'I've got it,' he told the herder, undoing the harness so he could help Sofia into the sled. 'But you can help me stow her skis and poles,' he added, because his hands were too clumsy to work with the bungee hooks.

'She's a tough young lady,' Hánas said, when Sofia was in the pulk and they were ready to push off again.

'You have no idea,' Erik replied.

*

179

'Pappa! Pappa, look at Čalmmo.'

He stopped and bent forward, catching his breath, and looked over his shoulder. Sofia was twisted around, looking over the back of the pulk into the eddying snow.

'He's seen something,' Sofia said.

Hánas materialized beside him, planted his poles in the snow and unslung the old Russian rifle. 'Could be lynx or a hare,' he said.

But it wasn't. Erik knew that.

Čalmmo barked at the darkness. Hánas hissed something at the dog and the dog didn't bark again. But it was excited and alert. The wind was at their backs now, so the dog might have caught the scent of something. Not something. Someone.

'I think it's the man who's been hunting you,' Hánas said.

'I think so too,' Erik said.

The reindeer herder pointed. 'See his tail? It's wagging more to the left. He does that when he doesn't like something . . . or isn't sure about something.' The dog was standing stiffly, its weight shifted forward, its tail high.

'Stay down, Sofia,' Erik said. She lowered herself back into the pulk.

'If it is him, it doesn't mean he's seen us yet.' Hánas was peering through his rifle scope. 'In this wind, and with the snow covering everything, Čalmmo could have smelled him from a long way off. Three, four kilometres perhaps.'

'Then we carry on,' Erik said, slinging his own rifle onto his back again.

Hánas nodded.

'Shout if you see anything moving out there,' Erik told Sofia. 'But stay low.'

She nodded, and they continued on into an icebound valley that seemed to close in on them. They passed gaunt, looming hills and barren slopes, and it seemed a dead world. A place where humans were never meant to go. Where people's concerns had no importance. He felt the crushing weight of this, because his charge *was* important. It was the only thing. His reason for drawing breath. And it angered him that her life meant nothing to the ancient ice beneath their feet, the lichen-laced rock sleeping beneath the snow, and the stunted, brittle birches on the slopes of the valley. It angered him, even though he knew how absurd it was.

Soon, though, he wasn't thinking much at all. He was just moving, his motor cortex sending electrical signals through his spinal cord and peripheral nerves to his muscles, causing them to contract. Again and again. Ceaseless as the snow coming down.

Vaguely, he considered that maybe his brain was beginning to freeze, his thoughts themselves thickening, the way that, if it's cold enough, tiny crystals will grow in sea water and come together, forming salty slush. Yes, that was it, he realized. His brain was turning to slush, yet his body was still going.

The wind moaned through the valley, but at least it was on their backs and not in their faces. Still, he was cold. Too cold. After the warmth of the tent and the water he had drunk to rehydrate, he had sweated, so that his under layers were damp. Now that sweat was freezing on his skin because his body was failing to warm it.

*Wake up!* he told himself, though he knew he couldn't actually be asleep. *You have to stay sharp. Wake up, you bastard!* His mind was shutting down. Maybe because he was lost in the repetitive action of pulling the pulk, or because his body was diverting all energy and resources to his muscles. But what if it was because he was beginning to get hypothermic?

*Wake. Up.*

He tried to think, about anything. But nothing whole would form in his mind. Just fragments, like the image in a shattered mirror. Then something did come to him. He thought of how a fish will sometimes flap for an hour or so after you've pulled it from the fjord, even after it's been gutted and the head removed. The nerves still firing after death. *I would be like that fish*, he thought. *If my heart gave up now and I died on my feet, I would keep going. I would keep pulling.*

Then Čalmmo barked again.

This time they did not stop.

'Čalmmo!' Hánas called, expecting the dog to bound up beside him. When it didn't appear, he called again, and Erik looked over his shoulder. He thought he caught a glimpse of Čalmmo running back the way they had come. A black form melting into the dark. A moment later there was no sign of the dog, and even his prints were filling with snow.

Hánas was looking off in the direction that Čalmmo had run, and Erik stopped beside him. For a moment neither spoke, but he thought he heard barking, the faraway sound of it fraying on the wind.

'We need to move faster,' Hánas said.

Erik nodded.

'How are your hands?'

'I can go faster,' Erik said.

Hánas held his eye for a moment. 'Then let's go.'

The herder turned and kicked off and Erik followed, grimacing as he got the heavy sled in motion again.

'Are you warm enough?' he asked Sofia. She said that she was.

His hands were claws of aching agony now, even inside the fur-lined mittens Hánas had given him. But he had perfected the technique of swinging the poles by their wrist straps and pushing down on the ends of the grips with the heels of his palms, and he got up to speed, skiing in the tracks Hánas carved out in front of him.

Some time later, he saw dawn breaking in the east. The night had seemed to stretch on and on, so that it had begun to look as if a new day would never come. Yet here it was, seeping up into the dark sky, slowly as if by stealth, hoping to go unnoticed by the night. And he didn't know whether to want it or not. He would take the two- or three-degree rise in temperature, though, and the sense of optimism that can germinate when a new day emerges from the darkness. But he knew that darkness had been useful to them and that now they would be easier to track.

As the pale sun rose above the peaks, Hánas led them along another valley, whose sides rose steeply in a series of curved terraces of snow, gleaming pink in the dawn.

'Every spring, this whole valley is swept by avalanches,' Hánas told them.

Erik's mind returned to those long minutes of being buried alive when he had fallen from the ridge and brought a cornice of snow down with him. He might be in that cold dark still, had Sofia not dug him out. She had not panicked. Or if she had, she'd not shown it.

This world did not deserve her.

The snow clouds, which had been swollen and sluggish since the worst of the storm had passed, were thinning now. Stretching on thin westerlies and breaking over the mountains. He did not think this a good thing. They needed the snow to fall into their tracks. Needed the wind to choke their trail with snow.

'It'll be dark again in six hours,' Erik said. But six hours was too long and they all knew it. They had stopped by a rock to rest briefly and look back the way they had come, while Sofia shared out some of the salted liquorice sweets she had in her pack.

'We don't want the storm to end, do we, Pappa?' she said, taking her water bottle and squatting beside him to fill it with snow.

'No, we don't,' he said.

Hánas was looking south-east, his blue eyes scanning the valley.

'Has the dog done this before?' Erik asked him. 'Just run off like this?'

Hánas shook his head. 'If Čalmmo was alive, he would be here.'

Erik caught Sofia's eye. Neither of them needed Hánas to say what he thought had happened to the dog.

'Ready?' Erik asked her, nodding towards the pulk.

But she wasn't listening. Not to him. She lifted her hat away from her left ear and tilted her head.

'What . . .?' Then he heard it too. The unmistakable percussive *thwop thwop thwop* of a helicopter.

They all looked up, eyes scanning the lightening grey, each looking at different parts of the sky, because the sound was swimming around in the valley, making it impossible to pinpoint the source.

'There,' Sofia said, pointing north-east to the crest of the valley side, which was comparatively bright beneath a slash in the cloud. He saw it – a flash of red and the dark blur of rotor blades. Then it vanished below the ridge.

'It's going down,' Erik said. 'Landing – has to be.' He turned to Hánas. 'What's over there?'

The herder's eyes were narrow slits as he thought, moving the liquorice around in his mouth like a man who suspects that what he's been given has been poisoned.

'There's nothing over there,' he said. Then he turned and took in their surroundings again, as if to check his internal compass bearings. 'Nothing I know of anyway.' He lifted his pole and pointed with it. 'There is a climate research centre to the north. Two hours by snowmobile. Sometimes helicopters go there.' He stared up at the ridgeline beyond which the helicopter had disappeared. 'There's nothing else. Nothing so close. No one is allowed to build here.'

Erik turned to Sofia. 'Can you still hear it?'

She listened. 'No.'

He looked back at Hánas. 'A helicopter wouldn't just land out here in the middle of nowhere. Unless it was a Search and Rescue.'

'Bad weather to fly,' the Sami said.

'Could they be looking for us?' Sofia asked.

Hánas thought about it. 'It's possible. But then, why land over there?'

'So there must be something there,' she said, 'and if there are people there, they can help us.' She raised her eyebrows and her dry, cracked lips were parted, but she didn't say any more, and it hurt Erik to see that any hope she had was a small and fragile thing now, and that she was trying to harden herself against it in case giving it voice made her weak also.

'Can we get there?' Erik asked Hánas. Looking up at the peaks, he didn't see how he and Sofia could climb so high. Not in their condition. And Hánas himself was not a young man.

'I think there is a pass between the mountains,' the herder said. 'Still a climb, of course, but not like going over. Nothing worse than we've done already.'

'We can do it, Pappa,' the girl said. 'You won't have to pull me. I've rested. I'll be strong again.'

She did not look strong.

'Ride in the sled a little while longer,' he said.

'But, Pappa—'

'Just until we get to the pass. Then you can ski.'

She frowned. Nodded.

When she had clambered back into the pulk, he looked at Hánas.

'We're ready.'

Those narrow eyes looked back at him. Seemed to be weighing something inside him. Then Hánas turned and kicked off and glided across the snow like an apparition. And Erik followed, pulling Sofia behind him.

# 12

THEY CAME OUT onto another glacier. A wide and almost featureless landscape but for a fissure here and there and, to the east of the plateau, several columns of ice rising at the intersection of two crevasses.

'There's nothing here,' Erik said. He was breathing hard from the climb. They all were.

'But there has to be,' Sofia said, eyes scouring the white expanse, not ready to accept that they had taken the strength-sapping detour for nothing.

Before them, snow and ice swept across the surface in frigid gusts, the landscape like some frozen planet still in the process of being formed. And if Hánas told them no man had ever set foot here before, Erik would believe him. It was a desolate vista devoid of any reference to the human race, and now he could feel that shaping wind clawing at him too, trying to fuse *him* to its bleak creation.

While they were still in the pass, they had seen the

helicopter again. It had lifted into the grey above the mountains, rolled to the right, dipped its nose into the west and beaten away. They had watched it dematerialize, not even wasting the energy on waving their arms, because they knew it was too far away.

He had not known what to expect when they emerged from the pass, but it wasn't this. Not this nothingness. And he felt it like a blow to his stomach.

'What do we do now?' he said, to himself as much as to Hánas. He almost did not dare look at Sofia for fear of the disappointment in her face.

The reindeer herder stood before the land, his eyes reading it like a page in a book where he was taking in every word.

'That way,' he said, lifting his chin to the east.

'Why that way?' Erik asked. The left side of his face was numb, yet he was aware of the wind lashing ice crystals against him, coating half of his body in a white crust. Sofia was shielding her face with one hand, her eyes screwed up as she searched for some building, some cabin or tent, anything to explain what the helicopter had been doing there.

'There's something there,' Hánas said.

Erik could see nothing and neither could Sofia.

'What can you see?' he asked the herder.

Hánas lifted a pair of snow goggles from inside the neck of his fur coat and put them on.

'I don't know yet,' he said.

Erik had no wish to turn back. Nor did he want to stay still and watch the three of them become part of the glacier. He fished out the compass watch but the display was blank. The battery dead.

'Then let's go,' he said.

As they skied on, they began to see what Hánas had spied with those eyes well used to sifting through a snowbound world. Strange blocks of ice. There were five of them in all, irregular in shape, formed in tall pinnacles on a slope at the eastern edge of the glacier, each the height of a house. Seracs, they were called, and he knew they were dangerous. Remembered reading in the papers a few years back about a bunch of climbers being killed on Everest by a falling serac. And now, as they skied closer, these columns loomed above them, their shapes ill-defined against the white backdrop. He couldn't see the crevasses themselves, but knew they must be getting close, so he told Sofia to be careful, to keep her eyes on the ground in front of her.

Then she saw it.

'There, what's that?' she called.

He could see nothing but the snow on the ground and on the slope and in the air, and the columns of ice rising like monoliths erected by some long-extinct alien race.

But Hánas had seen it. He lifted a hand in a gesture that told them both to stop and they halted just behind him.

'See it, Pappa?' she asked.

'No,' he said. Was he going snow-blind? There was no sun to be seen, just a halo of cold light somewhere in the ashen sky above, so it seemed unlikely that ultraviolet light could have burned his corneas. But maybe it was still possible.

'A building, Pappa. There.' She was pointing with her pole. 'There, in the ice.'

'I see it,' he said at last.

'And see there,' Hánas said, pointing to the snow nearby. 'Where the helicopter landed.'

189

Erik saw the impressions left in the snow by the chopper's landing skids, even the shallow indentation that its underbelly had made as the landing gear sank in. These signs were vanishing before their eyes, but the building fifty or sixty metres away was obvious now he knew it was there. It looked to have been built into the slope, into the ice and rock. The door and about a foot of rusting metal were the only parts visible, so it was impossible to know the size or structure of the building itself, but there it was.

'What could it be?' he asked Hánas.

He wanted to ski right up to the place and hammer on the metal door. Get out of the cold, put steel between themselves and the Russian. But a wiser part of him advised caution, because whatever this place was, it had been designed to be just about as inconspicuous as a building could be.

'I've seen something like it before,' Hánas said. 'On Andøya.'

'And what was that?' Erik asked.

The wind was gathering strength again, sweeping the snow across their skis and lashing the falling snow across their cheeks. 'An old listening station,' the herder said, planting his poles in the snow, 'left over from the Cold War.' He pulled his reindeer-skin mittens off with his teeth, unslung the old rifle from his shoulder, drew the bolt and poked a finger into the breech to double-check that it wasn't loaded. Then he tucked the mittens inside his thick coat and held the rifle down in front of him, as he had when they had met him out in the storm. 'They were early-warning stations from the Aleutians to Greenland. A chain of them along sixty-nine degrees north latitude.'

'Listening for what?' Erik asked.

Hánas shrugged. 'The one on Andøya was full of radar screens. The men and women stationed there were looking for slashes of green light representing Soviet bombers headed southward from the pole.'

'Bombers loaded with nukes,' Erik added for Sofia's benefit, and he might have shivered at the thought, were he not already shivering.

'Of course, most of these stations became obsolete when the Soviets developed long-range missiles,' Hánas said, 'but more and more are being found up here in the Arctic because the ice is retreating.'

'Are there people in there now?' Sofia asked.

Erik looked at Hánas, who lifted an eyebrow.

Sofia kicked forward, drawing level with the reindeer herder. 'There must be, right? If the helicopter came here.'

The wind moaned across the plateau. 'Wait here,' Hánas said. He threw his rifle onto his back again and skied up to the door, stopping five metres or so from it. He took off his pack and his skis, unstrapped his snowshoes and put them on, then walked the last few steps, pointing out the security camera in its white steel housing to the left of the door, which Erik hadn't seen.

Hánas lifted his rifle and thumped its butt against the door, the metallic clang of it incongruous in this land of snow and ice. Nothing happened. He hit the door again, three times. Still nothing.

'There must be someone in there, Pappa. Why would there be a camera?'

Hánas looked up at the camera now and waved his hand in front of it, then banged on the door again.

The cold was in Erik's legs now that they weren't moving.

It was filling the big muscles in his thighs and creeping up into his groin. His feet were growing numb. He knew it because he was trying to crunch up his toes, but couldn't tell if they were curling or not. He looked at Sofia and saw she was shivering hard. The snow on her hat and on her shoulders wasn't melting.

'Come on,' he said, kicking forward and pushing down with his poles, and she went with him, the two of them skiing side by side up to the hidden building and Hánas, who turned and nodded.

'Let the camera see you,' the herder said, stepping back to let Erik get closer. 'Maybe they don't like the Sami.'

Erik turned his skis and sidestepped up to the door, where he looked up into the black lens of the camera. He needed there to be someone sitting in a room on the other end of that closed circuit. He was weak and cold and didn't think he and Sofia could survive another night out there.

The door did not open.

'Lillemor,' he said.

Sofia sidestepped up to join him.

'Look into the camera,' he told her. She did, and he saw her face reflected in the lens. Small and seemingly far away. He saw the anguish in her face. The hope too. Still there. Flickering like a flame in the darkness. 'Take your hat off. Just for a second,' he said. She did. Whoever was hiding in this relic from a war of espionage and embargoes, propaganda and technological advances, which had ended before Sofia was born, maybe they were not the kind of bastards who would leave a thirteen-year-old girl out in a blizzard to freeze to death.

But the door did not open.

He couldn't make a fist and so he slammed his forearm and wrist against the door. The muted *thump, thump, thump* was barely audible. 'Open up!' he yelled. 'Open this fucking door!'

Sofia had pulled her hat back on and stood there with her arms crossed over her chest, trying to keep some warmth in her body.

'Maybe there's no one here,' Hánas said. 'Maybe whoever was here left with the helicopter.' He turned and started to walk back over to his skis.

'There has to be someone here,' Sofia said, refusing to give up on the place. She unclipped from her skis, thrust one of her poles into the snow and took the other to the door, which she hammered at with the end of the grip.

'We should go,' Hánas said. 'We want to get down into the pass before full dark.'

'Open up!' Sofia screamed, striking the door again and again. 'Whoever's in there, open up. Please – we're freezing out here! There's a man trying to kill us! Please! Somebody!'

Erik looked back the way they had come, eyes scouring the swirling white world for any shape, any colour that didn't fit. The tall man was out there still. He knew that. Chances were the man had also seen the helicopter, and if he had, maybe had guessed they'd come this way looking for help.

*He'll see us out here on the glacier. He'll see us and even if we run, we won't lose him again.*

'Sofia, enough,' he said. 'We need to go.'

But she kept hitting the door. 'Please! You have to help us.'

'Sofia.' He took a sidestep and reached out, putting his hand on her shoulder. 'We *have* to go.'

She turned her face to him and he saw the wild fear in her eyes. And if he knew one thing in this world, it was that this fire he saw in her now was the last of it and this scared him more than anything.

A sound then. The clunk of a bolt being drawn. Sofia looked at him and he looked at her.

Then the door opened.

The man standing there was grey-faced, grey-haired, and wore a white lab coat with pens lined up in his chest pocket. The entire world's characterization of a scientist. The eyes on the other side of his black-rimmed glasses were pale blue and watery, and he took a moment to examine the three strangers at his door before ushering them inside.

'Bring your skis. Bring everything,' the man said, in an accent that Erik recognized as Finnish. 'We have a place for them.'

Erik thanked him and sent Sofia in while Hánas helped him with the pulk, before fetching his own skis, and then they were inside, following the man into a dimly lit interior far bigger than he would have imagined from the outside. They put their gear in a concrete and metal store room that reminded him of a boot room of a one-star hotel at some budget ski resort. The man introduced himself as Dr Kotilla and led them along a narrow corridor lit by a single LED strip running the length of the wall. Their boots clanged on the serrated steel floor grating.

Sofia took Erik's hand in hers. 'We made it, Pappa,' she said quietly.

From somewhere came the low drone of a generator.

'We made it,' he said, then they turned and took another

passage and came into the heart of the place, a room lit only by the screens of computer monitors at half a dozen work-stations arranged around the walls. Two of the desks were occupied, and both technicians twisted in their chairs to watch these strangers who had brought the cold breath of the blizzard into their secret world, and whose clothes and boots now dripped meltwater onto the floor. A pine and steel changing-room bench was set up in one corner of the room, as if it were a school cloakroom or gym. Hanging from the pegs above the slatted bench were four yellow haz-mat suits. From this central area, the three arrivals were led along another corridor, past two unlit passageways disap-pearing off into darkness, towards a door that looked old, though the handle mechanism did not.

'What is this place?' Hánas asked, before Erik's thawing jaw could shape the words.

'We conduct monitoring and research activities for the Ministry of Climate and Environment,' Dr Kotilla said, pull-ing a key card out on its retractable cord and slotting it into the lock. He pushed the door open and held out his arm, inviting them into the office. 'Come, let's get you warm and comfortable.'

Sofia went in first, then Hánas, while Erik lingered for one last look at the main room, at the test tubes, tongs and racks, the safety masks and boiling flasks and hazmat suits. At the computer monitors, glass partitions and low lighting. Hánas might have been right about it being a rusting Cold War relic, but it looked like a modern research laboratory now.

'After you,' the doctor said.

Erik nodded and walked into the office. Dr Kotilla closed the door behind him.

'We need to use your phone,' Erik said as Kotilla pulled up another chair alongside Sofia and Hánas.

'Not possible, I'm afraid,' Kotilla said, going around the desk to sit in his own chair. 'Our comms are down because of this storm.' He looked from Erik to Hánas and back to Erik again. 'A hazard of the job out here, as you can imagine.'

'Damn it,' Erik said, sharing a look with Hánas, who whispered something in his own language.

Kotilla picked up the phone and spoke in Finnish, then put a hand over the mouthpiece and half turned to Erik. 'Internal comms work fine, though,' he said, and Erik understood enough to know he was asking someone to bring two coffees and a hot chocolate.

'So,' Kotilla said, frowning as he placed the receiver back down. He took off his glasses and wiped them on the sleeve of his lab coat. 'Tell me what has happened. What on earth were you doing out there in this weather?'

Erik exhaled. 'A couple south of the Koppangsbreen glacier, Lars and Karine Helgeland, were murdered,' he said. 'Men came to their house offering them money if they would stop their protesting against the re-opening of the old copper mine. Things got out of hand.' The memory of it flashed behind his eyes and he flinched. The fear was still in his chest, tight and cold. 'They killed the Helgelands,' he said.

'God above,' Kotilla muttered, his pale watery eyes wide as he put his glasses back on.

Erik took a breath. His hands were agony. The pain made it hard to find the words. He felt like a man standing on lake ice, hauling on a line stretching down into the glacial dark water. 'My daughter and I were in the house at the time, but that's another story. We got out. Luckily.' He glanced at Sofia.

'The men who killed Lars and Karine have been hunting us through the mountains.'

'*Far* killed three of them,' Sofia said, her eyes round. She sat huddled as though she were still out there in some snow hole, making herself small so the wind couldn't find her. 'But there is still one man,' she told Dr Kotilla, a shiver running through her, 'and he never stops.' She was wringing her red hands together and he didn't know if it was because they were itching with chilblains, being in the warm, or if it was some manifestation of the mental trauma she had suffered.

Kotilla looked back at Erik, scratching at the grey stubble on one hollow cheek. 'Are you a military man, Mr . . .?'

'Amdahl,' Erik said. 'No. I'm a carpenter.'

The doctor blinked incredulous eyes.

'We got lucky,' Erik said. 'And we found Hánas. He helped us.' He nodded to Hánas now, knowing it was the closest he had got to thanking the man. If it weren't for Hánas, they would probably still be out there, wandering through the blizzard. If they would have been alive at all.

Kotilla looked across at the reindeer herder as if expecting him to add his part of the story.

'Karine Helgeland was my sister,' was all Hánas said. He looked different in this place of steel air-conditioning ducts and metal flooring and concrete walls and computers. He looked older. As though the cold LED lighting leached some of his essence, whereas the flamelight in his tent had fed him something.

The doctor shook his head. 'I am sorry for your loss,' he said. He sat back in his chair like someone who needs a moment or two alone with the things he's heard.

'Why did it take you so long to open the door?' Erik asked.

'Someone must have seen us on the camera. Someone must have heard us banging.'

Kotilla shook his head. 'The camera is not manned. And, of course, we don't hear anything through the walls and the ice. We . . . don't get many visitors up here. None that aren't expected.'

'And there's no way to call the police or get word out?' Erik asked.

'Not until the storm passes. In the meantime, I can send a distress signal. We have an EPIRB—' he lifted a hand as if in apology '—Emergency Position-Indicating Radio Beacon.'

'Like they have on boats,' Erik said.

Kotilla nodded. 'Of course, we cannot specify the nature of the emergency, but once we activate the beacon someone will come. They'll send a helicopter if they can. Snowmobiles if not.' He looked at Sofia and smiled thinly. 'The important thing is you are all safe now. Whoever this man is,' he said, jerking his head towards the wall, 'he will not find us here. And even if he did, he wouldn't be able to get in.'

Sofia looked at Erik as if seeking confirmation of the doctor's assurances.

He nodded confidently in return.

'Well,' Kotilla said, standing and nodding to him and Hánas, 'I'll activate the beacon and have a room prepared for you.' He gestured at Erik's hands. 'We'll have a look at your hands and see if there is something we can do.' He looked at Sofia. 'Are you hungry?'

'A little,' Sofia said.

'I could eat,' Erik said.

Hánas nodded.

'Nothing makes a person so hungry as skiing,' Kotilla

said, though he didn't look to Erik like a man who had ever put on a pair of skis. 'I'm sorry to say the food here is nothing to write home about, but it'll be warm at least.' He looked at Sofia and lifted an eyebrow conspiratorially. 'I do have some chocolate.'

She humoured him with a smile, and only now did she pull the pink hat off her head, as though signalling to all three of them that she had at last decided to stay.

'Don't go anywhere,' Kotilla said, which they all agreed with a shared look was a pretty lame joke, then he left the room, closing the door behind him.

Erik reached out a hand to Sofia beside him. She cradled it between her own on her lap, her wind-cracked lips pressed tightly together. She said nothing.

'We made it, Lillemor,' he said gently.

Two minutes later, a woman, also wearing a lab coat, brought them steaming hot drinks. As she placed the tray on Dr Kotilla's desk, Erik asked her what they were doing out there in the lab. There was the slightest frown, before the woman apologized in accented English and explained that she was from Lithuania and spoke no Norwegian. She smiled at Sofia as she put the hot chocolate down in front of her and then hurried out again, leaving the three of them alone with the intermingling smells of fresh strong black coffee and piping hot chocolate, and the comfort of knowing that, one way or another, people in the outside world would soon know what had happened.

'Good coffee,' Hánas muttered into his mug, and he was right. Erik thought he had never tasted better, and that it was worth the burn he would likely sustain on the palms of his hands, gripping the mug, though he felt nothing. But while Sofia waited for her hot chocolate to cool, she sat forward on the edge of her chair and reached out, picking something up off the desk in front of her. It looked like a green rock, being used as a paperweight.

'Know what that is, Sofia?' Hánas asked her.

She shook her head, turning the rock this way and that.

'The green metal,' Hánas said. 'Copper ore.' He said it like the words themselves tasted bad.

Sofia hefted the weight of the thing. 'From the Koppangen mine?' she asked.

'Could be,' Erik said.

'That mine sits on land through which many thousands of reindeer travel each year on their way to the summer pastures,' Hánas said. 'It's in the middle of the area where the calves are born in the spring. If they open the mine again, it will interrupt the calving process. And how will the female reindeer raise and protect their young?'

'That's not fair,' Sofia said, frowning at the lump of rock in her hand.

'No, Sofia, it's not fair,' Hánas said. 'But they tell me it is . . . progress.' There was a weariness in the way he said this, a resignation, as though it was a fight he had long since given up on. And yet, to Erik's mind, he surely hadn't. He still herded reindeer, as his ancestors had. He lived in the mountains, free as the wind, while other men and women trudged into their offices each morning, sat down in front of computer screens and did the bidding of others, until time and age wearied them and they themselves were put out to pasture.

'The mine will never open again, Hánas,' Erik said. 'Not

once everyone knows what happened to your sister and Lars. And what those men tried to do to us.'

'Look, Pappa,' Sofia said, putting the lump of copper ore back on the desk and picking up a sheet of paper. She turned the document so he could see it more clearly.

'What is it?' he asked.

She put the paper down, unzipped the chest pocket of her coat and took out the folded piece of paper her mother had given her the day they set off. This time she showed her father the other side, upon which was a typed letter – the one Karine had handed Elise the night they went over to the Helgelands' house for dinner.

'See?' Sofia said, picking up the other sheet and holding them side by side. 'I knew I'd seen that before.'

She was talking about the logo. It comprised two upper-case Ns interlinked to resemble mountain peaks and valleys, above the words Novotroitsk Nickel in the same blue. Beneath that, the correspondence was all in Cyrillic script, which none of them could decipher.

Erik leant forward and looked more closely at the pile of correspondence on the desk. Using the side of his hand, he spread it out across the table, instinctively glancing back at the office door. 'Look at that,' he said, because at least five of the papers had the same letterhead: the mountain peaks and Novotroitsk Nickel in blue. 'All from the mining company.'

'So *they* know about this place,' Hánas said.

The sound of feet rang out on the metal floor beyond the door and Erik hastily piled the papers back together.

'Put Mamma's letter away,' he said.

Sofia frowned, opened her mouth to say something, but

then the door opened. In came Dr Kotilla with a pile of blankets in his arms.

'Here,' he said, giving one to Sofia, then another each to Hánas and Erik. 'I can take your outer clothes and hang them to dry.' He walked around his desk and sat down again. 'We use the server room to dry our coats and wet boots.' He dipped his head and looked at Erik over the rim of his glasses. 'Just don't tell the IT guy.'

'So what exactly is it you do here, Doctor?' Erik asked. Sofia had taken off her jacket and was slurping at her hot chocolate, while Hánas was on his feet, removing his great reindeer-skin coat.

'We work for the Norwegian Polar Institute,' Kotilla said, steepling his fingers on his desk. 'We are just a small team here, but we study the climate – environmental pollutants. Also biodiversity.'

'You want to know about the climate, just ask me,' Hánas said, lifting his chin and challenging Kotilla with his eyes. 'In the past, my reindeer could always forage for food through the snow. Now the winters are warmer and the top layer of snow sometimes melts, then freezes again.' He leant forward and rapped his knuckles on the desk. 'It makes a blanket of ice and the reindeer can starve.'

Kotilla nodded solemnly. 'Temperatures in the far north have risen by more than two degrees Celsius since the industrial revolution. I can only imagine how hard it is to try to hold on to the traditional ways of your people.'

Hánas batted the air with a gnarly hand. 'Mining, power lines, wind power. They tell me it's all in the name of progress. For the future. But tell me, how can it be sustainable to destroy nature itself?'

Dr Kotilla lifted his hands in a don't-ask-me gesture, which struck Erik as odd, because surely anyone studying climate change should be advocating for electrification. For wind turbines, electric vehicles, the end of fossil fuels. And green technology needed copper, which had to be taken out of the ground. Strange for a scientist to be taking the side of the indigenous people against the drive to help the world economy move beyond carbon.

'Why do you need the hazmat suits?' Erik asked. 'That's some serious gear you've got out there.' The yellow suits he had seen were the real deal, fully encapsulating chemical entry suits with self-contained breathing apparatus. Almost identical to the one he had seen Elise wearing in a photograph taken by her colleague when they were in Siberia and had to protect themselves from contact with radioactive pollution from used nuclear fuel.

'Ah, they're just a precaution,' Kotilla said. 'You know what insurance companies are like.' He thumbed his forehead as if wiping away sweat. 'In 2012 a polar team taking ice cores in Siberia came across the carcass of a woolly mammoth trapped in the ice for forty-five thousand years. The carcass was largely intact. Flesh, skin, hair. They even found its blood, trapped in the ice below the body.' He took off his glasses and waved them through the air. 'But there was concern that there might still be living organisms present – a virus or parasite perhaps.'

'I think I saw that in a TV show,' Sofia said. 'People got infected and started killing each other.'

Erik looked at her and she shrugged it off. 'I didn't watch the whole series. I just saw a bit of it at Anette's house.'

He gave her his sceptical face. 'Of course you did,' he said.

Kotilla shook his head. 'Well, that's TV for you.' He pinched a finger and thumb together. 'They take a grain of science and bury it in nonsense.'

Hánas was saying something about TV being the thing he missed most of all up here, but Erik wasn't really listening. He was still thinking about the hazmat suits, all hung up like that ready to go.

'Doctor,' he said, interrupting Hánas, 'you must have attended the Climate Conference in Oslo last year?' Saying the words drew a knot in his chest, because while Elise was at the conference he had taken the girls to London, to spend a few days with his father, and they had gone to the climbing wall in Greenwich. If they'd gone anywhere else. *Done* anything else. 'Maybe you know some of the people my wife has worked with,' he said. 'She's with Friends of the Earth Norway.'

Kotilla sat back in his chair and drummed his fingers on the armrests. 'Sadly I was unable to attend the conference,' he said, returning Erik's gaze. 'But as I always say, I would rather be working up here than talking down there, if you know what I mean.'

Erik nodded. 'Still, it's a shame you missed Professor Edwards' keynote speech. My wife said it was truly inspiring. Wouldn't stop talking about it!'

Kotilla shifted in his chair. 'The professor is a brilliant man,' he said earnestly.

Erik nodded again. In truth, Elise had barely spoken about the conference afterwards, what with the accident and its hideous aftermath, but at some point in the last year he had seen a photo on her phone, taken by her colleague, of Elise shaking hands with Professor Edwards in the Oslofjord Convention Center foyer. And Edwards was a woman.

*Why is he lying? And what about those hazmat suits?* Erik knew there must be some connection between this lab and the Koppangen copper mine, but he couldn't make the link.

The phone on the desk rang. Kotilla lifted a hand to Erik in a *one second* gesture, picked up the receiver and listened, turning his head away and burying the receiver in the crook between his neck and his shoulder. He nodded. Swallowed. His eyes flicked to Hánas and then back to Erik, then he said, '*Toropit'sya*.' That was all. Then he put the phone down, pushed his glasses back up the bridge of his nose and pressed his thin lips into a smile.

'So,' he said, standing, 'I'll take you—'

The rest of the sentence never left his lips, because Erik stood abruptly, grabbed the rock on the doctor's desk and slammed it across his temple, breaking the circuits in the man's brain so that his legs buckled and he dropped to the floor in a disorganized pile, his glasses skidding across the tiles.

'What the hell?!' Hánas said, jumping up from his chair in shock. Sofia hadn't moved, but now stared up at him, her mouth hanging open, her eyes bulging in her exhausted face.

'He's lying,' Erik told them. 'We have to get out of here.'

'Lying about what?' Hánas said, stepping forward to look down at Kotilla, who lay there unconscious, blood bright in his grey hair.

'Everything,' Erik said. 'The word he said on the phone was Russian.'

Hánas nodded. 'He said *hurry*.'

'And who do you think he was talking to?' Erik asked them both.

'Shit,' Hánas said.

Erik took Sofia's coat from the back of her chair and thrust it at her. 'Put it on. Quickly.'

'What's happening, Pappa?' she asked as she put the coat on again.

Erik bent down by Kotilla and took the key card off the retractable reel attached to the doctor's trouser belt loop. Then he stood and put his hands on Sofia's shoulders. 'We're leaving now,' he said. 'It's not safe here.'

'But we can't go back out there,' she said, desperation thick in her throat.

'We can't stay here. I think the tall man is coming. I think that's who Dr Kotilla told to hurry. This place has some-thing to do with the copper mine and the people who murdered Lars and Karine.'

A tear rolled down his daughter's cheek and she looked at Hánas. Hoping.

'Your *far*'s right,' he told her. 'We need to get out of here.'

She nodded. Looked down at Dr Kotilla, who was com-ing round, groaning pitifully.

'Stay together and stay calm,' Erik said. He took a deep breath, opened the office door and the three of them stepped out into the dark corridor.

# 13

HE LED THEM along the passage, back the way they had come. Abruptly, he stopped and stuck out an arm to grab Sofia. People were coming. He could hear them talking and the clatter of their shoes on the metal grid floor, growing louder as they came closer.

Hánas lifted his chin to indicate a dark corridor leading off on their left. Erik nodded, following Hánas into the dark with Sofia. Suddenly the LED lighting along the passage flickered on. Hánas stopped dead.

'It's on a sensor,' Erik said, gesturing for Hánas to go on. He glanced over his shoulder to make sure no one was behind them, but when he turned back around, Hánas had not moved.

'Pappa,' Sofia whispered. She and Hánas were standing by a door, looking through a rectangular glass viewing panel. One of Sofia's hands was at her mouth, her other stretched out towards her father, who joined them at the door. Hánas stepped away to let Erik peer through.

It was a small room beyond some sort of inflatable ante-room. Almost empty. Dark but for a shaft of light reaching through the glass from the corridor. There was a steel table and on it lay a body. A skeleton almost, with dark skin like tanned rawhide stretched tight over tendons and the sharp angles of the bones beneath. One arm bent across its rib-cage. Black slits for eyes, shrunken lips and gums pulled back from the teeth in an eternal expression of savage glee. A mummified corpse lying in a haze of what Erik guessed to be liquid nitrogen, pumped in from somewhere to preserve the body. He could feel the cold coming off the glass and the door itself.

'What the hell has this got to do with climate research or biodiversity?' Erik muttered under his breath.

They moved on to the next door and looked through the window. Another steel table. Different corpse. As gnarled and twisted as the first, this one had a mane of brown hair and a tuft of beard jutting from its chin. The lips looked to be gone but the teeth were there, fixed in a terrible grimace, as if enough of the human spirit yet clung to the body to be resentful of the cold it was being made to endure. Its eyes were wide open, greyish white and swollen in their sockets.

'What's going on, Pappa?' Sofia said, still looking through the glass.

He shook his head because he had no answer to give her.

Hánas growled something. He was peering through the glass of another door further along the passageway, and now he turned to Erik, his dark brows drawn together over narrowed eyes.

Erik had a bad feeling. His hand found Sofia's and together they crept to the next door.

The three of them gazed through the viewing window and the PVC anteroom window beyond. This body lying in the dark was different. Only the face was exposed, the torso and legs covered with blankets. But this face was not mummified like the others. Pale and gaunt, yes, eyes closed, yes, but without the sunken, empty-vessel look of the dead.

Hánas lifted his hand and tapped his knuckle against the glass.

'What are you d—? Oh God!' Erik's blood ran cold, because the man lying in the dark had opened his eyes.

Hánas gripped the door handle but it wouldn't turn.

'We've got to go,' Erik hissed.

Then the man sat up, or tried to, but Erik could see now that he was strapped to the table.

'Hánas, we have to go.'

The man in the dark was straining against his bonds now. Thrashing this way and that like a fish on a hook. His head, though, remained still, his bulging eyes fixed on Hánas. The movement drew Erik's attention to the intravenous drip in the captive's arm and the bag of fluid swinging on its stand in the shadows beyond. The man was shouting but the sound was muffled behind the thick metal door.

'I know him,' Hánas said. 'His name is Ivvár.'

'You know that man?' Erik's mind raced.

'He's a guide for the mining company, last I heard.'

'Novotroitsk Nickel?' Erik said.

Hánas nodded and Erik looked back through the window. The man looked beyond terrified. But already his strength had drained away and he could barely hold his head up from the steel table he was strapped to. 'You can imagine how that went down with my people,' Hánas muttered.

'We've got to go,' Erik said. He pictured Dr Kotilla back in his office, clambering to his feet now, stumbling to the door to raise the alarm.

'What have they done to him?' Hánas said, pressing his palm against the glass.

'Hánas,' Sofia said, tugging at the sleeve of the herder's coat.

He looked at her and nodded, and the three of them continued down the hall and turned a corner. This brought them to the back of the dimly lit lab. Four metres away, a man sat at his desk with his back to them, intent on a document on his computer screen. They trod as lightly as they could on the metal floor, all watching the man's minor movements as he focused on the monitor. Hearts pounding in their chests, they tiptoed as lightly as they could over the metal floor, past the banks of little blue and green lights.

The man coughed and they froze in midstep, holding their breath. He turned and slid open a drawer, delved inside for a tissue and hawked into it, before dropping it into a metal bin.

His attention returned to the screen ahead and, after a moment's further pause, Erik and the others continued across the rest of the lab unseen. They turned down another hallway and came to the boot room.

Ahead of them, another door swung open. Into the room came a woman carrying a mug of steaming coffee. She faltered in her step, surprise written across her face.

Erik gave a broad smile. 'Dr Kotilla said we could make another hot drink,' he told the woman, nodding towards the small kitchen area behind her.

'Well, I would stick to the filter coffee if I were you,' she said with no discernible accent, smiling back at Erik and then at Sofia. Hánas, she seemed to ignore. 'The machine will make a cappuccino but it's all foam.'

Erik thanked her for the tip, and she headed past them and along the corridor. When she was out of sight, they slipped into the boot room and gathered their skis and poles as well as the pulk and their rifles.

Erik made sure Sofia fastened her jacket properly and put on her gloves and hat, before carrying the pulk round to the exit with Hánas. For a moment they stood there, the three of them sharing a few seconds of silence and unspoken questions, and he wanted to curse a god he didn't believe in for forcing him to take his daughter back out into the freezing dark. A foreboding flash of the one-eyed man appeared to him and he blinked it away.

Then he fumbled at the handle with the better of his two traitorous hands and opened the door and the cold air was a ferocious slap in his face.

'Ready?' he asked Sofia.

She nodded.

They stepped out into the snow. Erik felt first the hairs in his nose freeze and then the sear of the air in his lungs. He strapped the pulk harness on while the others clipped into their skis, and despite the inner panic rising in his belly at being back out in the snow-whipped twilight, there was some strange comfort in fastening on the pulk and stepping into his own ski bindings. Perhaps this was his purgatory, he thought, and he was doomed to endure it for ever. But it wasn't fair on Sofia. He looked across at her. She was standing ready, her poles planted in the snow. Looking at him. Waiting for him.

'He's here,' Hánas said.

Erik's guts twisted. He looked up at the high ground where some pale light lingered as if reluctant to cede to the night. 'Where?'

Hánas was holding up his old rifle, scoping the ridge. 'Two o'clock. Knows what he's doing. He's moved off the brow of the hill to hide his outline.'

Erik brought his own rifle up, sweeping it from left to right. Then he saw him. A dark shape a quarter of the way down the dusky slope.

'Go!' he told Sofia. 'Go!'

She performed a perfect kick turn, thrust down with both poles and he saw the snow thrown up on the spot where she had stood just a heartbeat before.

'Go, Sofia!' he shouted again, taking off after her as the suppressed report of the tall man's rifle rolled down the hill in their wake. Hánas fired the Mosin-Nagant, flame blooming from the barrel like the Devil's tongue, noise filling the world, echoing off the lab and the ice like a thunder crack.

'Faster!' Erik called after the girl. He was moving fast himself now, racing after her, and heard Hánas behind him working the bolt of the Russian rifle. The next shot rang out, making him duck instinctively and throwing him off balance, but he stayed on his feet and kept going. Kick and glide, kick and glide. Because the bastard had been aiming at Sofia and that thought was an adrenaline syringe pumped right into the hot beating muscle of his heart.

He saw another gout of ice thrown up by a round hitting the snow a foot to Sofia's right, but now he had caught up with her and got as close as he dared without running the risk of fouling her skis and sending them both face first into the snow.

'I'm here!' he called out, holding himself more upright than was comfortable, staying as tall as he could because he needed to shield her. 'I'm with you.'

Then he glanced to his left because Hánas was off his shoulder, skiing in his fluid, economical style, seemingly unencumbered by his thick reindeer-skin coat.

'I didn't get him,' Hánas said.

'Where are we going?' Erik asked.

'The ravine I told you about. We can still make it.'

'Hánas,' he said, driving on, watching the girl in front of him, not letting more than a metre of ground grow between the back of her skis and the front of his own. 'If I don't make it . . . you keep her safe.'

'Pappa!' Sofia said.

'You'll make it,' Hánas said.

'But if I don't—?'

'You'll make it.'

He gritted his teeth, hating himself for letting the girl see his fear. His weakness. But he had needed to say it. He was already breathing hard. The adrenaline was wearing thin and soon it would be gone. His legs felt empty. His arms too. The muscles in his stomach were screaming, but it was OK. Pain was OK. Pain was good. What he feared was his body failing him. Betraying him as his hands had done. In his mind he could go on for ever. He could love her for ever. Even after he was gone. He didn't know how it worked. He didn't know if anyone else had ever made it work and he didn't care. But he would love her still when he was nothing. Love was not reliant on his body, his muscles and tendons, his beating heart and his lungs inflating and deflating like bellows fanning a fire. Sooner or later, though, his body would be unable to go on. The fire would go out. Then what?

'Keep going, Sofia, we can make it,' he said, ploughing through the deep snow. 'We're strong. We are not the kind of people who give up.' He grimaced, feeling the cold on his teeth. Thinking about his next words. They came up into his throat and for five or six strides he kept them in his mouth.

'And Emilie is with us now,' he said. 'I know you feel it too.'

It came out of him like someone had ripped his soul from his body. And there it was, in that small space between them, so that he could almost see it. And tears came to his eyes. 'Your sister is with us now, Lillemor, and we're strong.'

Sofia didn't answer. But her stride lengthened. Maybe it was his imagination, but it seemed that her poles landed with more strength behind them.

She led them into the blizzard. Into the teeth of the wind.

He couldn't see how they could get away from the tall man now, because he would be on their trail before their tracks silted up. Was probably skiing in their tracks now, saving himself the effort of breaking new snow. But maybe, if they could stay ahead of him until dark, there was a chance. The Russian knew they were armed. Two rifles against his one. If they could make it until dark, they could set a trap for him. Lay a trail into the night, then double back and lie in wait and put him down like an animal.

That thought warmed him. The hate in it.

They skirted the base of a steep bluff which rose above them into the darkening sky, then Hánas led them south.

After passing a series of gentle gullies, the reindeer herder pointed up ahead to the location of the hidden ravine.

'It leads down to the glacier,' he reminded them when they reached the top and stood staring down into the void.

Erik looked at Sofia. She was regaining her breath, faster than him perhaps. And they couldn't linger long.

'It's steep,' she said warily.

He nodded. 'It is. Can you do it?'

She thought about it. He could see her hands opening and closing on her poles.

'Yes,' she said.

'Side-slip, remember?' he said.

'I know. What about the pulk?'

'I'll take it slow.'

'Leave the pulk,' Hánas said. 'You don't want to risk a broken ankle.'

'I'll take it slow,' he said again.

Hánas nodded and slipped over the lip and into the ravine.

'You go next,' Erik told Sofia. 'Be careful.'

She turned her skis across the fall line and started to slip down the slope, her skis sending loose powder snow cascading, Sofia stopping now and then by leaning her knees and ankles inward towards the uphill side.

'Good girl,' he said, 'that's it. Perfect.'

As she faded into the shadow, he took one last look behind him, then edged over the lip. He kept his legs fairly straight, pushing his heels outwards and his toes inwards, making a wedge with his skis, their tips some thirty centimetres apart, his torso bending forward at the hips. The pulk behind him was impatient, trying to push him downhill, so he had to work hard to control the speed of his descent, bringing his knees towards each other, his thigh muscles quivering with the effort.

Down and down they went. The only sounds were their breathing and the soft tumble of snow dislodged by their skis and, now and then, the scrape of their skis on patches of ice. It took them a long time, but eventually the ravine levelled out onto the glacier and they were able to straighten up and let their skis run normally for a few minutes, which was as good as a rest.

In his exhaustion, the hiss of his skis and the effect of passing through the falling snow was mesmerizing, putting him almost in a sort of hypnotic trance, so that when he came to a stop he felt as though he'd been experiencing an out-of-body episode. He stood there in the blizzard, his face as numb as his mind, and found he couldn't remember getting down the mountain.

'Are you OK, Pappa?' Erik looked up. Sofia was waiting for him. Hánas stood a little further on, looking back at them through the falling snow.

'I'm fine,' he said. He looked back up the ravine. The darkness welled between the steep valley sides, like black water caught in a tide pool. He couldn't see the tall man but that didn't mean he wasn't there.

Then he gazed out across the almost featureless glacier, so that even in the failing light he could see Hánas, or the bulk of him at least. Three of them out there on the glacier would be impossible to miss.

'We don't want to be caught out here,' he said.

'My legs are shaking,' she said. 'I need to lie down.'

'No,' he said, shaking his head, 'you can't.'

'I know. But I can't go much further.'

He couldn't go much further himself, he knew, but didn't say it.

'We'll find somewhere to lay low on the other side,' he said. 'We'll keep watch with the rifles and you can rest. OK?'

Her teeth were savaging her bottom lip. 'OK,' she whispered.

'Let's go.'

'Pappa.'

'What?'

'What do you think happened to Čalmmo?' She wiped her eyes but he couldn't see if she was crying. 'Hánas's dog.'

He shrugged. 'Maybe the tall man got him.'

She nodded. 'That's what I think,' she said.

'But he won't get us,' he said.

She looked back up the ravine.

'Sofia, we've got to go.' He lifted an arm. 'Keep in Hánas's tracks as best you can. I'll be right behind you.'

She looked towards Hánas.

'OK?' Erik asked.

'OK,' she said.

She set off and he followed her.

Waking dreams now. Memories and random thoughts swirling in fragments in his mind. Elise in a bath, her breasts half hidden by the foam. Her eyes level with his, so he knew he must be in the bath with her. The hot water. The scent of the sandalwood and sweet almond oil that she liked. The four of them at the pizza restaurant that was always Sofia and Emilie's choice whenever he suggested eating out. The day they had driven up to the cabin. Him lighting the fire in the stove and holding his hands up at the glass like a supplicant before an idol.

Images came and went in a montage over which he had little control. His mind and his body seeming separate, each going their own way. Some part of him knew he was skiing still. Knew that he had become almost an extension of his daughter, his own skis beginning where hers ended. But his mind was untethering. He knew that too. Was as passively aware of it as he was of the snow whipping around him and into his face, and the wind in his right ear, the distorted roar of it through the wool of his hat, and the hiss of the skis beneath his feet and the thrum of the blood in his head. To all of it, he was more than just a spectator, and yet less than the subject.

A holiday in Fuerteventura. His feet sinking into the hot sand. The rhythmic murmur of the sea. The sound of his girls laughing. The best sound he'd ever heard. Standing on the beach, watching Emilie take a windsurfer out. Falling in, over and over, but never giving up, until at last she caught the wind and made a hundred metres before falling again. Sofia jumping up and down with excitement because her big sister had *mastered* it.

So long as he stayed with his girl. So long as he did not fall.

Then his body stopped moving. Some instinct had taken hold of his mind and was shaking it now, like a dog with a soft toy in its jaws, tossing the thing from side to side in some imitation of its wolf ancestors killing prey.

His vision sharpened, the white world forming around him, sound and sight coalescing into a coherent whole.

'Pappa, look at Hánas.' Her voice was small in the drone

of the wind. Fifty metres ahead of them, Hánas stood in the swirling snow. He was facing them, his rifle raised, its butt nestled in his shoulder.

'Sofia, get down!' Erik yelled. She ducked, but Hánas just stood there. *What are you doing?* he thought, then Hánas took his hand from the stock and beckoned him and Sofia on, and Erik saw that the Mosin-Nagant's barrel was pointing past them. Was aimed at something behind them. 'Ski!' he shouted. 'Ski, Sofia!' They were moving again and he saw the flame leap from the rifle, felt the round pass them by and heard the whizz of it, followed by the report itself.

Erik skied towards Hánas as the herder worked the bolt and drove it home and fired again.

'Keep going,' he cried into the wind, and when they were less than fifteen metres from Hánas, he felt the heat from the muzzle flash before he knew Hánas had fired again. Then Sofia was past the herder, with Erik following in her tracks.

'Go!' Hánas roared, their eyes meeting for a fraction of a second, but in that half moment he saw the fire of hate in the Sami's eyes, before Hánas turned his gaze back to the north and drew the bolt, chambering another antique Soviet cartridge, and fired again. The *crack* of it was impossibly loud, rolling across the glacier after him in an avalanche of sound. It occurred to him that the tall man wasn't firing back. At least he hadn't heard any other shots.

He bent forward, thrusting his poles down as best he could, and as his skis hissed along behind Sofia, he looked back over his shoulder. He couldn't see their pursuer, but as he straightened and rammed the poles down again, he heard another shot, the sound of it far away. He looked back again and saw Hánas throw his rifle onto his back and turn to follow.

The three of them skied for their lives. Into the blizzard like sacrificial victims willing to appease the gods of ice, so that spring might one day return. They wanted to lose themselves in the white flakes. Wanted the snow to come down behind them like a wall.

*Let me give my life for her – please*, Erik thought, though he didn't know to whom he was thinking this.

After a while he called to Sofia to stop because he didn't want to lose sight of her while he waited for Hánas to catch them up.

'You OK?' he asked the older man, because he knew, even before Hánas came into focus, that something was very wrong.

'Keep going,' Hánas said. His face was grey. His lips had a blueish tint to them that Erik didn't like the look of. He looked behind Hánas and saw the blood in his tracks. Hánas read it in his face and turned and saw the blood too. His own blood. A trail of it in the snow, stark in the ebbing light. He swung his eyes back to Erik. 'Keep going,' he said again, lifting his chin towards the snowstorm.

'You've been hit,' Erik said.

'It's nothing.' Hánas looked down at himself. There was a hole in his big coat halfway down. Just a little thing. He pulled his mitten off with his teeth and fumbled at the horn buttons. Pulled his coat open.

'Shit,' he said, then looked up at Erik. 'It doesn't hurt anyway.'

'We need to stop the bleeding,' Erik said. There was a bloom of blood on the man's woollen sweater, on the right side of his stomach, and a hole at the centre, like the dark heart of a rose that hasn't fully unfurled. Blood had run down the inside of his right leg, down his calf and onto his boot, where it glistened now, inky and ominous in the dim light.

'We don't have time,' Hánas said.

'Let me see it,' Erik insisted. Hánas lifted the jumper and Erik turned to Sofia. 'Keep watch,' he told her, gesturing back into the north. But she was staring at the wound. At that little hole, malevolent and black and steaming. Blood was welling from it, trickling down over the white skin of Hánas's abdomen and into the waistband of his trousers. 'Sofia, I said to keep watch,' Erik told her again. She tore her eyes away and looked back the way they had come, one mittened hand shielding the side of her face against the snow.

'It doesn't hurt?' Erik asked.

Hánas was looking down at himself, his teeth clenched. 'It burns a little,' he said, then looked over his shoulder, and then at Erik. 'There's no time.'

But Erik was already undoing the sled harness. He unclipped from his skis and went over to the pulk to fetch the first aid kit and for a moment he was back in the tent on the first night out, when Sofia had cut her hand and he had bandaged it up before they had set off for the Helgelands' house. Before all of this.

'Erik, you're not listening. We have to go. Now.'

Erik gave Sofia the packet holding the antiseptic wipe because his fingers would never get it open, then he gestured for Hánas to hitch his jumper up higher. 'Keep still,' he said, taking the antiseptic back and pressing it to the entry wound. The dressing turned from white to red in an instant. Then

Erik pressed five gauze pads against the wound and told Hánas to hold the wad in place while he handed the adhesive tape to Sofia so she could find the end.

'We have to stop the bleeding or you'll lead that bastard right to us,' Erik said. He looked Hánas in the eye and something unspoken passed between them. Hánas nodded. Erik passed the tape around his midriff once, twice, then the tape spooled out and he pressed it down as Hánas winced in pain. There was no exit wound in his back, meaning the bullet was still lodged in there, but Erik didn't know enough about human anatomy to say where it could be or what damage it had wrought. Was it in his intestines? Higher, if he had to guess. The kidney? Or the liver perhaps? Or maybe it had pierced his stomach, which would not be good. None of it was good. He had seen enough movies to know that people who were shot in the gut didn't usually die straight away, but die they did.

He went back to the pulk and found the leather-bound hip flask full of bourbon that he had imagined himself sipping in some cosy DNT hut beside a blazing fire, while Sofia blew into her mug of hot chocolate and they made plans for the next day of the trip. Hánas reached out and put the offering to his lips. He let the whisky stutter into his mouth for five whole seconds. Maybe it would help with the pain. Maybe not.

Erik looked to the north, eyes half closed against the blizzard. 'Can you get us somewhere safe?' he asked. He was worried for Hánas, for what ruin that bullet had done to him. But the girl was his charge. Only the girl.

Hánas returned the hip flask and Erik tucked it into a pocket.

'It's not far now,' Hánas said, looking out across the virgin snow. Clouds of white rolled like sea fog. 'We'll drop down off this glacier and keep the storm behind us.'

Erik clipped back into his skis and Sofia helped him into the pulk harness.

'Will he be OK?' she asked, looking at Hánas, who had already set off ahead. He was leaning forward and slightly to the right, as if his whole body was being drawn into that entry wound. As if it were a black hole that would suck the man into it and he would be gone from this dimension to some other.

'He's as tough as they come,' Erik said, 'and we bound the wound nice and tight. He'll be OK if we can get him to a hospital.' He realized how unlikely that was even as he was saying it, but if Sofia had doubts she kept them to herself and they kicked off after the reindeer herder, keeping in his tracks, glancing over their shoulders from time to time like people afraid of their own shadows.

# 14

HÁNAS WAS DOWN again. Erik could see the boulder-like shape of him up ahead through the slanting snow, but Sofia got to him first. She was pulling him back onto his feet when Erik came up on them.

'Don't think I can do it,' Hánas told them, slurring the words. His eyes had a heaviness about them and he opened them wide a few times, like a man who is trying not to fall asleep.

'You can do it,' Erik said, nodding at Sofia to help him steady Hánas on his skis.

'Pappa, we can put him in the pulk,' she said.

'No, Sofia,' Hánas said. His face was grey now, and yet his brow was sheened in sweat.

'Why not?' she asked. Erik could feel her eyes boring into him. Judging him.

'Your father needs to save his strength,' Hánas said.

Shame rose inside him but Erik didn't contradict Hánas.

The man was right. He was exhausted. Any strength he could still call upon was not now of the body but of the mind and the heart and the soul. He had nothing else to spare. Not even for himself. Only for his daughter.

'Let me check it,' he said, and they opened Hánas's big coat and saw that the blood hadn't soaked through the dressing, which was good. Maybe the cold had helped, he thought. But the external cold could not stop the internal bleeding, and surely there would not be enough blood going to Hánas's heart. His fluids would be too low and his kidneys would fail. And who knew what else was going on behind the scenes? Maybe gastric acid was leaking into places it shouldn't. Maybe his bladder was spilling its contents, poisoning him.

'I don't know what to do,' Erik admitted. In that moment he was struck with the realization that he knew far more about timber and the various properties of wood than he knew about the human body.

'I'll go on as long as I can,' Hánas said, 'but if I can't keep up, you leave me.'

'No!' Sofia said, looking at her father for support. But she found none and so she sidestepped up to Hánas, pressing herself against his left side. 'You can lean on me,' she told him, and took his arm and put it around her shoulder. 'We'll kick our skis at the same time. My left and your right, then my right and your left, but at the same time.'

Erik watched her, feeling as proud of her as he was ashamed of himself.

'I'll do it,' he said, moving into position as Sofia sidestepped away. Yes, he only had strength for her, but this *was* for her. 'It'll be easier for me because we're more or less the same height.'

'I can take the pulk then,' she said.

He shook his head. 'Ski just ahead of us. We'll need your eyes.'

They set off again, and for a while it worked, his and Hánas's legs moving in synch, their skis running parallel, carving their passage through the deep snow. But then Hánas started coughing. Thirty seconds later he went rigid and started retching, then pulled away from Erik and bent over and vomited blood. It came out of him in a crimson gush, spattering into the snow and onto his skis, and so bright in the dark.

'Jesus,' Erik said, because there was so much blood. It steamed for a few seconds before the heat from it was lost.

'Do something, Pappa,' Sofia pleaded.

He nodded. 'Keep watch,' he told her, pointing back the way they had come. He went to Hánas and put a hand on his shoulder.

Still bent over, Hánas turned his face up to him.

'Can't . . . breathe,' he said. He spat more blood, then waved an arm weakly in their direction of travel. 'G—' he coughed and spat again. 'Go.'

Erik shook his head. 'It's OK. You'll feel better now the blood's out. We've got to keep moving.'

Hánas shook his head. Straightened. Dragged an arm across his mouth. 'Go,' he said.

Erik looked at the blood in the snow. So much blood. How far could Hánas go in that condition? Truth was, he wanted to leave him there. He wanted to take Sofia and go. Maybe the two of them could reach the outskirts of town and raise the alarm. Send help back up here to bring Hánas down. Maybe they would come across a police patrol on snowmobiles, or the mountain rescue, or a DNT hut where there were other people sheltering from the storm, people with phones that worked. But even if he could justify it to himself, he knew he couldn't justify it to Sofia. She would know, and he couldn't live with her knowing a thing like that. Not yet.

'Let's go,' he told Hánas, who grimaced and nodded and dragged cold breath into his lungs and reached out and took hold of Erik's arm.

*What would you do for her?*
    *Anything.*
    *Anything?*
    *There is nothing I would not do.*
    *Would you kill?*
    *Yes.*
    *Would you murder?*
    *Yes.*
    *What about leaving a man to die in the snow?*
He thought about that, though he knew he didn't need to think. But something about the one-eyed man demanded a sort of introspection. A show at least of having considered the answer deeply, rather than spitting it out like an olive stone.
    *Yes, I would leave a man to die in the snow.*
    *Even if he's helped you?*
    *Even then. I told you, there's nothing I wouldn't do.*
    *What if it made her hate you? What then?*
This time, he did think about it. *I would still do it.*
    *Then do it.*
'Which way?' Sofia had stopped, looking back at them through the swirling snow.

227

'Just keep going,' he called. She nodded and turned and kicked off again.

He didn't know where they were. He had no recollection of the last kilometre. Hánas was leaning on him still, skiing still, though his head was slumped forward, his bearded chin resting on his chest. His eyes might even have been closed – with that great hood over his head, there was no telling while they were in motion. But they had covered a lot of ground since Hánas had puked up all that blood. Their outer arms poling, legs moving together, skis carving through the snow in perfect harmony, so that he thought they must resemble some weird automaton, a machine in mockery of men programmed to follow a predetermined sequence of operations.

Erik wondered if Hánas was in fact helping him, rather than the other way around. But how was the man still skiing at all, having lost so much blood? With a bullet inside his torn flesh? Perhaps to a man like that, a man who had skied thousands of kilometres in his lifetime, the act was just about the same as breathing. The only thing that could stop him doing either was death itself. That wouldn't be long now. Couldn't be.

Would Hánas even know if they stopped here, wherever *here* was, and Erik gently laid him down in the snow? That's what the one-eyed man had been getting at, wasn't it? That's why he had come. Didn't even need Erik to be asleep now. He'd just show up. And if a god can't do that, what's the use in being a god?

*I'm still here*, the god said now. Proving a point.

'What do you want from me?' Erik asked him.

He got no reply. The wind keened across the glacier and

there was another sound too, and he realized Sofia had shouted something.

'What is it?' he called.

Again, the wind, the sound of it like a dirge for the lost.

'There's something there,' she said.

He looked in the direction she was pointing her pole. It was getting very dark and with so much snow in the air he couldn't see what she had seen. But as he skied on, whatever it was took form, and his stomach tightened with a feeling of hope.

'Where are we?' Hánas said, his head still bowed so that the words – the first he had spoken for a long time – came from inside his reindeer-skin hood.

'There are buildings,' he said. 'Halfway up a slope. But they're old.' Not just old, he realized now, but derelict. 'They're on legs.' The hope he had felt shrivelled inside him now because he could see that the place was abandoned.

'The old mine,' Hánas said, even before he found the strength to lift his head.

'The copper mine?' Sofia asked. 'The one they want to reopen?'

'Yes,' Hánas said.

'We'll find no help here,' Erik said, looking up the slope. There was enough light reflected from the snow to make out three main structures. A clutter of long timber-plank build-ings with corrugated iron roofs, in three rows, one seemingly on top of the other and all running parallel to the craggy mountain face behind them. Where the hillside fell away, the buildings stood on stilts, an ancient and fragile-looking lat-ticework that put him in mind of some 1920s wooden roller coaster.

'What now?' Sofia asked, pulling at the cuff of her mitten and huffing warm breath into it. She looked so small, her face pale, but for the dark pools of shadow beneath her eyes. In actual fact, she looked sick. Like she had in the weeks after Emilie died. She had said it was her fault, because it had been her idea to go climbing.

'We made it this far,' he said. Maybe Hánas's legs were giving up, or maybe his own strength was finally spent, but he was now more aware than before of the weight of the man leaning on him. He knew that if he stepped away, Hánas would collapse and they would never get him up on his skis again. He looked to the east. 'It can't be far to town from here. Five kilometres to the outskirts. Maybe six.' Even saying it broke his heart because he knew it was too far.

'I'm done,' Hánas said.

Erik swallowed and straightened his spine, lifting his shoulder and, in turn, Hánas, whose arm lay across it. 'We can make it,' he said.

Hánas shook his head. 'Leave me.' His head sagged again.

Erik looked at Sofia. She shook her head.

'We could leave him there,' he said, lifting his chin to indicate the old mine buildings up the slope. 'He'll have shelter. We'll get to town and send the police and medics up here to fetch him.'

'Pappa, I can't do it,' she said.

'He'll be OK,' he said.

She shook her head and he saw the tears in her eyes, and knew she wasn't talking about Hánas now. 'I can't,' she said. 'I can't ski any more, Pappa. I can't.'

'I know, Lillemor. It's OK.' He wanted to go to her and

hold her, but Hánas was a dead weight hanging off him. 'It's OK. Come here.'

She took two strides and now he was close enough for the fog of her breath to drift over his face on the freezing air and, with it, the faint scent of the sweat from her head.

'We can rest here,' he said, looking back up at the deserted buildings. A line of cableway towers stretched into the dark to the east like the skeletal remains of giant robots or some long-defunct technology. 'We can rest. Eat something. Gather our strength for the last push.' The words themselves were like sustenance in his mouth.

'What about the man?' she said, peering off into the gathering night.

He looked back and could barely make out their tracks, though that didn't mean they weren't there. 'We'll rest and be ready. We'll find a place where we can keep watch. We have the rifles, remember. If he comes, we'll kill him.'

She thought about this. She looked beyond exhausted. She was shivering with cold and no doubt fear too. She nodded. 'OK, Pappa,' she said.

'Come on. Help me get him up there.'

*Good to get her moving again*, he thought, as she came round on Hánas's other side, and put his arm over her shoulder.

'Ready?' he asked her.

'Ready,' she said.

And together they carried Hánas up the slope, towards the abandoned mine buildings. Towards shelter.

They hid their skis and the pulk in the first building they came to, then found a place in the topmost shed to lay low.

It took what felt like the last of their strength to climb up there, dragging Hánas, who had little left to give. But Erik wanted a better view of the approach to the mine. He told Sofia it might also give them more warning if the tall man came and they didn't see him, because they might hear him searching the two rickety sheds beneath.

From their vantage point, he saw other buildings behind the main processing plant beyond the edge of the mountain. He supposed they had once been administration offices or bunkhouses for the men who laboured here. It looked like a Wild West town in an old movie, somewhere that had started as a camp for brave prospectors before some rich railroad man bought up the land and turned it into a frontier town with its own laws separate from civilization and God. Now it was a ghost town. But it was their only sanctuary from the storm and from the man who preyed upon them.

They chose the room with the fewest holes to allow in icy gusts, but with a window looking out over the patch of ground where they had been standing twenty minutes before. It was empty but for some broken pieces of rusting machinery whose purpose he could not begin to imagine. Kids had been up here over the years, their impotent rebellion immortalised in spray-painted tags on support timbers and wall planks. Nonsensical words in blocky blue script and yellow bubble-style lettering, or unreadable names formed of arrows, curves and spikes. The stylised signatures of young people who had most likely long since settled down to jobs and families and social conformity.

They wrapped Hánas in a foil survival blanket from the pulk and propped him upright against the timber wall nearest the mountain behind the mine, where it was warmest, and Erik told Sofia to make sure their companion didn't go to sleep.

'But he needs to rest,' she said, looking at Hánas sitting there, his lips warped with the pain he was trying to exorcize from his body with mumbled prayers or curses or whatever it was he was saying to himself in his own language.

'I know, but if he goes to sleep, he won't wake up again,' Erik told her.

She gave a solemn nod, a gesture of understanding that he felt, with a jag of pain, should have been beyond the repertoire of a thirteen-year-old girl.

They shared out some of the dried reindeer meat Hánas had brought with him, but the herder refused his share.

'He can't eat,' Erik said in a quiet voice, in answer to the look in Sofia's eyes as she glanced over at the man.

She nodded and then the two of them fell to their own food, ripping the leathery slivers with their teeth like starving people. They withdrew to the silent world of their own heads as the wind outside moaned and rattled some of the old timbers around them and hissed through the holes in the walls.

'Good?' he muttered after a while, the meat fibres separating, his mouth flooding with salty saliva.

She nodded.

He sat on a stool at the window, the glass of which he had rubbed with snow and wiped with an abandoned rag until he could see out. He was shivering. Did that mean his body was still fighting? That even now it possessed some hidden energy or will to try to warm itself? Because he was so tired. He couldn't have gone on, and he wondered if he should tell Sofia, so she didn't think that it was her weakness, her

exhaustion that had made them hole up here like some creature run to ground to await the inevitable. But he held his
tongue, because he didn't want her to know he was done.
He couldn't allow her to know that his legs had nothing left
to give. That his lungs were blown. That his bones and flesh
were riddled with the cold like the inexorable conquest of
some wicked cancer. And that his mind and his body had
long since started to go their separate ways.

*You said you would do anything.*

He startled and looked around. The god was standing in
the shadows between a rusting industrial engine and a coiled
pile of iron cable. He was wrapped in a black cloak and
wore a floppy, wide-brimmed hat as black as a raven's wing,
so that it was hard to make out where he ended and the
shadows began.

*I would*, Erik said in his mind, resenting the intrusion. He
needed to keep watch, not sit there being interrogated by
some deity whose time was long past. A spectre from men's
dreams who had long since been overthrown and replaced
by newer gods.

*Then go on*, the god said. *What's stopping you?*

Erik held up his hands. *These.* There was no pain in his
hands now. Nothing compared with before anyway. But
they were almost useless. The first three fingers on his right
hand were turning black. *And this.* He gestured with those
traitorous hands at the rest of him. *I'm empty. I've gone as
far as I can.*

The god lifted his bearded chin and Erik saw the eye
patch in the shadow beneath his broad hat. The other eye
was bright, like an ember glowing in the dark. Fixed on him.

*What about the girl? Haven't you always told yourself*

*you could walk to the ends of the earth for her? Haven't you always told yourself that you could carry her for ever?*

He clamped his teeth together. *What do you know of it?*

The god shrugged. *I know what you tell yourself. When you fear that you're growing old. When you fear your own mortality.*

He let that revelation sit a while, gathering layers upon itself like snow. Like the cold which his grandmother always said sits in the walls of a place.

'Pappa . . . Pappa!' Sofia shook him by the shoulder and he focused his eyes on her. She stood there in the blanket he had put around her, her hat with its igloos, snowflakes and polar bears crusted with bobbles of ice, her breath fogging the air between them.

'What is it?' he said.

She was silent a moment but the look on her face betrayed concern. Had he been talking aloud?

'I think we should give him more of your whisky for the pain. I've been talking to him but he keeps going quiet. Like he's . . .' She swallowed. 'I think he's giving up.'

Erik fumbled at his pocket and managed to scoop the hip flask half out so she could grab it.

'Don't let him drink it all,' he said. 'Just a mouthful.'

She nodded.

'Do you want some?' he asked.

She frowned.

'It'll warm you up from the inside,' he said. 'Or at least it'll feel like it's warming you.'

Now she *really* looked worried about him, as though he'd actually lost it.

He smiled in spite of everything, thinking how fucked up

it all was. That somewhere out there was a man trying to kill them, that his little girl had witnessed murder, seen her own father kill men, had skied her heart out and endured hardships she would never have imagined, yet here she was, shocked because he'd given her permission to take a sip of bourbon from his flask.

'What will Mamma say?' she asked, a sad, far-off look in her eyes, as though deep down she knew they would never find out. She lifted the flask and unscrewed the top and sniffed the contents. By the twist of her face anyone would have thought she'd got a nose full of sewer fumes or worse.

'It's too good for girls anyway,' he said, at which she narrowed her eyes, lifted the flask to her mouth and let some of the liquid find its way through her pursed lips. It took a second, then she pulled her head back, wrinkled her nose and drew up her top lip.

'Yuk!' she said, shuddering while he laughed, the sound seeming to come from another time and place.

He shrugged. 'I told you.'

She grimaced and offered him the flask. 'How can you drink that?'

He lifted a hand. 'Save it for him.' They looked across the hut to where Hánas sat, his head slumped forward, eyes closed.

Sofia screwed the top back on. 'He's dying, isn't he?' she said in a quiet voice. Her eyes on him were as piercing as the god's eye had been. If he lied now, she would trust nothing else he said.

'Yes, I think he's dying,' he said.

She nodded.

'Get some sleep if you can,' he told her.

She looked out of the window. 'I can watch for a while.' The snow was coming down thick. Big flakes like duck down spilling from a pillow. It made it hard to see far beyond the old window pane. In reality, the tall man could have been standing down there, looking up at them now, and they probably wouldn't see him. Although he probably wouldn't see them either.

'I'm fine,' he said. 'Get some rest.'

'I thought you wanted me to keep Hánas awake.'

'I'm awake,' Hánas said, surprising them both. They looked at him. He lifted his head and grimaced, and even in the dark Erik could see there was blood on his teeth.

'Your father and I will talk to pass the time,' he told Sofia. 'I'll make sure he doesn't fall asleep on watch.'

She turned back to Erik, needing his consent. He nodded. 'You lie down.'

'Pappa . . .'

'Yes?'

'The man out there.' She was looking out the window again. 'He's not going to give up, is he?'

A gust of wind rattled the glass.

'No, he's not,' he said. 'But neither are we.'

She thought about this. Then she leant forward and kissed him on the cheek, her dry lips rough on his skin. And he loved her so much it threatened to overwhelm him.

'Rest,' he said.

She walked away, shivering and hugging the blanket around her, and found a place to lie down beneath another window, where the weak light from the veiled moon fell upon her like a cold caress. Like she had been chosen for something.

And Erik turned his face to look back out into the night, his breath fogging on the glass.

He awoke, or became aware, like someone emerging from a coma. Like a person buried alive digging their way up through wet earth or deep snow. Consciousness returning in instalments. A sense of having been somewhere far beyond the experience of the physical body, while having no recollection of where that plane was or what had occurred there. He felt impossibly heavy, as though his limbs were iron and his blood was molten lead and everything was pain. But even the pain retreated before a cold rising panic. *How could I have fallen asleep? How could I put her in that danger?* He looked at her. She lay still and silent, and he remembered all those nights when she and Emilie were little and he would sneak into their bedrooms and stand for a while, listening, letting his eyes adjust to the dark until he could be sure they were still breathing, because often they made no sound.

He did the same thing now, watching her until he was confident that he had seen her blanket move up and down, four, five times. Then he looked over at Hánas, who was awake. The herder acknowledged him with an almost imperceptible nod of his head, and there was something about his gesture that made Erik think that maybe he'd not properly fallen asleep as he feared. As though Hánas was saying, *you went for a minute there, buddy, but good to have you back.*

They had been talking before, about whatever he could come up with to keep Hánas conscious and thinking. They'd talked about the football, and he'd been surprised to learn that Hánas knew more than he did about Tromsø Idrettslag's current squad, though the herder admitted he was a long-time fan of Liverpool F.C. Then he'd asked Hánas how many reindeer he had, despite remembering Sofia's warning about what Lars Helgeland had told her – that you mustn't ask a reindeer herder unless you wanted to insult him. Hánas had coughed until blood came up, then curled his lip.

'How much money do you have in your bank account?' he had asked Erik, which proved Lars's point. But the strategy seemed to be working. If the man was talking, he was alive. Then, inevitably, like skis in a trail laid out by a snow groomer, the conversation had come round to recent events. They talked about the research lab and what it might have to do with Novotroitsk Nickel. This ruin which was now their sanctum away from the malevolence of the storm and the man. The connection was there, they both knew it, but neither of them could come up with an explanation, or a reason why Dr Kotilla had lied about what he and his colleagues were doing up there, and why they were keeping mummified corpses in the lab. Nor, come to that, what the hell had happened to Ivvár, who had been employed by Novotroitsk Nickel as a guide.

Even Hánas, grievously wounded, bleeding internally and most probably dying, looked healthier now than Ivvár had done, tied to the bed, eyes bulging in his sweat-drenched, skull-like face.

'Ivvár was a troubled man,' Hánas had said. Every word took great effort, but he made the effort. Knew the game. 'He and his brother had their own herd once, but they fell out. Over money. I don't know the details, but Ivvár drinks too much. That's no secret. He started making money taking tourists out. Skiing. Snowmobiles. Salmon fishing in late summer. Whatever. But then I heard he got a job for the mining company. Collecting the directors, board members, engineers, whoever, at the airport. Bringing them up here. Maybe helping them scout new places to dig.' Hánas had shaken his head then. 'You can imagine how this went down in our community.'

'I can imagine what your sister thought about it,' Erik said, remembering the steel in Karine Helgeland's voice when she had defied the tall man and refused the company's bribe. Her courage had got her and her husband killed. Her brother too, most likely. Might yet get them all killed.

Hánas winced in pain and shifted his position. 'She said Ivvár had betrayed us all. But I think she pitied him more than hated him.'

Soon after that, Hánas had fallen silent and Erik had drifted away. But the fear that he had fallen asleep sharpened his mind now and he looked out into the night, shielding his mouth with his hand so that his breath didn't fog the glass.

'Maybe you hit him,' he said, looking back at Hánas.

'I don't think so,' Hánas said. 'The range was too far for me.' He brought the hip flask out from under the foil blanket and raised it to his lips with a trembling hand which Erik saw was slick with blood. 'Not too far for him, though,' he added, with something close to respect.

'We should change the dressing,' Erik said.

'You have more pads?' Hánas asked.

'No.' He had taped the whole wad of them onto the wound, but the blood must have soaked all the way through by now. 'I can use something else. I think we still have some clean clothes in the pulk.'

Hánas arched his brows. 'Are you on lookout or not? We'll do it when she wakes.'

Erik nodded and they both looked at the girl. Her face was mostly hidden inside her hood, except for part of her cheek and her mouth. Those lips which had never yet kissed a boy.

*Sleep*, he willed her. *Every minute you can. Dream of home. Of your mother. Your sister. Dream of happy times when we were all together, unafraid and unbroken.*

# 15

HE WAS OUT behind the long hut, relieving himself against the black mountain face, when he heard it. It took his sluggish brain a while to recognize it, but then the realization came upon him like a rockfall. Snowmobiles. Several of them, whining out there in the snowstorm, the pitch of each engine rising and falling with its rider's use of the throttle. He ran around the side of the building to the front and stood on the deck, looking out, his head turned so that he could focus his concentration into his left ear.

Maybe it was a search party out looking for him and Sofia because Elise had somehow known something was wrong and raised the alarm. Or maybe someone had found the Helgelands and, knowing there was a murderer on the loose, the police were visiting all the homes and cabins in the mountains to make sure everyone was accounted for. Elise would tell them that he and Sofia were out on a trip and the police had come looking. Maybe they had found the bodies of the men Erik had killed and there was now a major manhunt operation going on. It was possible, wasn't it?

He saw the lights before he had pinpointed the sound of the engines. Seven sleds coming from the south-east. Still a way off, the beams from their lights strobing in the falling snow as they negotiated the gullies and mounds between the mountains. He unslung the rifle and lifted the scope to his eye but it was impossible to focus on any of the machines well enough to see if they were police or mountain rescue, and the fog of his own breath wreathed his head, misting the glass of the telescopic sights.

He went back inside and told Hánas, then woke Sofia gently, so as not to scare her.

'What is it, what's happening?' she asked, sitting upright, her features screwed up like some snug creature pulled out from hibernation too soon.

'People are coming,' he told her.

'Who?'

'I don't know.'

He helped her up, she cringing with her own aches and bodily anguish, and together they shambled to the door.

'Don't let them see you,' Hánas said, without lifting his head.

'But it can't be him,' Sofia said, glancing at her father for confirmation.

'He's right,' Erik said. 'We stay out of sight until we know who they are.'

The snow on the exposed part of the deck was two foot deep and they trudged through it and descended the external iron staircase that provided access to all three of the long buildings nestled against the mountain, keeping within their earlier footprints wherever they could. They didn't descend all the way, instead entering the first building and feeling their way in the dark past old machinery and relics of a bygone age to the windows on the right, which were washed white by the light of the snowmobile lamps. Erik waited until the windows fell dark again, then looked out through an empty frame, Sofia alongside him, peering through a square of clouded glass.

'Who is it?' she whispered.

The cold air bit at his face. 'I can't tell,' he said.

The sleds had driven across the front of the old mine buildings and pulled up on the side by the other shacks and the three office buildings roofed with corrugated iron. Only now did he see the tent there too. One of those large fabric basecamp tents used on expeditions or by polar researchers. He couldn't miss it now, because they had set up the snowmobiles in an arc and left their lamps on when they killed the engines, so that the area that evidently concerned them, which included the shacks and the big tent, was flooded with light.

'It's not the police,' Sofia said.

'No, not the police,' he agreed, the words following in the wake of his hope, which had already dissipated on the air like his breath.

'Or the mountain rescue,' she added.

'No,' he said, lifting the rifle, carefully pointing the barrel out of the empty window frame so that he could look through the scope. 'They're something to do with the mine, or the lab, or both.'

'So we can't let them know we're here.'

He didn't answer, because he was watching them through

the sights. Some of them must have doubled up on the sleds because there were twelve of them, men and women. They were in a hurry, some going into the huts, others into the tent, and all moving with an urgency and an efficiency born of something more than just the desire to get a job done and get back into the warm. He moved the rifle across, focusing the scope on a man wearing a thick black down-filled parka who was barking commands, his words lost in the roar of the wind. He had a rifle slung over his right shoulder.

'There are more coming,' Sofia said.

He could hear the engines but kept the scope on the huts or the tent, turning only his head to see three more snow-mobiles arrive, these ones with trailers hitched to them.

'What's happening, Pappa?' Sofia asked.

'Wait,' he said again. Then, 'Looks like they're packing up.'

'Packing what up?'

He moved the scope onto a woman emerging from one of the huts. She was carrying something.

'Computer monitors. Files,' he said, then moved the rifle barrel a few centimetres to the right. 'Hazmat suits.'

'Like the ones in the lab?'

'Yes.' There was a man lugging a jackhammer, struggling with it through the deep snow, and another with arms full of pickaxes. Two were carrying a generator between them, while two others were bringing fuel cans out of the left-hand hut. All of it was being loaded onto the trailers behind the newly arrived snowmobiles.

'What were they doing here?' Erik asked himself under his breath.

'Are they packing up because of us?' Sofia asked.

He turned his face and looked at her. 'Why would it have

anything to do with us?' He knew why, but he wanted to hear her say it, wanted to hear the way she had pieced it together on her own.

Sofia frowned, knowing he was testing her. 'Because this old mine has something to do with the hidden lab and the bodies, and that man Ivvár. And we escaped from the lab, so now they're worried that we'll tell the police, and whatever they're doing won't be a secret any more.'

Erik put his eye back to the scope. 'I think you're right,' he said, placing the crosshairs on the bossman, who was now standing at the entrance to the big tent, holding open the door flap, so that light from the parked sleds flooded its interior. A man and a woman were standing either side of a hole in the ground, a square-cut trench into which they were laying a tarpaulin with the careful efficiency of people who mean to find whatever they're concealing in the same condition when they return.

'Pappa.'

'Yes?'

Sofia said nothing and so he tore his eye from the rifle sights to look at her.

Even with her hat on and in the near-dark he could see the vertical crease between her eyebrows which was all Elise. 'Maybe they're not bad people. Maybe they would help us. Help Hánas.' She stood with her arms wrapped around herself, small and vulnerable. Shivering like someone for whom that physiological reflex has become the natural state. 'If they knew he was dying, they would help him. They could take him down the mountain on a snowmobile.' She shrugged. 'Maybe they're not like the other ones.'

'But what if they are?' he asked her. 'Whatever they're

trying to hide, it must be very important to make them come up here in this storm.'

She considered this. 'But shouldn't Hánas get to choose if he wants to take the chance?' she asked, and he was taken aback by her wisdom and by the kindness of her heart. She was right too. Hánas was the one who was dying and, faced with that, wouldn't he rather take the risk? Even a ten per cent chance that these people would help him was better than the odds of him surviving the night otherwise.

'OK. We'll let Hánas choose,' he said. 'If he decides to go to them, you and I stay hidden. We watch, see what happens. But we don't show ourselves. Agreed?'

She nodded. 'Agreed.'

'Come on.' They edged back from the window and made their way to the rear of the building and out onto the stairway, staying low as they ascended, every step requiring an effort of mind and body because his legs were spent, hollow and yet heavy, and it felt as though gravity itself was pushing him down with a force three times stronger than he remembered.

They found Hánas trying to stand, white-faced in the gloom and grimacing.

'I was beginning to think you had left me here,' he told them, winking at Sofia as Erik helped him to his feet.

'Keep watch,' Erik told Sofia. She went over to the side window and looked through the glass while he told Hánas what was going on outside and laid out the options as he saw them.

'We can't trust them,' Hánas said.

'No. But you need to be in a hospital,' Erik countered.

Hánas shook his head. 'They know about us, that there are three of us.' He brushed Erik's steadying hand away and stood by himself. 'Once they see me, they'll come looking for you.'

Erik knew that was true. Which was why he was glad that Sofia was over by the window. He said in a low voice, 'I can't risk that happening. I can't put her in that danger.'

Hánas answered him with a resolute look of agreement.

Then another idea came to Erik. 'What if I could steal a motor sled? They've left the lights on, so the keys are probably in the ignition. If I can get close enough without being seen. Even if I have to put a gun to someone's head.'

Hánas grunted. He was hunched forward, hands pressed to his wound, but he looked up at Erik from beneath arched brows.

'And that's not risky?' he asked. 'The others would jump on their sleds and catch you when you stopped to pick us up. And anyway, could you drive with those hands? I doubt you could even turn the key.'

Erik exhaled in frustration. 'Shit.'

Sofia hissed at them from across the shed and he looked over to see her waving her arm in the universal *come quick* gesture. He joined her at the window.

'There,' she whispered, pressing her mittened hand against the grimy pane.

'I see him,' he said. A man had wandered away from the main group and beyond the wash of illumination from the snowmobile headlights.

'I think he was having a pee,' she said.

'Don't eat the yellow snow,' he murmured.

She was still looking out the window. 'What's he doing now?' she asked.

Something like pain announced itself in Erik's stomach. 'Move!' he said. 'Grab the gear.' Because he knew the man had seen their tracks, or what remained of them. His head lifted and he was peering towards the mountainside and the mine buildings. 'We've got to get to the skis before he finds them.'

They put on their packs and he put Hánas's arm over his shoulder. 'Ready?' he asked him. Hánas looked anything but ready, but he nodded and they went out into the storm, their boots crumping in the snow on the metal stairway, Hánas's laboured breath smelling of Erik's favourite whisky.

Eleven steps took them down to the middle level, where they stopped and listened for a moment, peering into the dark for any sign that they had been seen. Nothing but the wind. Then a distant voice, wind-whipped to their ears from the huts where the clean-up operation was well underway.

'Go,' he told Sofia, and he and Hánas followed her down the next set of stairs and slipped into the bottom shed, where he eased the rotting door shut behind him, relieved that it didn't creak as he had expected, while Sofia hurried over to the window. Then she turned away from it and sank down to her haunches, her eyes round and bulging in her gaunt face.

'He's coming!'

For several heartbeats Erik had no idea what to do and stood there frozen, Hánas all but hanging off him. He looked into the shadows where they had stashed their skis and the pulk beneath a thin sheet of rusted metal. There was no time. He eased Hánas to the ground against the wall, then took the rifle off his shoulder. 'Stay down,' he hissed at Sofia, then opened the door and stepped out, keeping his body pressed against the timber planks of the hut. He took a deep breath and then peered around the corner of the building.

The man was less than three metres away. Cocooned in a thick black North Face puffa jacket, black hat pulled down and a fleece neck warmer hitched up to just below his eyes – *none of which does much for his peripheral vision*, Erik thought.

The man was looking at the footprints on the stairs. Looking up at the top of those stairs and at the long building running across the mountainside, and probably wondering if whoever had made those tracks was up there now. If he looked more closely, he might be able to tell that the fresher prints were coming back down again and leading into the lower shed. Either way, he had only walked off to relieve himself and was probably not motivated enough to go exploring up there alone. No. He'd go and tell the others. He'd tell the man with the rifle, and they would come. They would find them.

Erik could not let that happen.

His heart was thumping in the empty cavern of his chest, the rhythm of his blood gushing deep in his ears, the sound seeming to grow louder as he girded himself for action.

*Am I really going to do this?*

Gripping the rifle diagonally across his body, right hand on the girth behind the trigger guard, left on the forestock, he edged out, barely breathing, committing himself for better or worse. Either the man heard something, or the primeval feeling of being watched had come upon him, because he started to turn.

Erik took three plunging strides through the snow and threw his arms and the rifle over the man's head, and the man yelped but Erik hauled the weapon back with all his strength, pulling the man against his own body.

'I'll kill you,' Erik growled into the snow-laced wool of his hat. 'I'll fucking kill you. Don't do anything, don't try anything.' He was dragging the man backwards now, like some animal pulling its prey back to its den. 'I'll shoot you in the face, you bastard,' he snarled, panting with the effort, his arms straining to maintain the pressure, to give the man no sense that he was anything other than helpless, completely at the mercy of his captor.

When his back struck the door, Erik turned his head and snarled for Sofia to open it. He pulled the man back into the shed and threw him onto the floor as Sofia shut the door behind them.

'Don't open your mouth, you bastard, or I'll kill you,' he growled. The man, lying face down, eyes down, held up his hand in a gesture of compliance and deference. Erik raised the rifle to his shoulder, gasping for breath, and was surprised to see Hánas back on his feet, the Mosin-Nagant trained on their captive, his face a grey, sweat-glistened mask, his eyes dark points of pain.

'Nod if you understand,' Erik said, gesturing with his chin to Sofia to resume her vigilance at the window.

The prisoner nodded.

'Good,' Erik said. They didn't have long. Eventually someone would realize he was missing and come looking for him. 'What's going on here?' he asked.

The man didn't answer, so Erik stepped forward and dug the muzzle of the rifle into the thick jacket at his shoulder.

251

'You can talk now. Turn over. Keep your hands behind your head.'

The man did as he was told, rolling over on his back and shuffling up against the wall and pressing himself against it, as if he would have retreated further if he could. As though by wishing it with all his mental power he could make every molecule in his body solvent and pass through the timbers in some feat of human osmosis. And there he half sat, half slouched, cowering in the shadows, his fingers laced behind his head.

Erik went back over to him, this time using the barrel of the Remington to drag the man's neck warmer down off his mouth. Then he stepped back and lifted the rifle, and the man cringed before it, whimpering like a kicked dog. Erik asked again, 'What are you people doing here?'

He could see the prisoner's face for the first time. He was young, late twenties, early thirties, and clearly scared out of his mind. But Erik could feel no pity for him. He was beyond empathy now. Only his daughter mattered. 'We don't have time for games. You tell me what I want to know and you live. You bullshit me and you die.' Some part of him was aware of how easily those words came to him now and of how crazy that was.

The young man nodded, shifted, pushed himself more upright. 'We're scientists,' he said, his eyes flicking to Hánas and then coming back to Erik. 'Well, I'm on my way to being one. I start my fellowship next year.' He grimaced, glanced down at himself, and Erik smelled it then. He had soiled himself. Erik supposed he couldn't blame him – who wouldn't, when some wild-looking, rifle-wielding stranger jumps them out in the dark?

'What kind of scientists?' Erik asked.

'Immunologists. Pathologists. Molecular biologists. Researchers in environmental virology. Two medical archaeologists. There's a professor of genomics and bioinformatics.' The qualification meant nothing to Erik, but it didn't matter.

'What are you doing here? You're part of what's going on up in that lab in the ice, right?'

'You were there,' the man said. Not a question. A statement.

'Not for long,' Erik said.

'What happened to Ivvár?' Hánas asked the man.

Erik gave Hánas a look saying that this wasn't the most pertinent question at this point, but Hánas ignored him, drawing the bolt on the old Russian rifle to confirm that he wanted his question answered.

'Well?' he asked the man.

The man looked from Erik to Hánas. 'He's infected,' he said.

'Infected with what?' Hánas asked.

The prisoner screwed up his face as the battle waged between the him who wanted to spill it all and the other him who thought that would be a very, very bad idea.

'Look, if you let me go, I swear I'll say nothing. You can stay in here or, if you don't trust me, you can leave. But either way, I swear I won't tell anyone that I've seen you.'

Erik tipped his chin towards Hánas. 'See my friend here? Does he look like he's ready to ski off into this blizzard?'

Hánas turned his face and spat out a wad of blood.

'Who's chasing us? A tall man. Mean-looking bastard.' Erik put a hand to his own lips. 'Scar here,' he added.

The man shook his head. 'Someone you don't want as an enemy,' he said. He swallowed. 'Please!' he begged. 'I have a little boy. You don't have to do this.'

Erik jerked the rifle. 'If you don't start telling us what we want to know, I'm going to shove this deep into that nice thick coat and I'm going to pull the trigger. Your friends won't even hear it over this wind.'

Maybe true. Probably not.

He felt Sofia's eyes on him but he didn't look at her.

The prisoner nodded. 'OK, OK.' He looked like he was about to throw up. 'In 2016, in a remote part of Siberia, a twelve-year-old boy died and many others were hospitalised because they were infected with anthrax. The anthrax bacteria came from a reindeer that had died over seventy years previously.'

Hánas nodded. 'The reindeer had thawed out of the permafrost,' he said. 'We all heard about it.'

'Right,' the young man said. 'We already know that glacier ice is cryogenically preserving bacteria and viruses that could be . . . hundreds of thousands of years old.' He nodded down at the floorboards. 'Here, we're on top of permafrost.'

'Frozen soil?' Erik put in.

'Essentially, yes,' the man said. 'Almost a quarter of the Northern Hemisphere is underlain by permafrost and, thanks to global warming, it's melting to a deeper and deeper layer. It's only a matter of time before thousands of graves will be uncovered. The victims of smallpox, diphtheria, bubonic plague. And the pathogens that killed them will come back into the light. Diseases we thought we'd seen the back of . . .? Well, maybe not.'

Hánas jerked the Mosin-Nagant. 'What does any of this have to do with Ivvár? What happened to him?'

The young man dipped his head submissively. 'There are burials here,' he said, tilting his head towards the window where Sofia stood. She looked at him, but Erik jerked his head to the window and she turned back to it. 'You've heard of the 1918 flu?' their prisoner said.

Erik nodded. 'The Spanish Flu.'

'An H1N1 virus originally passed on to humans from birds. Killed more than fifty million worldwide, maybe as many as one hundred million. Nearly a third of the world's population became infected.'

'Talk faster,' Erik said.

The man swallowed. 'In 1918 some local Sami caught the virus and died. Normally, the Sami would leave their dead in scree graves near sacred sites.' He looked to Hánas then, perhaps for his blessing to talk about the man's people, but the reindeer herder just watched him through narrow eyes, as though by half closing them he was keeping his pain from spilling out and drowning him. 'But the families of these dead Sami men and women were afraid of the disease.'

'Understandably,' Hánas said.

The prisoner looked back at Erik. 'They thought they should bury the bodies deep. But that's not easy when the ground is frozen hard. So they brought them here, to the mine, and paid some men to do it. Or at least to dig the graves.' He looked back at Hánas. 'Ivvár knew about this. Turns out his great-great-grandfather was one of the men who paid for the burial. One of the miners left diaries which recorded details: what the Sami brought as gifts, the payment itself and what they spent it on.'

'Get to the point,' Erik said.

'They needed Ivvár to help locate the graves. To identify the bodies as Sami—'

'Who needed him?' Hánas asked.

'Novotroitsk Nickel,' Erik answered, before the young man could.

'I don't know the details,' the man said, 'but the mine is a front. It's not about copper. I don't even think they'll reopen it.'

'So who's your employer?' Erik asked.

The prisoner shrugged. 'A biotech company,' he said, as if it should be obvious.

'Russian?'

'I don't know. I think so.'

Erik looked at Hánas, who looked at him. His expression said: *what the hell is going on here?* Erik turned back to the scientist. 'And the bastard hunting us?'

'His name's Maksim. He's Spetsnaz,' the man said. 'Or was.'

'Special forces?' Erik said.

'More like special purposes,' the man replied. 'Airborne Forces. VDV. Their insignia is some crazy-looking lone wolf.'

Erik thought back to that first day in town and the tattoo on the back of the tall man's hand.

'I don't know the man, but I heard he was kicked out of the military,' the young scientist went on. 'There was some hostage situation in Beslan. The wrong people died and Maksim took the fall.' He shook his head vigorously. 'From what I've seen, he's a professional, but they say his brother's a maniac.'

*Not any more, he's not*, Erik thought.

His hands still meshed behind his head, the prisoner pushed his elbows out wide. 'That's all I know. I'm telling you, that's all I know.'

'Pappa, something's happening.' Sofia huffed on the glass and rubbed it with her mitten. 'I think the others are looking for him.'

Erik nodded. 'Keep watching,' he told her, then he drew the Remington's bolt for effect. 'What does your employer want with bodies that were put in the ground over a hundred years ago?' He saw in his mind those corpses laid out in the lab, their features preserved by the permafrost all these years, so they still looked like people he might have known in this time, in his own life.

'We're not the first who've tried to recover a sample of living virus from the lung tissue of Spanish Flu victims,' the young man said. 'They tried it up in Longyearbyen, but the virus wasn't viable. In Alaska, they recovered the body of an Inuit woman and enough of the viral RNA to sequence the 1918 strain in its entirety.'

Erik thought about this. 'So if it's been done already, what are you doing here?'

The man looked uncomfortable, seemed to squirm inside his Michelin Man coat. 'If . . . if we can examine the virus, we can prepare for, possibly even prevent, future pandemics.'

'But you just said it's been done. The sequencing.'

The man shook his head. 'It's complicated.'

'Humour me.'

'They couldn't make the virus live again. Not that it's alive as you might understand it, but you get my meaning. They could study it but they couldn't make it grow.'

GILES KRISTIAN

'Why would anyone risk bringing back a virus that killed millions?' Erik asked.

For the first time, the young man unclasped his hands from behind his head and spread his fingers. 'I'm a nobody,' he said. 'I told you, I'm just helping out. They don't tell me anything. I couldn't even ask. They made me sign all sorts of shit. NDAs.'

'You don't know why you're digging up the dead?' Hánas asked him. 'Why you're trying to bring to life one of the most lethal viruses the world has ever known?'

'No, I swear it,' the captive said. 'I don't know.'

But Erik did. Suddenly he understood it all. 'So Ivvár is infected?' he asked.

The man nodded.

'By accident?' Hánas asked.

'I . . . I don't know,' the young man said. There were tears in his eyes.

'Pappa!' Sofia said, and this time there was a note in her voice which had been absent before. She looked at him and he saw the purest terror in her face, her mouth moving though no sound came. She stood there rigid, straight as a ski pole, her mittened hands balled at her sides. 'It's him,' she said. 'He's here.'

# 16

'GO,' HÁNAS TOLD him. They looked into each other's eyes and Erik said nothing. Hánas nodded. 'Go, Erik,' he said. 'People need to know what's happening here.'

Erik opened his mouth to speak. Closed it again, tightening his jaw, then turned and went to the pulk and lifted the steel sheet off, placing it to the side as quietly as he could. He grabbed the harness and dragged the pulk over to the door.

'We can't leave him here, Pappa,' Sofia said, looking from him to Hánas.

Their prisoner sat drawn into himself, trying to make himself small, invisible, like he was hoping they might forget he was even there.

'Get your skis,' Erik told her.

'But, Pappa . . .'

'Get your skis,' he said again.

She looked at Hánas.

'It's all right, Sofia,' Hánas said.

'Now!' Erik said.

She fetched her skis and poles and carried them to where Hánas stood, his old Russian rifle still trained on the frightened young scientist.

'Come with us,' she said. 'Please.'

Hánas fastened his eyes on hers and shook his head. 'I can't,' he said.

'You can try,' she said.

'No, I can't.'

'Why not?'

'Because I'm ready.' He managed a smile. 'But you still have far to go.'

She shook her head.

'Sofia, listen to me.' There was fresh blood on his lips. 'Your father needs you. You must help him now. You must go.'

She turned to Erik, tears brimming in her eyes. 'Pappa, please.'

'He's right, Lillemor,' he said. 'We need to go now.'

Hánas hauled himself over to the window and looked out. 'He's coming, and he's not alone,' he said, then turned back to them. 'Go!' He nodded at Erik again, giving his final permission, and Erik nodded back, knowing he would never see Hánas again.

Then he opened the door and stepped out. Sofia followed, but stopped on the threshold and turned back and said, 'I'll never forget you.'

If Hánas spoke again, Erik didn't hear it, and then they were out in the freezing night once more, the icy wind biting into his cheeks, making his eyes water, reminding him that they faced another enemy, just as relentless, just as cruel. As fast as he could, he strapped on the pulk and they clipped into their skis and kicked off down the slope into the blizzard. Sofia was light enough that her skis did not sink deep, but stayed on the surface, which the wind was turning into an icy crust even as new snow fell. He watched her bend forward, almost crouching, her poles tucked beneath her arms.

'Go!' he called after her, ice crystals like little needles stabbing his face. 'I'll be right behind you.' Then he stopped and twisted, looking back up the hill at the old mine as a gunshot rang out, the report amplified by the mountain behind. Shocking in its loudness. Then another shot, even before the echo of the first one had died.

'Kill the bastard,' he said, because he knew those shots had been fired by the Mosin-Nagant. That Hánas was fighting for them. For his sister. For Ivvár.

Erik turned and skied after Sofia.

'We need to cut across over there,' he said when he had caught up with her, lifting his arm towards two sharp black peaks surrounded by night. She didn't reply but made the turn and set their new course. Another rifle shot reverberated amongst the mountains. If nothing else, Hánas was buying them time, so they needed to honour his courage by putting as much ground between themselves and the tall man as humanly possible.

*But you haven't got it in you*, the god said. *Maybe once. Even just a few years ago. But not now.*

They came onto flat ground, skiing south-east, the snow driving across their fronts, numbing the right side of his face.

*This is the way of it. Strength fades. Nothing lasts for ever.*

261

'But she needs me,' he murmured into the wind.

*You cannot fight time.*

'I must.'

Maybe it would have been better had they not taken shelter in the old mine, but had expended their last reserves of strength and will in getting down the mountain, even with Hánas in the pulk. Because the brief respite had taken a terrible toll on him, he realized now with the sharpened awareness of flight. The short reprieve had fooled his body into thinking it was over, that it was time to submit to exhaustion, to rest and to heal. A cruel deceit. Like a palm-fringed oasis appearing to the thirsty wanderer in the desert being no more than a mirage. He needed his body to work again and it was unwilling. His arms and legs no longer felt part of him. They were moving, but driven by muscle memory rather than his own commands. The poles hung from his wrists on their straps and struck the snow without conviction, the rhythm of alternate arm, alternate leg now a parody of its one-time mechanical perfection. He had a sense of himself as if from the outside or from overhead, looking down upon some grotesque creature shambling through the dark in a poor imitation of a man.

*Will you not face up to the truth?* the god said. *There comes a point when you have to acknowledge the way of things. You must fade but she will go on. Look . . . look at her. Would you hold her back?*

He did look. He had fallen behind. Before, he had tasked himself only with keeping pace with Sofia, being aware of her as a presence in front of his skis that he must cling to like a shadow. But now he saw she was twenty metres ahead and skiing well. So maybe the rest and the food had helped her. Maybe her young body, her young mind, had been better able to make use of them.

'Good,' he murmured, giving that small word to the cruel wind. Watching her arms and legs do all the things she had learned. Everything *he* had taught her. *My girl. I am so proud of you.*

There was a time he would have squared himself to the wind and relished the force of it in his face. When he would have accepted the unspoken challenge and pitted himself against it with all the arrogance of his masculine strength. Now he bent forward under his rucksack, like some broken, humpbacked thing, turning his face away as though the storm was an alpha predator and he sought to acknowledge its dominance and avoid confrontation.

The cloud cover was dense, hazed above them with cold moonlight by which he could make out an infinity of mountain shapes and peaks looming all around them in their timeless indifference. It made him feel a fool for ever having bought into the illusion that his life, that their lives mattered. Were of consequence. The truth was shocking and savage, and he felt like apologizing on behalf of the entire human race for its vanity. Its pretensions. But to what or to whom should he apologize? If the mountains were indifferent, and religion was a construct born of human fears and conceits, who would hear him now?

*What about me? I'm still here,* said the god. *I am called Father of Men. Frenzied One. Lord of the Dead. Far Wanderer.*

He didn't know if the voice was in the wind or in his own head. But where before he had resented it as an unwelcome intrusion, now he accepted it.

*Then I'm sorry*, he replied in his mind. *I am nothing. We are nothing.* He looked at Sofia up ahead, her birthday backpack covered in snow, her stride matching the thump of blood in his ears. *But if we are nothing, then let us live. Why not let us live? Damn you, let her live!*

The god didn't answer, but his own muscles and flesh and bone kindled the anger in his belly and it flickered there, hot and hungry. He wasn't done yet. The girl would go on and that was the way it should be. But fuck the god if he thought her father was ready to let her go on without him.

*Come on – move! Ski, you son of a bitch*, he willed himself. Commanded himself, trying to restore authority over his own rebellious limbs and his wayward mind. There was order in rhythm, he knew, and so he fought for the cadence of movement that had previously come without thought, and metre by metre he gained on Sofia until he was skiing in her wake, close enough that he could feel the dissipating warmth of her outward breaths on his cheeks. And behind him, the pulk slid over their tracks, blurring them, and the wind unwrote what remained, and the falling snow turned a fresh page.

'I'm just here,' he called. 'I'm right here, Sofia. We're strong, you and I. We can do this. I promise we can do this.' He said it for himself as much as for her.

'OK, Pappa,' she called back, her voice thin and small, and there were no more words between them for a long time.

They climbed up a narrow valley, side-stepping, stopping every few metres because they had so little strength left.

*That murdering bastard must be feeling it too*, he thought, looking back into the night as he sucked in each cold breath. The tall man had not rested in Hánas's tent or in the lab as they had. Nor had he sheltered in the old mine. Somehow they had managed to stay one step ahead, and Erik hoped that wherever he was, he was suffering as they were. Maybe he was dead. That was a warming thought. Of the three shots Hánas had fired from the window of the mine shack, maybe the tall man had only heard two, because the third bullet had taken his life before the sound reached him. It was possible, wasn't it? But even if he *was* dead, they needed to get to shelter or else the storm would kill them. The cold would stop their hearts, even ones as fierce and full as theirs, and the snow would bury them and there they would lie, like ruins swallowed by shifting Saharan sands. Relics of a father's failure.

After another downhill run they came onto open ground across which the wind howled, driving the snow into them and almost stopping them in their tracks. Sofia wasn't using her poles now because she was holding her arms up in front of her face, shielding herself from the spite of it, so he went in front of her, the wind thumping into his chest, driving him back on his skis if he did use the poles.

He turned his face and the wind roared in his left ear.

'We need to find shelter,' he called.

She didn't reply. He stopped and turned and took her in his arms, wrapping himself around her. She was shivering violently inside her clothes.

'We'll find shelter,' he said. Still she didn't answer. 'You're OK, Lillemor. It's OK.'

Still holding her, he straightened and looked around them,

his eyes trying to make sense of the world through the dizzying blur of the blizzard and the darkness and their own fogging breath.

Then he saw it. A dark mass, low on the horizon to the south-west. Fir trees. 'We can get to those trees and make a shelter,' he said. 'One more rest before the final push. OK?'

She didn't reply, and he was worried. He took her head in his hands and put his face against hers, so that their breath mingled and their noses were almost touching. 'We'll make a shelter,' he said. 'Get warm. We just have to get to those trees over there. You can do it. I know you can.'

Her eyes were full of trust and it hurt him deeply.

'OK,' she said.

'Good girl.' He pressed his forehead against hers. 'Good girl,' he said again. Then he slid backwards on his skis and turned towards the distant woods.

'Soon be there,' he said.

When they came amongst the trees they were both shivering uncontrollably. He fetched their snowshoes from the pulk and Sofia put her own on, then helped him with his because his fingers were useless on the straps and buckles. Then he took the snow shovel and began to dig.

*Hurry*, the god said. *She's freezing.*

He thrust down with the shovel while looking at the girl. He was very worried about her now. She stood there small and silent, surrounded by birch and spruce, her arms down by her sides. A trembling thing in the dark.

'Help me, Sofia,' he said, because he needed her to keep moving.

She just stood there, maybe watching him dig, maybe not.

'Sofia, I need you to help me. You still have the knife? The one Lars gave you?'

She jerked her head, as if hearing him for the first time. Then she nodded.

'I want you to take the knife and cut some pine branches. Can you do that?'

She nodded again.

'Hack them where the branch meets the trunk, OK?'

She took off her pack and found the big knife and went over to the nearest spruce and started hacking.

'Take no more than one or two branches from the same tree and try to do it so no one would notice.'

Down came the Sami knife. Two, three times, and off came another slender bough thick with green needles.

'Good girl,' he whispered. Her body would be generating heat and soon they'd be inside their improvised shelter conserving that most precious resource.

'Be careful of tree wells,' he said.

'I know,' she replied.

On another snowy day, a day of easy ski trails and spring sunshine, and hotdogs and French fries for lunch – a day from a different life – he had told the girls about a boy he had known growing up who had died in a tree well, where leaves and branches had prevented snowfall from building up around the base of a trunk. Maybe the boy had become tired, or acquired a cramp from walking in deep snow, but he went to sit at the base of a tree and fell head first into the well, and the surrounding snow had caved in, suffocating him. Emilie had been horrified imagining the boy struggling upside down, in the freezing cold, slowly running out of air. But Sofia had sat quietly, thinking, and after a while she had said if the same thing ever happened to her, she would create a space in front of her face to breathe, then dig upward, slowly, carefully, to avoid more snow caving in.

Well, it was all caving in on them now. And the weight of it was too much.

Down went the shovel. Not much muscle behind it, nor could he thrust it into the snow more than three or four times before having to stop and catch his breath and summon the energy. He was digging a trench and it wasn't lost on him that it looked like a grave.

When the ditch was about forty centimetres deep and wide enough for them both to lie down flat, they started laying the spruce boughs in it to insulate them from the snow beneath, then he took their skis and poles and laid them across the trench to make a basic frame. After that he fetched his ice axe from the pulk and cut more branches until they had enough to spread across the frame. He covered the whole thing with snow, then half buried and covered the pulk too, so that in the end there was no sign of either. They had not come far into the woods, so their own prints from the snow-shoes would be covered by falling snow soon enough, he told her, as she got down onto her front and crawled into the den.

He stood for a moment, listening, looking at the dark woods around him, aware that for all he had lost in terms of his physical capabilities, his night vision was better than ever. *I'm like an animal now*, he thought, *not a man*. Then he dropped to his knees and onto his belly and crawled in after the girl. Through an act of contortion that should have been beyond him at his age, he managed to drag their backpacks in to block the entrance.

'It's cosy in here,' he said inside the dark space. It was almost silent, the moan of the wind beyond the woods far away, as though it were looking for them out there. 'You OK?'

'Yeah,' she said. Their bodies were close enough that he could feel her shivering through all their respective layers.

'You'll warm up soon, I promise.'

'I know,' she said.

'We'll stay here for just a little while. Get warm again. Maybe get some sleep.'

'You think we're safe here?'

'Yes.'

'Because he won't be able to see it?'

'*I* couldn't see it and I was standing over it,' he said.

They lay still and quiet in the dark, but he thought he should keep her talking, at least until he knew she was warming up.

'You can't beat the smell of a Christmas tree,' he said, because the air was fragrant with spruce.

'We must smell very bad,' she said.

'We must,' he agreed. 'We're OK so long as we don't unzip. Deal?'

'Deal.'

'I should have lined the sides with branches too.'

'We'll do that next time,' she said, and he knew that was her attempt at a joke and loved her for it.

'So what shall we talk about?' he asked her.

'I don't know.'

He thought for a moment. 'What would you eat now if you could have any food in the world?'

'You mean like a last meal? Like someone on death row

269

in America?' she said. 'I saw a programme about that. They can choose whatever they want.'

'No, not like death row,' he said. 'But when we get home. You choose. Whatever you want.'

She was quiet for a time and he thought maybe she didn't want to indulge him. But then she said, 'Grandiosa. A big one to myself. With pepperoni and meatballs and peppers.'

'Pizza?' he said. 'You can have anything in the world and you choose pizza?'

He could feel her frown even if he couldn't see it.

'It's my choice,' she said. 'And anyway, you dreamt about pizza. The night before we set off.'

'That's true,' he admitted. 'OK, that's what we'll have. Three large Grandiosas.'

Silence again. And he knew it was because it was three pizzas, not four. He could feel his words hanging in the dark space between them, unable to escape into the forest.

*You idiot*, he thought.

'Mamma probably thinks we're having the cosiest time in some DNT hut waiting for the blizzard to stop,' she said.

'With you cheating at cards.' He sensed her smile.

'And you reading by the fire with your eyes closed,' she said.

Thirty seconds later she said, 'I miss Mamma.'

He moved his arm until his hand found hers. 'Me too.'

'So . . . why is that drug company trying to bring back that virus if it killed millions of people?' she asked.

He weighed the answer in his mind. He'd always tried to shield her from the horrors in the world. Would turn off the news if it reported a murder or a terrorist bombing, because he didn't think there was any rush for the young to see how grimy the world really was, to know what people will do to each other in the name of their god, or for greed, or in anger, or just for the hell of it. But now? Now Sofia had seen it with her own eyes and the genie could never be put back in the bottle.

'It could be used as a weapon,' he said. 'If they've recovered the virus, they can study it. Maybe adapt it. Make it mutate, or whatever it is viruses do. Make it even more deadly, while at the same time developing a vaccine. You could hold the world to ransom that way.'

'How?' she asked.

'Vaccinate your own population, release the virus, or threaten to, and sell the vaccine.'

'That's evil,' she said. 'Who would do something like that?'

*Plenty of people*, he thought, but did not say.

'What about that man? Ivvár?' she asked.

'Maybe he got infected when they dug up the bodies. Or maybe they tested the virus on him. I don't know.' He moved, trying to get comfortable because a fir branch was sticking into his shoulder blade, and a trickle of snow fell onto his face. 'But we have to get back so we can tell the police what's happening up here. The world needs to know.'

For a while the silence was heavy in their little den, beyond which the white storm raged between the mountains like a caged beast.

'We'll tell them after the pizza,' she said.

He smiled in spite of his aching body and his swimming mind and the cold in his blood.

'Yes, after the pizza,' he said.

\*

He slept for a long time and did not dream. The girl lay still beside him, the two of them like some ancient burial complete with grave goods: all the things they would need in the next life. A sad tale that some future academic would uncover and rewrite for themselves.

In the moments before waking, he was struck by a wave of panic and confusion and fear. It was like before, when he had been buried in the snow. He couldn't breathe. He started to dig, to claw at the cold tomb around him, but his hands could find no purchase, his fingers would not cooperate, would not close around the snow.

Then he opened his eyes and couldn't see, and remembered where he was.

'Shhh, Pappa,' Sofia hissed in the dark beside him. 'He's here!'

He listened. He could feel her fear. His own now too. It filled the snow trench like a poison and neither of them breathed. He heard a voice, the sound muffled by the snow above them. Someone was out there. He could hear their footfalls, the crump of each one. Could feel the faint vibration of them.

*What have I done? I've killed us. I've killed her!*

The tall man had found them and now they would die.

'Don't . . . move,' he whispered.

*Please, God. Please.*

Maybe there was a chance the man wouldn't see their hiding place. The whole thing must have been covered with more snow by now, surely?

*I've killed us and buried us*, he thought, sick in his stomach with the guilt and horror of it. Slowly, so slowly, he moved his left hand to the rifle lying beside him, though he didn't think his hands were capable of using it.

A scraping sound then. Close. Over their faces.

*Bastard. Why not just shoot us through the snow? Why make her suffer?*

'Pappa, I'm scared,' she whispered. Her mittened hand was squeezing his right thigh. He could feel each of her fingers pressing into his flesh. Her breathing came in short jagged gasps.

'It's OK, Lillemor,' he whispered. 'It's OK, Pappa's here.'

He got his right-hand mitten off and gripped the rifle in both hands now, the stock resting on his groin, the steel barrel cold against his cheek.

Snow was tumbling in on them, finding its way through the spruce boughs. He blinked some from his eyes.

'Here! This is the place,' a muffled voice said from above, then hands were pulling the spruce branches away and he saw the face of a man looking down.

'Holy shit!' the policeman said. 'Lene, over here! Here! Holy shit!' The man was on his knees, ploughing the snow and foliage away with his forearms. 'It's OK, we've got you,' he said.

'Wait, stop, we're coming out,' Erik said, and the man moved back. 'Come on, Sofia, it's all right. They've found us.' Then he rolled over onto his stomach and looked at her face in the shadow. She hadn't moved, but lay there looking back at him with round eyes. She seemed to be holding her breath. 'It's all right. They're the police.' He smiled at her. 'Come on, we're going home.' He pressed his hand against her arm, then he crawled backwards, every movement like slow motion, putting on his mitten and kicking their backpacks out to unblock the entrance.

He emerged and slung the rifle onto his shoulder, but

stayed on his knees to help Sofia out. Then the two of them climbed to their feet, looking at each other and then turning to the two police officers, whose eyes seemed to grin at them through the blizzard.

The man pulled down the front of a fleece ski mask to uncover his mouth. 'Erik Amdahl?' he said.

'Yes,' Erik replied, then nodded at Sofia, who was holding his hand in hers. 'And my daughter, Sofia.' He heard his voice crack as he said the words, because the emotion of the moment was almost too much. It rose in him, a wellspring of relief that he had felt only twice before in his life, when first Emilie and then Sofia had been born, and Elise had come though the ordeal of childbirth.

The female officer came forward on her snowshoes and swung her backpack onto the snow and fetched from it an emergency blanket. 'Here, Sofia,' she said, wrapping the foil sheet around Sofia's shoulders. 'You poor thing, you're freezing.'

'Thank you,' Sofia said, allowing the woman to try and rub some warmth into her shoulders.

'I'm Officer Johansen and this is Officer Haugen,' the male officer told Erik. 'Mr Amdahl, we've been looking for you for the last two days.'

'Did my wife call you? Is she OK?'

The officer put a hand on his shoulder. 'Your wife is fine. Worried about you both, of course, but she's fine.' He pointed down at the ruin of their shelter. 'Come on, let's get your things and take you somewhere warm.'

'His hands are bad,' Sofia said.

Erik turned his mittened hands up.

'Frostbite?' Johansen asked.

'A little,' Erik said.

The policeman nodded. 'We'll have a doctor look at it. In an hour from now, you'll both be warm and eating some hot food.' He and Officer Haugen gathered up his and Sofia's rucksacks, while the two of them picked up their skies and used the ends of their poles to free the bindings of snow.

'I can take the pulk,' Johansen said.

'I've got it,' Erik said, putting the harness on, he hoped for the last time. 'I need to tell you what's happening,' he told the officer, as he and Sofia clipped into their skis. 'The Helgelands—'

The policeman raised a hand. 'We know about Mr and Mrs Helgeland,' Johansen said. 'Their daughter found them.' He shook his head. 'Poor woman.'

Officer Haugen looked at Sofia. 'You must have been terrified.'

Sofia glanced from Haugen to her father with a *they have no idea* expression on her face as she planted her poles in readiness to kick off. And the scene of that bloody night flashed once again behind Erik's eyes. Karine running out into the snow, her nightdress flying behind her, exposing her white skin. Then her lifeless body, face down in the drifts.

'They were good people,' he told the officers as they moved off, he and Sofia trudging more than skiing through the deep snow, keeping pace with the officers on their snow-shoes. He was so stiff, he wondered if his blood was turning to ice in his veins.

'The investigating team found your phones in the Helge-lands' spare bedroom,' Johansen said. 'They figured you'd climbed out of the window and escaped on skis.' He pointed south through the trees as they walked. 'Our snowmobiles are that way, just up the hill. Don't worry, no more skiing, you'll be riding home in style.'

Erik looked at Sofia and she looked at him. 'That sounds good, hey, Lillemor?' he said.

She nodded, and her expression – he would have bottled it if he could.

'How in the hell did you find us out here in this?' Erik asked them.

Johansen gestured at his partner. 'You have Officer Haugen to thank for that,' he said.

The policewoman smiled, and even her ski mask couldn't hide the pride in her pretty face. 'We use a drone,' she said. 'I'll show it to you, Sofia.' She smiled at her, turning her face away from the icy wind. 'It's very cool. It has a thermal imaging camera.'

'A camera that can see heat?' Sofia said.

'That's right,' Haugen said. 'We saw you and your father as an emission spectrum. A kind of heat map made of different colours.'

'It wasn't the clearest picture,' Johansen said, lifting his voice over the moan of the wind. 'Another three centimetres of snow on that den of yours and the drone wouldn't have seen a thing.'

'I'm surprised it would even fly in this,' Erik said.

Johansen gave his partner a knowing look. 'We're not meant to fly it in these conditions. If we break a one-hundred-and-eighty-thousand-Kroner drone, our boss is not going to be happy.'

Haugen looked at Erik. 'I don't think she'll mind that we took the risk today,' she said, as they came out of the trees and started up a gentle slope.

WHERE BLOOD RUNS COLD

Up ahead, he could make out the yellow hoods of the two police sleds in the weak first light of dawn. He didn't know how many police officers were in the mountains looking for them right now, but he did know that the chances of them being found in the dark and in this blizzard must have been slim to none. It was a miracle. With a little help from cutting-edge tech.

'Our colleagues called your wife from your phone,' Johansen said, shooting Erik a questioning glance. 'They deemed the situation warranted unlocking it without your consent, Mr Amdahl. You understand, I hope?'

He nodded. He hadn't known they had the technology to do that, but the ethical connotations were the last thing he cared about at this point.

'Just a little further, Lillemor,' he said, turning to encourage Sofia because she was finding the slope hard going now and had stopped to catch her breath.

'Your wife told us you were out here on a trip,' Johansen said, calling behind him as he trudged up the slope, 'but she was surprised to learn that you'd been at the Helgelands' house. They found a medical dressing with blood on it. Didn't take them long to figure out the blood was not from Lars or Karine. Until more testing could be done, the best guess was that one of you two had cut yourself out here and so you'd skied to the Helgelands' to get help.'

'You've been busy,' Erik said.

'Ah, not us,' Johansen said, turning to grin at him. 'We've just been out here freezing our arses off looking for you.'

'So they've found him?' Erik said. 'The Russian?'

Johansen frowned, his breath clouding in front of his face. 'The Russian?'

Erik felt something squirm in his stomach. 'The man who killed Lars and Karine,' he said, 'and who's been trying to kill us. He's been hunting us from the moment we jumped out of the Helgelands' window.'

Johansen and Haugen looked at each other, the woman's gloved hand instinctively going to her holstered Heckler & Koch P30.

'He's still out here?' Johansen asked, looking around, eyes searching the pre-dawn gloom.

Erik felt sick. 'We need to get out of here.'

'We'll call it in,' Haugen said. No grin on her face now. 'Come on, Sofia, nearly there. You can ride with me, OK?'

'OK,' Sofia said, glancing at her father, who nodded to reassure her that it would be all right.

They came to the top of the slope and Johansen helped Erik hitch the pulk to the back of his sled, while Officer Haugen took their skis and poles and strapped them to the pulk.

'I'll show you the drone later, Sofia, OK?' Haugen said, placing a hand on the hard black case strapped to the rear of the seat on her sled, while Johansen took out his radio and twisted the knob to bring it hissing to life. He thumbed the talk button.

'All units, this is Vikter Six. Anyone hearing this? Over.' He released the button and nothing came back through the static. He tried again. 'This is Vikter Six. We've found Erik and Sofia Amdahl. Any of you hearing this? Over.' Nothing. 'Ekkoh Seven, this is Vikter Six. Berg? Gundersen? Can you hear me? Over.'

'It's the storm,' Haugen explained to Sofia, 'and the mountains.' As if to prove her point, the wind seemed to change

278

direction, a vicious gust hurling snow sideways at them, so that they all had to turn their faces away.

Erik moved closer to Johansen. 'Do you know about the lab?' he said.

Johansen lifted a *wait a minute* hand to him. 'Any patrols?' he went on. 'This is an urgent call. I repeat, an urgent call, over.' He released the talk button and looked at Erik, the radio hissing. 'What lab?'

The static crackled, then before Erik could say more, the radio bleeped and out of it came a voice that sounded as if it were from someone on the moon.

'Vikter Six, this is Ekkoh Seven. Go ahead, over.'

Johansen looked at the radio in his hand as if he'd never expected anyone to answer, then lifted it to his ear.

His head exploded in a spray of blood, bone and pink gobbets of brain. Then they heard the liquid whip of the bullet and the suppressed report and, for a full three seconds, Johansen stood there, the radio still in his hand, his face gone and in its place a mess of raw flesh. Erik saw a red mist vanish on the wind.

'Get down!' Haugen screamed, pulling Sofia down to the snow beside her.

Erik turned towards the sound of the shot but could see only slanting snow and the softly glowing mantle and the distant mountains, beyond which the sky was grey with dawn.

'Pappa!' Sofia screamed.

'I'll get the sled going, then you jump on!' Officer Haugen yelled. Then she was on her feet, keeping low, her pistol in both hands as she got to the sled and crouched behind it, eyes scanning the gloom.

'Pappa, get down!' Sofia screamed.

Haugen was on the sled now. She pulled the start cord, turned the key, pumped the throttle once, twice, three times, then let the engine purr. 'Come on!' she called over her shoulder. 'Get—'

She slumped forward onto the handlebars, her head against the windshield as the buzz of the round that had killed her rang in Erik's ears. She was gone, just like that. A life extinguished in half a second.

# 17

HE STOOD IN the sunless dawn. A metre away, the body that had been Officer Johansen lay in the bloodstained snow. Five metres away, Johansen's erstwhile partner, Officer Haugen, sat slumped against the windshield of her snowmobile, just as dead.

He was aware of time passing, like sand spilling from his fist. He was aware too that the sand represented his own life, his own breaths, his own heartbeats, and that the last trickling grains of it would soon be gone and he would be no more.

Even so, he thought about Elise. Pictured her in his mind. Older and alone. Her faded distant eyes haunted by ghosts. He thought of Emilie and wondered if he really had seen her those nights ago. If they had really spoken, or if it had just been his mind, his own conscience trying to heal itself.

Was someone screaming at him?

He looked at the blood on the snow. Blood was in his

mouth too. He could taste the metal of it. How long since the first shot that blew Johansen's head apart? Two minutes? Two seconds?

*He'll kill her*, the god said. *If you don't get your shit together right now, he's going to kill your little girl.*

'Pappa!'

His mind found traction again and he was moving.

'Get on!' he told her, shielding the girl with his body as he bundled her onto the seat of the snowmobile and pushed her head down onto the handlebars. 'Stay down.' Then he plunged through the snow to Haugen's machine and stopped the engine, and a bullet *thunked* into the hood and he dropped to the snow, his back to the sled, but reached up and pulled the keys out of the ignition and hurled them away into the dark.

'Start it up!' he yelled, getting up and running back to Sofia, who turned the key. Nothing happened.

'I don't know what to do!' she screamed.

He climbed up behind her, giving her Johansen's helmet which had been left on the seat, then he leant forward and hammered his fist onto the red kill switch. 'Choke the engine, there.' He pointed at the lever and she pulled it out. 'Turn the key again,' he said. She did.

As she put on the helmet and clipped the safety tether to her jacket, he leant forward on her other side and tried to get hold of the start cord but couldn't grip it.

'I'll do it.' Sofia pulled the mitten off her left hand and grasped the pull handle.

'Wait!' He grabbed her by the wrist, clamping on with his thumb. 'One, two, three, now!'

They pulled together and the machine purred into life. He

looked over his shoulder and thought he saw a figure strid-ing towards them through the squalling snow. Turning back, he put his mouth against her helmet. 'That's the brake—' he pointed to the lever on the left side of the handlebars '—and that's the throttle,' he added, pointing to the other side. 'I'm going to need you to help me, OK?'

She nodded and took hold of the handlebars, bending forward so that he could put his hands over hers.

He flicked on the headlamps. 'Let's go!' Together, they squeezed the throttle until the transmission engaged and the machine growled, throwing snow up like bow waves before the front skis, and then they were moving, really moving, the thousand-cc engine driving the long lug tracks through the drifts.

He heard the hiss of a bullet as it passed the right side of his head.

'Stay down!' he yelled to Sofia, who hunched over even more as he turned to the right, then snaked left again, throwing up great gouts of snow, trying to make them a harder target. Then he pushed the throttle and the engine roared and the sled powered away, bumping over the ter-rain, and he could barely see where they were going because of the wind and the snow in his face. And suddenly a hole appeared in the windshield, but he kept going and veered left and then right, then faked left but went right again.

He glanced at the hole in the right of the windshield and his heart kicked inside him because there was blood around the edge of it and a trickle of blood being dragged by the wind up the polycarbonate.

'You OK?' he yelled.

The helmet in front of him nodded.

The sled screamed. The jaundiced throw from the halogen headlamps was poor, but though it wasn't yet day, it was no longer night, and it was enough. He swerved to the left and aimed the machine at a stand of birch trees that were revealing themselves in the distance.

'You sure?' he shouted.

This time he heard her shout yes.

*Thank God*, he thought. Then he thought, *we must be out of range by now. That bastard.* He headed for the trees. He could see both sides of the birch stand now and decided to head to the right of it, through a patch of scrub between the trees and the mountain. It looked the most direct route down the valley.

He glanced at the hole in the screen. The wind had scoured it almost clean. He looked down at himself. Saw nothing untoward, but then it was hard to see anything with all that snow in his eyes and in the weak dawn light. 'We're going to slow down,' he called. 'Keep it steady.' He eased back on the throttle and the engine tone dropped an octave, though he guessed they were still going north of sixty kilometres per hour. 'Have you got it?'

'I've got it,' she called.

'Just aim for that gap to the right of the trees.'

She nodded.

He took his right hand from hers, leaving her to control the throttle, while he kept the left handlebar steady and moved his other hand around his chest. Nothing. He patted himself down, moving to his right side, trying to line up the hole in the windshield with his own body.

Nothing.

'Good girl,' he told her, slurring the words because his

face was numb, and they flew through the blizzard, and the effect with the snow in the headlamps was like an intergalactic space cruiser hitting light speed.

He replaced his right hand on her right hand and took his left hand from the bar and pressed it against his upper right arm and took it away and looked at it. There was blood on the reindeer-skin mitten. It was already crystallizing, and some had frozen as the wind had tried to whisk it away, and now stuck out like a blood popsicle. He leant forward over the girl, reaching out to replace his hand upon hers as part of his mind screamed in panic and fear. He'd been shot, and the realization of that was at once both profound and surreal. *I've been shot.*

*At least it's not the girl, so that's good*, the god said. And he agreed. And he could feel no pain from the wound.

*So keep going.*

They came to the scrub poking up through the snow and he kept the pressure on the throttle because the vegetation wasn't dense enough to obstruct the sled, though he looked behind now and then to make sure the pulk was still with them. He imagined the distances they were covering in terms of the length of so many soccer pitches, one after another. Every pitch they could put between them and the bastard who had shot him gave them a chance of survival.

'I remember this place,' she called.

He hadn't recognized it himself. Or perhaps he had, but his subconscious had dared not believe it. But she was right, he realized when he looked carefully at the skeletal scrub poking through the snow between the birch wood and the mountain. Beyond it was a narrow strip that fell away on the left, down to a stream valley where folk would fish for salmon come summer. They had passed this place on the first day of the trip. He was sure of it, even in the snow-blurred twilight world of the Arctic dawn.

They followed the foot of the mountain round to the south and Sofia lifted her left hand and pointed towards a spruce wood whose trees were heavy and inert beneath their cocoons of snow. 'That's where you made the snow bench,' she called. 'And we saw that eagle catch the hare.'

He heard her but couldn't reply, because his teeth were clamped together to stop him from yelling in pain. It had come upon him unannounced but with an acute and terrible intensity. It felt like someone had taken a red-hot piece of metal, like a fire iron, and thrust it through his upper arm. Pretty close to what had actually happened, he supposed, only it had been a small lump of lead and copper.

Sofia's body jerked to the left. 'Pappa!' she shouted, her voice muffled by the helmet, and he lifted his right hand from hers and blood flew from his wrist because it had welled in the cuff of his mittens and now the wind whipped it away. It was all over his right leg too, and in the footwell. Sofia's sudden movement had alerted him, but it was his own shock at the sight that distracted him. His own fault that he didn't see the birch stump sticking up out of the snow just beyond the yellow wash of light from the head-lamps, until it was too late.

The sled's left ski hit the log and the machine lifted and then they were flying, the snowmobile completing half of a barrel roll and flinging the two of them clear.

He hit the snow with incredible force, and even in the split-second white chaos of it, he heard the crack.

*

He lay in the snow. In the crater of his own creation. A kind of snow mould for the making of a broken creature. He lifted his head and rolled over, gasping for breath. For one panicked moment he thought he was blind, but it was just the snow that had driven into his eye sockets and into his mouth and plugged up his nostrils. He tried to call to Sofia but his words were unintelligible. His soul screamed at him to get up, to go to her, to make sure she was alive, and so he tried to stand, but he fell before he was halfway up, and the screaming now was all from his own mouth because he had never known pain like this. It wanted to swamp him. It was a blackness pushing in at the sides of his vision, shrinking the world.

*No!* his mind yelled. He tried to force the agony down before it ruled him completely, though he knew it was a battle he would not win, and he sat up and looked for the girl. She was five or six metres away, sitting up in the snow and looking around as if she had just woken and was trying to figure out how she had got there.

'Are you OK?' he called to her.

She looked over at him and nodded, blinking, then turned her head and looked at the motor sled, which was lying on its side a little way off, silent now because the safety tether had done its job and stopped the engine.

'I'm going to need some help, Lillemor,' he said. He had lifted his left trouser leg and was now wishing he hadn't.

Sofia climbed to her feet, still dazed and unsteady, and trudged towards him, taking the helmet off while he took the opportunity to examine his leg before she saw it herself.

'Yeah, this is not good, baby,' he told her. 'Maybe you shouldn't look.'

But she was already looking. Truth was, he didn't want to look at it himself, so he lay back in the snow and gazed up at the sky for a while, as if by ignoring it there was a possibility it might all go away.

'Told you it was bad,' he said, lifting his head.

She was bent over, throwing up. When she had finished, she said, 'Sorry, Pappa,' then picked up some clean snow and licked it to take the bad taste away.

'It's OK,' he said. 'I feel a bit like that too.'

He knew how cold it was. The air was biting his exposed skin, and yet he could feel beads of sweat breaking out on his back between his shoulder blades and on his forehead. As if there was so much pain inside him, it was bursting out in physical form.

Between the bullet wound and the leg, the leg was worse.

'There's a lot of blood,' she said.

'I know.' There was blood staining the snow where it had run down his right arm and out. More blood was spreading in the snow beneath his leg and the jagged piece of his broken fibula, which was sticking out of his calf. The wound wasn't large, about a centimetre across, but there was a thumb-length section of bloody bone protruding from it, heat rising from it like steam.

'It must hurt so much,' she said, the pity in her eyes hurting him almost as much as the broken calf bone.

'It's only pain – enjoy it while it lasts, hey?' he said through gritted teeth, because he had always said that to the girls when they hurt themselves. When they had stubbed a toe or scraped a knee. He took a ragged breath and grabbed a handful of snow and placed it on the bone and around the wound, hoping to numb it.

He didn't know if he had struck his leg on the motor sled when they had been airborne, or if he had broken it on impact hitting the snow. Either way, he was in trouble.

'What about your arm?' Sofia said, falling to her knees beside him.

Keeping his leg still, he twisted at the waist to get a look at his right arm. There were two holes in the sleeve of his jacket just down from his shoulder.

'The bullet went in and out,' he said. 'I think that's a good thing. But we need to stop the bleeding.' He pointed at the pulk, which was upside down in the snow near the motor sled, its poles bent. 'See if you can find something to tie it with. Something for my leg too.'

She nodded. 'What about the rucksack straps? We can use them.'

'Good idea,' he said.

As soon as she turned to go, he lay back down and concentrated his efforts on trying to master the pain. The wound in his arm felt like fire, but the broken bone poking out of his flesh was a different kind of pain. It swept him with waves of nausea and brought tears to his eyes which he didn't want Sofia to see, though he knew she had already.

*You know what you have to do*, the god said.

'We can fix this,' he murmured through his grimace.

*There is no fixing this. He's coming. You know it. Don't waste the time. Think of the girl.*

'We'll fix it,' he growled.

The figure in the broad hat glared at him a moment with his one eye, then retreated, fading like breath on the air.

Sofia came back with a handful of straps of varying

lengths, which she had cut from their packs using the Sami *stuorraniibi*.

'The wide one,' he said. 'Nice and tight, just above the wound.'

She passed the strap around his upper arm and tied it off. Shook her head. 'It's not tight enough,' she said.

'We're not finished. We need something to wind it with. About this size.' He stretched out the finger and thumb of his left hand. 'A stick if we had one.'

'My pocket knife?' Sofia said, pulling out her Swiss Army knife.

He nodded. 'Good girl. Put it on top of the knot and tie it on.'

Her hands were shaking but the knot was good.

'Now turn it,' he said, 'and keep going until I say.' She turned it three times, then stopped to look at him. 'More,' he said. She rotated the pocket knife three more times and he gasped, swearing under his breath. 'Good,' he told her. 'I'll hold it. We need a carabiner to stop it unwinding.'

Sofia fetched one from the pulk harness and he looped it through the ring at the end of the pocket knife. Then she took a thinner piece of strapping, passed it through the carabiner and tied the strap around his arm so the knife couldn't unspin.

'Good girl,' he said through gritted teeth. 'Now the leg.' He would have dealt with the leg first, because of all the blood. But there was a chance he would pass out from the pain, so better to sort the arm out before that. 'We need to do the same thing there,' he told her. Sofia looked at the leg and looked at him, chewing her bottom lip, brows drawn together. 'You can do it,' he said. 'We need to get this done. Try not to think about it.'

She clenched and unclenched her hands, as though steeling them to the next task.

'Don't think, just do it,' he said.

'Just like with the arm?' she asked.

'Just the same,' he said, scooping more snow onto the jagged piece of his fibula because the last lot had melted already. He shoved more into the bullet holes in his jacket sleeves, pushing in as deep as he could. 'First we need to improvise a splint with one of my ski poles. Think you can cut it?'

'Yes,' she said, and she took one of his poles, laid it on top of her backpack and drew the Sami knife from its leather sheath.

'Careful now,' he said, and she had enough awareness of the absurdity of that to turn and cock an eyebrow at him. Then she lifted the knife high into the snowy air and brought it down onto the pole, putting a dent in the aluminium. The second strike cut it part way through. She grunted for good measure with the third strike and it was done.

Erik swallowed his pain, though the snow had maybe numbed it a little. 'You're scary with that thing,' he said.

Sofia smiled.

'I want you to lay the strap over the bone that's sticking out. The wound is small, so I'm not too worried about the bleeding, but we need to pull the bone straight or I won't be able to walk on it.'

Sofia fetched a dinner fork for the windlass, but when she went to unclip another carabiner from the pulk, he told her he had something else she could use. 'In my pocket,' he said, patting the breast of his jacket.

She unzipped the pocket and took out his wedding ring,

and he knew from her face that she was thinking of her mother. 'Good idea, hey?' he said.

'We're a good team,' she said.

But when she wound the strap, she stopped before it was tight enough.

He looked at her questioningly.

'I don't want to hurt you,' she explained.

'We have to do it,' he said. 'Same as before.'

She waited.

'It'll hurt, but I can take it. You know your pappa is tough, right?'

'I know.'

'Now there's a chance I may pass out,' he said, then forced a smile. 'Even as tough as I am. If I do, wake me up again. Slap me. Throw snow in my face. Whatever it takes to bring me back.'

She shook her head. 'I can't do it, Pappa.'

'Yes, you can,' he said. 'I know you can. Look what you've done so far. Look what you've been through and you're still going.' He jerked his chin at his left lower leg. 'This is nothing.'

She didn't agree but she took hold of the fork with both hands. Exhaled. Closed her eyes for a moment, then opened them. 'Tell me when.'

He took a deep breath and let it out slowly.

'Now,' he said.

She twisted once, twice, and he felt the bone driven back inside his flesh, then she put his wedding ring over the end of the fork and tied it in place while he screamed.

# 18

HE DID NOT pass out, but it was a close thing. He lay there a while, waiting for the blackness to recede from his vision, for the surging agony to retreat enough that he could pull his thoughts together. He knew he wouldn't be able to ski now. He might not even be able to stand. They'd find out soon enough.

'Here,' Sofia said, breaking off three squares of chocolate from the half bar she had found in her pack. 'The sugar and calories will help.'

He opened his mouth and she popped the chocolate in and he closed his eyes and let it melt on his tongue. Then she broke off two more squares and put them in her own mouth.

'How far ahead do you think we are?' she asked, looking back along the trail the motor sled had made. That trail was disappearing but not fast enough.

'I don't know,' he said, thinking about the ride. 'Four

kilometres, maybe five? Not far enough. I've been lying here too long. Grab my snowshoes and help me put them on.'

'You can't walk,' she said.

'I can't ski,' he corrected her.

She looked over at the pulk. 'I'll pull you,' she said.

He shook his head. 'No. I'm too heavy and you're too tired. You need to save your strength.'

'I'm tough too, you know,' she said.

He smiled through the pain. 'I know you are, baby girl. You're tougher than me. But the poles are bent. My snowshoes.'

She went to the pulk and fetched his snowshoes and strapped them on for him.

'We have to leave it behind, OK?' he said, meaning the pulk.

'I can try to pull it.'

'No. It'll be too hard now. Even if we could straighten the poles. It's served its purpose. We don't need it any more.'

She frowned. He knew why. He knew about Emilie's teddy bear, which Sofia had put in the pulk and which had been with them every step of the way.

'But he'll find it when he comes,' she said. 'I don't want him going through our stuff.'

'I don't want that either,' he said. 'Help me up.'

Using his other ski pole and with Sofia's help, he got up onto his feet, gasping and cursing with the pain of it, trying to keep his weight on his good right leg. 'Can you bring the pulk?'

She clipped into her skis and went off to bring it to him. He pointed in the direction they should go and put his left arm around her shoulder.

'Ready?' she asked him.

'Ready,' he said. Every time his left snowshoe touched down, he hissed with the sickening torment of it.

'They died because of us, didn't they?' she said. He knew she was talking about the police officers. 'If they hadn't been out here looking for us, they'd still be alive.'

'And we wouldn't be out here if it weren't for that Russian. It's his fault.'

She thought about that. 'Fuck him,' she said.

He winced, a low moan escaping his lips. 'Yeah, fuck him,' he agreed. If there was ever a time to let her get away with language like that, this was it.

'And not just his fault,' he went on, 'but the scientists messing with that virus. And the mining company.' He stopped so he could catch his breath and gather himself for the last few metres. 'But the one person whose fault it definitely isn't, is you. Do you hear me? None of it was ever your fault.'

Sofia looked down at the snow. She knew he wasn't just talking about the police officers and the Helgelands and Hánas and this whole mess. She knew he was also talking about Emilie. About that day at the climbing wall.

'Come on,' he said, and they came to the edge of the ridge and looked down at the narrow river valley. It was pure white, but for the odd fir tree on the steep slopes.

'We're going to let the pulk go?' she asked.

'Yes,' he said. 'Is that OK?'

She thought about it. They both knew what was inside it. A worn-out soft toy bear in a red sweater. But neither of them spoke of it.

'I don't want him to have it.'

'He won't,' he said.

Sofia gave a resolute nod. 'I'll do it.' Leaving him leaning on his single ski pole, she dragged the pulk to the edge and pointed its nose down the slope. Then she just stood there.

'You're sure?' he asked.

'We can't take it,' she said. 'And we can't use the backpacks without straps.'

'I know, but are you sure?'

She took a deep breath. 'I'm sure.'

'Then do it now.'

Sofia pulled the pulk forward and for a moment it teetered on the lip, so she gave it a shove and down it went, sliding fast and gathering speed.

Its final journey.

They set off again, he on his snowshoes, Sofia on her skis, unencumbered now by backpacks or the pulk. All they carried were the rifle across his back, the ice axe clipped to the belt of his over-trousers, and the big Sami knife, which Sofia kept sheathed inside her jacket, as well as a few items they had stuffed into their pockets: the last of the chocolate, some strips of dried reindeer meat, the matches and three tea lights, along with a few plasters from the first aid kit, which weren't much use for a bullet hole or a broken calf bone.

Still, they were getting nowhere. He was barely able to put any weight at all on his left leg, and he was pressing down on Sofia with every other step, though she made no complaint.

*He'll catch you now. You know it.*

He looked to his right and there was the god, walking

alongside him, plunging his staff into the snow as he went, his broad hat tilted up as he regarded a sky the colour of a wolf's pelt beyond the driven snow.

*You don't have long*, the god said.

Erik ignored him. If only they could have turned the snowmobile upright again. Sofia had tried but she wasn't strong enough, and he had been no help.

'What if he knows how to get it started without the key?' Sofia had said. 'Like with cars in the movies.'

He hadn't considered that as a possibility. 'If he could do that, he'd already be on Officer Haugen's sled,' he'd said.

'I suppose,' she said. But just to make sure, they had taken the ice axe and between them hacked off the front right ski of the sled, rendering the machine useless.

'Will we get in trouble?' she had asked, as he tossed the ski away for good measure.

'No, we won't get in trouble,' he said.

He looked behind now to see how far they had come. The sled was still in sight, even through the blizzard. There was blood on the snow, from his leg or dripping from his sleeve maybe.

*You might as well be laying out a ball of twine for him to follow*, the god said.

Some time later, he simply stopped. Stood there with his weight on his right leg, looking at the fir trees up ahead.

'We just have to keep going,' Sofia said. 'One foot in front of the other.'

'One step at a time,' he heard himself say.

He was so tired. And in so much pain. Now and then the pain helped to focus his mind, brought all his senses into overdrive so that he was startlingly aware of their situation and had full recall of everything that had happened since the night in the tent when Sofia had cut herself. At other times the pain was too much and his mind sought to protect him by numbing him with a kind of mental anaesthetic, so that the pain in his arm and his leg, and the events of the last days, all blurred together like their own tracks silting up in the snow.

It was like that now. He felt he was outside of himself. Like a cartoon soul drifting up from its body.

He looked to his right, but the god wasn't there.

*That's it, I'm losing my mind*, he thought.

*Just because you can't see me, doesn't mean I'm not here.* The god's voice came across him like the wind. *What are you doing, Erik?*

*What does it look like I'm doing?*

'Pappa?' Sofia said, thinking he was talking to her, though she kept her eyes on the ground in front of her skis. He said nothing and they kept going, step by awkward step.

*You said you would do anything for the girl. That she's the only thing that matters. But look at you. Limping along like a cripple. Leaving those snowshoe prints and a blood trail like an invitation to that bastard to come and kill your little girl. She's freezing. Can't you feel her shivering? You bastard. She's practically carrying you. Using up what little strength she has, just to lug you along. You bastard. You selfish—*

'Stop!' he said. This time he *was* talking to Sofia.

'We've got to keep going,' she said.

But he turned and stood in front of her, his hands on her shoulders.

'Listen to me, Sofia,' he said. 'This is no good. We're going too slowly and he's going to catch up with us. And you know what he'll do when he does.'

'So we keep going,' she said, a pleading edge to her voice.

'You're not listening. I'm done. I can't walk. And I can't let you carry me like this.'

'I can do it, Pappa,' she said. Her upper eyelids were raised and her brows drawn together beneath the rim of her hat.

'No, you can't,' he said, 'because I won't let you.'

She stared up at him and two tears slipped from her eyes and rolled down her cheeks. 'What are you saying, Pappa?'

He took a breath. He wasn't sure he wanted to say the words, because he knew once said, there could be no taking them back.

'Pappa?' she said.

He nodded. 'You need to go. You need to leave me.'

Her lips started trembling then, her whole face, her whole body suddenly done with trying to hide her fear. And this was another blade in his already dying heart, because even in the face of death she had not expressed the fear she now felt at the thought of not being with him. Not having him.

'I can't,' she said.

'You can. You have to,' he told her. 'Look.' He pointed in their direction of travel. 'See that mountain with the bite taken out of it? At the foot there. That's where we were when you had to stop for a pee and you were worried someone would see you, even though there was no one within three kilometres in any direction.'

She was looking, remembering, her chest rising and falling quickly.

'So we're nearly there,' he said. '*You're* nearly there. Just two more hours and you'll be home.'

'So we can do it together,' she said.

'He'll catch us,' he said. 'Think of Mamma. She'll be so worried. You need to get home to her.'

She was crying. Her breathing had changed. It was getting faster and he feared she was on the edge of panic, of hyperventilating, and so he took her head in his hands and put his forehead to hers.

'I need you to be OK, Lillemor. I need you to live. I need it more than you can possibly know.'

'I won't leave you, Pappa. I can't.'

'Someone needs to tell the world what's going on in that lab. You're the only one who can do that. Only you.'

'We're wasting time,' she said, but there was no conviction in her words.

'I love you, Sofia. You've made me so proud.' Tears came to his eyes then. He kissed her cheek, holding his lips there a long time. His throat was closing, trying to choke him. But he had words that needed to be said. 'I am the luckiest pappa in the world.'

She closed her eyes. 'Please,' she said in a small voice.

'Just keep going,' he said. 'That's all you have to do. Just keep going and I'll be with you. I'll always be with you. For all your life.' He was crying now. 'Even when you're old, I'll still be with you.'

He pulled her against him and held her a long time. As though he could pull her heart into his own. Even though she *was* his heart. Then he took the rifle from his shoulder and slung it over hers.

'You need to go.' He looked up at the sky. The wind was dying. The storm had blown itself out now. 'Just follow the valley and you'll make it. When you get home, you and

Mamma get in the car and drive into town. Tell the police everything.' His breath caught in his chest. 'And tell Mamma I love her. I love her so much. And I'm sorry.'

'OK.'

'You'll tell her?'

'I promise.'

He exhaled. 'OK. Good girl.' He hugged her and pulled her hat down and kissed her again. 'Now go.'

She put her hands through the loops of her poles and turned her skis around. Stopped. Turned and looked back at him, and he tried with all his might to smile.

'I love you, Pappa,' she said.

He felt his soul crumbling like powder snow. 'I love you, Lillemor,' he said, his breath stuttering in his chest. 'I always will.'

She turned away and bent forward and pushed down with her poles and moved across the snow. Kick and glide. Kick and glide.

He watched her until she was gone.

He made it another hundred metres, then slumped down to the snow and sat there shivering. The fir wood was still a way off, but there remained a part of him that dared to hope. If he could get to the trees, then maybe he could hide. It was a desperate hope and he felt it was unworthy. That by clinging to it, he was somehow weaker. Even if he could get to the woods, it wouldn't be enough, he knew deep down, because the blizzard was fading away and the wind was ebbing or moving on, so that his tracks were no longer being unwritten. The tall man would come. Even in the half-light he would follow those footprints easily.

*Still, why make it any easier for that bastard? Get to the trees. Do that at least. Make him work for his money.*

He climbed to his feet.

He thought of Sofia. Pictured her skiing. That silly pink hat with the fishing polar bears. It warmed him to think of her, but he missed her so much. He felt as if someone had ripped his heart out of his chest and it was flying further and further away into the cold dark. And in a way it was.

The god was nowhere to be seen now. Maybe he had done what he came to do. Said what he came to say. But Erik wished he would come back because he felt so alone.

He was so tired. Now Sofia was gone, he was empty.

And yet somehow full.

'She will live,' he said to himself.

*She still has far to go.*

After a while, he fell down again. But the wood was close now. He caught the faint scent of the trees.

*Just a little further.*

He lay on his left side and dragged himself along.

He kept the faces of his wife and his girls in his mind. As if he were crawling toward them.

Eventually he closed his eyes.

*He's here*, the god said.

Erik didn't open his eyes. He didn't know if he was asleep or awake, alive or dead. He knew he wasn't cold now and that felt good.

*He's here. You've come as far as you could. Now it ends.*

'OK.' He felt the word rather than heard it, as a breath across his lips.

He opened his eyes.

The tall man was standing at the edge of the wood. A black shape in the twilight world.

*Has it stopped snowing?*

The figure came closer. He looked like a wraith. Looked hungry and cold, but there was fire in his eyes. He was breathing hard but getting it under control, like an athlete after a race.

'This has been a good hunt,' the man said. 'We have come far.'

Erik leant his head back against the fir trunk. He thought of Sofia and he smiled. She would be nearly home now.

'You lost,' he said.

The man tilted his head on one side. 'You think so?'

'She's gone. You'll never catch her.'

The tall man looked off in the direction Sofia had skied, and for a second, fear stabbed Erik in the guts because he thought the Russian would take off after her. His hand went to the ice axe clipped to his trousers. But what could he do with that? He wasn't even sure he could hold it with his ruined hands.

The tall man didn't set off after Sofia. He just stood there.

'So it's just you and me,' he said, turning back to Erik. He unclipped from his skis and came closer, trudging through the snow, holding his rifle diagonally across his body, the stock almost level with his right shoulder. 'That's a shame. Your daughter . . .' He dipped his head. 'She is your daughter?'

Erik said nothing.

The tall man smiled, understanding. 'She's a good girl. Strong. Brave. I told you I will kill her, but I will do it quickly because I respect her.'

His hatred for this man rekindled the old fire in his chest. What he would give to make him suffer. But it was too late now. He breathed in, feeling the cold air in his lungs as if for the first time. Then he let the breath out and it plumed silver in the shadows. 'I beat you,' he said. '*We* beat you.'

The tall man looked up at a trickle of snow falling from a branch as he took the glove off his right hand and tucked it into his pocket. Then his eyes came back to Erik, as though he was trying to look inside his mind. 'How did you beat me?' he asked. By the look in his eyes, it was a genuine question. 'In a minute you will be dead.'

After a long silence between them, the man drew the bolt of his rifle and chambered a round, the sound unnaturally loud amongst the trees.

*Because she goes on*, the god said. *That's how you won.*

Erik smiled as the tall man lifted the rifle.

He put the butt into his shoulder. He didn't need to put his eye to the sights. Not at this range. He nodded. An acknowledgement of the end of things. Of this thing anyway. 'It was a good hunt,' he said again, placing the index finger of his right hand on the trigger.

Erik took another breath, this time through his mouth. Savouring the taste of it.

*Some men call me Killer*, the god said.

The tall man sensed something. He pulled his head back from the rifle, and over his right shoulder he saw snow spill from the bough of a fir. The girl was there, seven, maybe eight metres away amongst the branches, her breath like silver smoke in the night. The man started to swing the rifle around, started to turn, but the girl already had her rifle up, the butt in her shoulder as she had seen her father do it, the muzzle aimed. She squeezed the trigger, the recoil throwing her savagely back, and the sound of the shot filled the world as the rifle fell away.

The tall man looked down at his chest and saw the hole in it. Dropped his rifle. Looked back at the girl, who had been knocked down and lay in the snow, and stumbled towards her. Fell to his knees, spitting blood. Choking on it. Clutching his chest with one hand and reaching out for her with the other.

'Pappa!' she screamed, scrambling back against a fallen tree. She had nowhere to go and couldn't move for terror, as the man crawled through his own blood towards her.

'Run!' Erik yelled, hauling himself upright and making two lurching strides before he fell. He tried to get up but fell again, and so dragged himself after the Russian, who reached out and took hold of Sofia's boot.

'No!' Erik yelled, and Sofia screamed, kicked out with her other foot, but the man would not let go, and she fumbled inside her jacket and then the Sami knife was in her hand and she leant forward, screaming again, bringing the knife down, and three fingers fell into the snow, inert and somehow inhuman.

'Look away!' Erik yelled, pulling himself on top of the man, every muscle trying to force the Russian down into the frozen crust. 'Bastard!' he screamed again, an animal sound as he brought the ice axe down onto the man's skull. And the *crack* of it was loud amongst the trees.

For a moment he lay on the man, breathing hard, needing to know that the Russian was dead, but too exhausted to move. Then he lifted himself away and up onto his knees, like a man before God, and the girl threw herself at him.

'You were supposed to go,' he said between ragged breaths. 'You should have gone.'

'But we're a team, Pappa,' she said, sobbing, the two of them kneeling in the snow, her slight body pressed against his. He pulled her to him as if he would never let go again.

'Yes, we are,' he said, and they held each other in the nearly dark.

They ate the last of the reindeer meat and the chocolate, and with the Sami knife she cut a birch branch for him to use as a walking staff. They were both cold but neither of them wanted to take anything that had belonged to the tall man, who they left face down in the red snow.

The blizzard had passed. By the time they got halfway through the valley winding south towards home, it was early evening and the clouds were thinning and breaking so that they could see the stars, and the world seemed bigger.

They didn't talk about what had happened. Maybe they were too tired to talk. Or they didn't have the words.

Many times, they would stop and rest. The two of them shivering, holding on to each other until one of them said it was time to move again, and they stood and trudged on into the clearing night, like the last humans emerging from some cave at the end of the world.

The pain in his arm and his leg, in his whole body, was a trial by ordeal and he welcomed it because nothing could hurt him now. He would make it, or he would not. But the girl still had far to go, and when he saw another set of footprints in the snow beside their own, he thought she had seen them too, though neither of them spoke of it, and that was OK.

Eventually they came to a rise and looked up at the slope, which glowed and sparkled under the light of the moon.

'Nearly there, Pappa,' she said.

'I know,' he said.

'Look, Pappa.' She pointed up at the northern sky where the aurora played in green and yellow and blue. Cascades of light falling in broad veils, intense in one place, then cool, then hot. Like the breath of God.

'It's beautiful,' he said.

'Hánas said they are the souls of the dead,' she told him, her face turned upward in infinite wonder. 'Our ancestors.'

'Maybe he was right,' he said.

The cosmic dance held them spellbound for a long while, then they climbed the slope, each taking strength from the other, and when at last they came to the top, they stood beneath the frozen sky.

The man and the girl.

In the distance, though not too far, a house sat alone in the snowbound world. Silver smoke drifting up from the stone chimney. Golden light in the windows. Snow on the roof.

Home.

# Author's Note

## *A Writer's Tracks in the Snow*

BEING HALF NORWEGIAN on my mother's side, I spent many holidays on the fjord's edge in our cottage near Bergen on Norway's west coast, or in the mountains skiing.

The idyllic, jaw-dropping scenery there is rooted deep in happy childhood memories, and yet even back then I was always aware of a darker past lurking behind the stunning landscape. That darker past is known to most Norwegians simply as the 'war years' during the occupation of Norway by Nazi Germany (April 1940–May 1945). And it was on one such childhood visit that I became aware of the famous Telemark campaign of the Second World War.

I'll return to my own story and its evolution in a moment, but first it's worth a couple of paragraphs to learn about two extraordinary events that tested the limits of human heroism and resilience in the face of extreme danger – both manmade and environmental.

The Telemark campaign was brought to the silver screen in the 1965 film *The Heroes of Telemark*, directed by Anthony Mann and starring Kirk Douglas and Richard Harris. The aim of the real-life mission was to prevent the Nazi regime from building an atomic bomb by destroying the heavy water unit at the Vemork power plant at Rjukan. In February 1943, a team of SOE-trained Norwegian commandos parachuted onto a Norwegian glacier and linked up with an advance party on the Hardanger Plateau who had spent months surviving in a barren world of rock, snow and wind. With only the most basic equipment, a nine-man team scaled a cliff in the middle of the night and pulled off one of the most heroic sabotage acts of the Second World War.

This tale of daring, skill and determination stayed with me and when I was older I heard about another mission, this one involving a team of expatriate Norwegian commandos who sailed from the Shetland Islands back into Nazi-occupied Norway in March 1943. Their aim: to destroy a German airfield control tower at Bardufoss, and recruit for the Norwegian resistance movement. However, unlike the resounding success of the Telemark operation, Operation Martin ended in disaster. The men were betrayed and ambushed, their boat sunk by the Germans. Three were killed. One escaped. The one who got away was Jan Baalsrud. Soaked to the skin and minus a boot, he escaped via a snowy ravine, where he shot dead a German Gestapo officer before going on the run in the Lyngen Alps, where this book is set.

As told in the brilliant book by David Howarth, *We Die Alone*, what followed has to be one of the most remarkable survival stories of all time. Over nine weeks, Jan Baalsrud would endure hardships almost beyond imagining. His feet would freeze solid, he was buried up to his neck by an avalanche. Snowblind and frostbitten, he wandered lost in a snowstorm for three days, became entombed in snow for four days and was left abandoned for two weeks. To prevent the spread of gangrene, he cut off several of his frostbitten toes. Eventually he lay near death and, tied to a stretcher, was dragged up and down snow-covered mountains by teams of Norwegian villagers.

Despite all this, he somehow endured. Jan Baalsrud survived what would surely have killed anyone else. The man simply refused to die.

## The not-so-long ski and the initial inspiration for *Where Blood Runs Cold*

Those guys from Jan's generation were tough, almost a different breed. What they often lacked in equipment or intel, they made up for in guts, determination and a mindset to get the job done, no matter the cost. I admire them enormously from the comfort of my life and have always been intrigued by that part inside of us – which we *hope* is inside of us – that refuses to give up when all seems lost. I think it's fair to assume that we all have an animal instinct to survive. But instinct is not, I think, the same as the sheer determination – almost superhuman desire – that drives some people to carry on going when by rights they should long have given up.

These stories of Norwegian war heroes were in my mind when in 2003 I undertook a cross-country ski trip with my brother, James, and some Norwegian friends. The idea was that we would ski some 15 km, stop and build a five-man igloo to sleep in, and repeat the pattern over three days. I had worked hard on my fitness before the trip and felt ready. Eager and excited for the journey, we got off the train at Finse Station in a small mountain village in the municipality of Ulvik in Vestland county (at 4,010 ft above sea level, the highest point on the Norwegian railway network), strapped on our heavy packs and clipped into our skis. I set off after the others and must have made it all of twenty metres down the first slope when I lost my balance and completely wiped out, the iron snow shovel strapped to my back smacking me in the head as I landed in a tangle of limbs and skis. If I hadn't known it already, I knew then that I wouldn't have made it into Joachim Rønneberg's Telemark sabotage team in 1943! In all honesty, I wasn't even proficient enough to be with the Norwegian guys waiting for me on the other side of the slope, but they were too generous to say as much. I'm sure James was just glad it wasn't him lying there with a face full of snow. But at least the snow hid my blushes.

Anyway, the thing about a long ski trip is that you have plenty of time to think. There's a lot of space for the imagination to conjure in. Maybe the snowy landscape is a metaphor for the blank page, but I got to thinking (when I wasn't too busy trying to force my feet into frozen ski boots that I'd mistakenly left outside my sleeping bag on the first night), what if we were out here and someone was after us and wanted to kill us? That's all it takes if, like me, you suffer from an overactive imagination. The first tracks of a story were starting to appear in my mind.

As it turned out, though, a couple of days into the trip James and I cut out and made a break for it. Our fitness was good, but we just weren't experienced enough with the techniques of cross-country skiing, and we felt we were holding the others back. We had learned from two police officers passing on snowmobiles that there was a train station several kilometres away. And so, when the going got tough, we got going – only, in the other direction. The next day, we were back in our comfortable cottage by the fjord, fishing and drinking beer and very much playing to our strengths.

At that time, I was working on a novel called *Blood and the Saints*, set during the First Crusade of AD 1096. The novel was never published, but then a stag weekend in Oslo inspired me to start writing another book, this time about a young man with memory loss following a head trauma, who is taken in a Viking raid and grows to become part of the crew. I was writing part-time and so it took a while, and then in 2006 Sally and I moved to Manhattan, New York. Serious now about wanting to become a published writer (who am I kidding? I was desperate), I got myself a literary agent who saw the potential in *Raven: Blood Eye*. As we then learned, it was no easy thing getting a US publisher to see the potential in historical fiction, let alone a story set in the ninth century about Vikings.

Still, whilst I may have been raiding with Vikings in NYC, looking for a deal, I clearly had unfinished business with my failed cross-country ski adventure, because while *Blood Eye* was on submission, I started writing another story. This was a survival thriller set in the Lyngen Alps, about a man and his son who are on a ski trip when they get caught up in an attempt by American special forces to secure an underground oil resource deep in the Arctic Circle. I set the story in the future, in 2020 (which, by an incredible coincidence, is the year I started writing *Where Blood Runs Cold* – then titled *Far Wanderer*), where the United States of America is a dying superpower and, having been forced to relinquish its oil assets in the Middle East, is desperate enough to stake a claim on the largest underground oil reserve ever discovered in Europe, sitting beneath the Arctic wastelands of the far north of Norway. I had written the first thirty thousand words when, to my utter delight, my UK agent rang with the news that Random House were going to publish *Raven: Blood Eye*. My would-be editor was keen to see an outline of books two and three (I had pitched *Blood Eye* as the first of a trilogy), and seeing as I had no such outline, I got busy planning. The futuristic thriller was put on ice.

Eleven published novels later, in 2020, I had finished *Camelot*, the second in my Arthurian Tales series. That book, along with *Lancelot*, comprised nearly four hundred thousand words set in the post-Roman Arthurian world I had created. They were big books, and they took a lot out of me, emotionally, physically (because the body and mind are one) and creatively. I felt I needed to cleanse my creative palate. I wanted to write a different kind of book. In fact I needed to.

Those who know me only as a writer of historical fiction were probably more surprised by this than those who know me as a person. I've lived an eclectic life. From my days in the music business, to writing advertising copy, to doing the narrative design for video games, experimenting creatively has always been what drives me. So, to me it seems the most natural thing in the world that I should want to write in other genres, be that historical horror or, in this case, a contemporary thriller. I've never been just one thing, and perhaps that makes me a jack of all trades, master of none, but I prefer that to being crammed into a pigeonhole.

That's also why I didn't want to follow the normal procedure in such circumstances and publish this book under a pseudonym. I understand why some authors do this, and why some publishers insist on it, because they don't want to confuse retailers or readers when an author known for one genre writes a different kind of book. But I like to think that the cover itself, along with a quick read of the blurb, will tell my readers what this particular novel is about. And whilst the story might not be set a thousand years or more in the past, like some of my others, I think it still has all the elements that my readers would expect from a Giles Kristian book. Besides, I'm a storyteller and this is a story I've been wanting to tell for many years. Having built up a loyal readership over the course of my career, it felt to me completely counter-intuitive to publish it under a different identity, because my readers might not otherwise know I had a new book out. We authors spend years trying to build a brand, to get to the point where readers recognize our names on the cover. Why then suddenly use a different name and effectively have to start again? I think some authors enjoy the glamour and mystique of a nom de plume, and perhaps I will too at some point, but for now I'm glad that you found this book and took a chance on something different from me. Furthermore, I'm enormously grateful to Transworld for supporting this novel and for giving me the opportunity to flex my creative muscles. For allowing me simply to tell a good yarn that needed telling.

Returning to that story then, and its false beginnings in 2007. Had I written it back then, it would have been a very

315

different tale from the one you have in your hands, and not just because the premise was different. I daresay it would have taken the familiar shape of a chase thriller. There would undoubtedly have been guns and drama in the snow and it may even have been a good read, but I think it wouldn't have gone much deeper. Timing is all part of the creative process. We can go along for years with the seed of an idea rolling around in the back of our minds like a boiled sweet gathering lint in a jacket pocket. I wasn't ready to write 'the snow thriller' back then and I'm glad I didn't. Because now, with a few more years on my back, and being a father too, the story became what it was meant to be. For me it was an exploration: of physical suffering and the human will to survive, yes, but beneath this, another theme, of grief, and of a father's struggle to let go, and his child's struggle to go on without him.

I think we write different kinds of book at different stages of our lives. At least I've discovered that I do. Take *Raven: Blood Eye*, my first published novel. A story about a young man, an outcast, who falls in with a new crowd and tries to find his place in the world. Written by a twenty-something-year-old who had left a career behind in search of pastures new. At that point in my life, I was done with being moulded and pushed in this or that direction and I needed to forge my own future on my own terms.

Next came my Civil War books, *The Bleeding Land* and *Brothers' Fury*, at the heart of which are three siblings, each of them different, each pushed and pulled by issues of loyalty and conscience, yet all ultimately bound by blood. There's no doubt that as I was writing those stories, I was placing myself, my brother and my sister into the roles of

Mun, Tom and Bess, and using our relationships as a foundation upon which to build my characters.

I wrote *Lancelot* whilst grieving the death of my father, and I think that story is all about love and loss, and about trying to reconcile those glorious moments in the past with all that can now never be.

And then *Camelot*, about Galahad, a man trying to step out of the long shadow cast by his father. A man burdened by the past and questioning his freedom to shape his own destiny, and how much of his future is pre-ordained since he is, after all, his father's son.

Now, *Where Blood Runs Cold*. The story of a father's struggle to come to terms with his daughter growing up, with his own mortality, and his own weakness. Of the natural order of this, the way the strength of the parent must inevitably fade while the child grows and thrives and comes into her own. And the story of a daughter seeking freedom whilst coming to terms with her father's mortality and the unalterable reality of facing the world without him. A book written by a father who is not as young or as strong as he once was. A man plagued by fears for his children as he grows older and weaker, but determined to do what he can. Whatever it takes.

As for the spiritual element in *Where Blood Runs Cold*, that is of course open to interpretation. Is Odin (one of whose many nicknames was Far Wanderer) a literal – if spiritual – presence in the story? The Odin of Scandinavian mythology? Or is he some other supernatural presence manifesting itself in a guise that would be familiar to Erik as a child of the north? Could he be a creation of Erik's own troubled mind, some expression perhaps of his grief-stricken conscience? Certainly both Erik and Sofia 'wander far' physically, but it is in their minds that they wander the farthest.

Nevertheless, for someone who does not partake in organised institutional religion, I certainly do tend to flirt with ideas of spiritualism and personal belief in my books. From visions of the Norse Aesir in my Viking sagas, to the spirit-journeying of *Lancelot* and *Camelot*, to Erik's conversations with Odin Far Wanderer in *Where Blood Runs Cold*, it's clear that I enjoy dabbling in ideas of things behind the veil. Of other dimensions, either in reality or in a person's mind (those possibly being the same thing), which can, on occasion and with the right talent and/or training, be accessed.

This is also hinted at, of course, in the character of Hánas. Traditional Sami spiritual practices are based on what anthropologists talk of as shamanism – that is to say, beliefs based on a type of animism and polytheism. The nomadic Sami people of northern Europe believe that the animals, plants and rocks they share their land with possess a soul. I didn't want to go too far with this idea in the book. I didn't want Hánas himself to be a shaman as such, because it can come across as somewhat of a cliché – the wise, spiritual 'medicine man' as representative of an indigenous people. Someone who somehow knows more, 'sees' more than the other protagonists.

And yet it seems to me quite obvious that someone who lives and works with nature, who measures time in the passing of the seasons and for whom much of the year home is where the *lávvu* (tent) is set up on the migration trails, should be connected and more attuned to the natural world and mysticism than those of us who work in the city, in offices, in a modernised, industrialised world inexorably separating us ever further from nature. The Sami herders' semi-nomadic lifestyle is inherently tied to natural cycles, and for those who still make their living herding reindeer as their ancestors did, I can imagine it becomes ever more important to hold tightly to the past, as the modern world continues to encroach. And so, as one of the approximately six thousand five hundred Sami in Scandinavia engaged in reindeer herding, Hánas has one foot in the modern world (he owns a cell phone, a snow-mobile, probably has a modern home somewhere, equipped with Internet and television), and one foot in the traditional indigenous culture of his people. As such, he provides a bridge via which Erik can venture further into his own psyche than he might do otherwise.

It was important for me also that Erik should be stripped of the modern world, of technology and the trappings of twenty-first-century Scandinavian life, because I thought it would be easier for him to connect with himself and his emotions without all the distraction and noise of a city. The white canvas of the snowbound land gives him the space to think, and in a way, by going into nature, he goes back in time, which is something he needs to do to help him deal with his grief.

This stripping away is part of his journey. In their most desperate struggle, both Erik and Sofia learn about themselves, and that is really the point. Because the instinct to survive is perhaps inherent in us, as it is in all animals. But the unquenchable desire to overcome appalling odds, the unbreakable will to endure, to go on living for those we love and who love us, no matter the cost – well, those are human.

*Giles Kristian*
*4 May 2021*

## Recommended reading:

*We Die Alone* by David Howarth (Canongate, 2009; first published by Collins, 1955).

*The Real Heroes of Telemark: The True Story of the Secret Mission to Stop Hitler's Atomic Bomb* by Ray Mears (Hodder & Stoughton, 2003).

*Hunting the Nazi Bomb: The Special Forces Mission to Sabotage Hitler's Deadliest Weapon* by Damien Lewis (Quercus, 2017).

# Acknowledgements

Having built my career writing historical novels, I appreciate that this book is somewhat of a departure. (Hard not to use an 'off-piste' gag there.) And yet, when I pitched the idea to my agent, Bill Hamilton, he was on board immediately. Turns out Bill is partial to a snowy thriller, which was good news for me and straight away the two of us were bouncing ideas around. It was Bill who said I needed a deeper conspiracy buried within the story, and so I gave him one. He also took his red pen to the first twenty thousand words; a rather painful lesson for me in how my usual descriptive style would have to be pared down. It's all about momentum and action with a thriller. However, I've never been good at conforming, so I still had some fun with the prose. Thanks, Bill! Next, we had to convince my editor, Simon Taylor, because he would have the unenviable task of telling Transworld – which has successfully published ten Giles Kristian novels about Vikings, the English Civil War and the Arthurian legend – that I wanted to write something completely different. I wish I'd been a fly on the wall during Simon's publishing pitch. I was expecting a fight, but Simon has always been in my corner – with the sweat towel, the priceless advice and, at times, the smelling salts – for which I'm ever grateful.

I recall a slightly nerve-wracking conversation with my publisher, Bill Scott-Kerr, on 10 June 2020, during which he asked why I wanted to write this book and I made my case, and we talked about the industry and my career and all that jazz. I'm absolutely positive that many in Bill's position would have chosen to play it safe and turned down my proposal, if for no other reason than the inevitable challenges we would face trying to break me in to a new genre. Bill told me that he still believes publishing is a qualitative business, so whatever is good will rise to the top. As I write this, I cannot know the fate of *Where Blood Runs Cold*, but I do know how lucky I am that I was given the backing to write and publish it. Thank you, Bill! And thanks to Larry Finlay and everyone at Transworld for having the faith and for joining me on this very different adventure. Thanks to Richard Shailer for the cover, which I love, and to Phil Evans in production. Thanks to my publicist Hayley Barnes, Lilly Cox, and Tory Lyne-Pirkis at Midas PR for helping *Where Blood Runs Cold* find its way into readers' numbing hands. Which of course couldn't happen without the Transworld sales team, so thanks to them, too, and to Josh Benn and Vivien Thompson for managing the editorial side of things, and to Monica Byles for a copy-edit which made me question how on earth I'd managed to write eleven novels before now.

To Anthony Hewson, thanks for being the first set of eyes

after my own to read the manuscript and all which that entails, and to Grethe Moberg Widdowson for reading it with a Norwegian adventurer's eye and for letting me steal your grandmother's saying about the cold 'sitting in the walls'. To Phil, as ever, it's a privilege to talk stories with you. Thanks for being on the other end of the phone or across the pub table with a beer when I tie myself in knots on some or other plot point. To Sally, Freyja and Aksel, thank you for making me the luckiest husband and pappa. You know I would ski to the edge of the world for you.

And lastly, thank you to Tore Nordahl-Pedersen for taking me on that fateful cross-country skiing trip all those years ago. I may have failed the mission, but at least I got a novel out of it!

# About the Author

Family history (he is half Norwegian) inspired Giles Kristian to write his first novels, set in the Viking world. His bestselling 'Raven' and 'The Rise of Sigurd' trilogies have been acclaimed by his peers, reviewers and readers alike.

In *The Bleeding Land* and *Brothers' Fury*, he tells the story of a family torn apart by the English Civil War. He also co-wrote Wilbur Smith's No.1 bestseller *Golden Lion*. With his *Sunday Times* bestseller *Lancelot*, Giles plunged into the rich waters of the Arthurian legend and *Camelot* continued his epic reimagining of our greatest island 'history'.

His contemporary survival thriller, *Where Blood Runs Cold*, won the 2022 Wilbur Smith Adventure Writing Prize. Giles lives in Leicestershire.

To find out more, visit www.gileskristian.com and you can follow him on Twitter @GilesKristian and Facebook/ GilesKristian.

Conn Iggulden called it 'a masterpiece' while *The Times*
hailed it 'a gorgeous, rich retelling of the Arthurian tale' . . .

# LANCELOT

In Britain, Rome's legions are but a distant memory.

And Uther Pendragon is dying.

Enemies stalk the land.

Into this uncertain world a boy is cast – an outsider,
plagued by memories of those he's lost.

Under the watchful eye of Merlin, the boy begins
his journey to manhood. He meets another outcast,
Guinevere – wild, proud and beautiful. And he is dazzled
by Arthur – a warrior who carries the hopes of the
people like a flaming torch in the dark.

But these are treacherous times, and the fate of Britain
rests on a sword's edge. This young man becomes a lord
of war: loved, hated, admired and feared. He is a man
forsaken but not forgotten.

He is Lancelot.

**Available now in paperback, ebook and audio**

The epic, heart-pounding and heart-wrenching sequel
to the bestselling *Lancelot* – 'a vital, glorious story:
rich, rewarding, and utterly revealing of our times'
said Manda Scott.

# CAMELOT

The Saxons have returned and their war bands stalk the
land. The lords of Britain look only to their own survival,
unable or unwilling to unite as they once did under Arthur.

And in a monastery hidden in the marshlands of Avalon,
a novice monk prepares to take his vows. However, two
strangers – the wild-spirited, Saxon-killing Iselle and the
ageing warrior Gawain – will pluck him from his sheltered
existence and his world will be turned upside down.

Together they will go in search of the last druid, to find
the cauldron of a god, and to raise an army to hold the
darkness at bay.

And as they journey, so the novice will cast aside
his training and embrace his legacy.

For he is a warrior born.

His name is Galahad. And he is the son of Lancelot . . .

**Available now in paperback, ebook and audio**